CHINOOK

A North-Western Story

Also by Max Brand™
in Large Print:

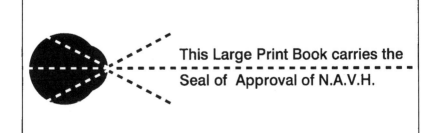

This Large Print Book carries the
Seal of Approval of N.A.V.H.

Max Brand™

CHINOOK

A North-Western Story

Thorndike Press • Thorndike, Maine

Published in 1999 in conjunction with
Golden West Literary Agency.

Thorndike Large Print® Western Series.

The tree indicium is a trademark of Thorndike Press.

The text of this Large Print edition is unabridged.
Other aspects of the book may vary from the original edition.

Set in 16 pt. Plantin by Al Chase.

Printed in the United States on permanent paper.

Library of Congress Cataloging in Publication Data

Brand, Max, 1892–1944.
    Chinook : a north-western story / Max Brand.
      p.   cm.
    ISBN 0-7862-1167-9 (lg. print : hc : alk. paper)
    1. Frontier and pioneer life — Alaska Fiction. 2. Alaska
  — Gold discoveries Fiction. 3. Sled dogs — Alaska Fiction.
  4. Large type books. I. Title.
    [PS3511.A87C48 1999]
    813'.52—dc21   99-21870

CHINOOK

A North-Western Story

Chapter One

Dogs and Men

Withdrawn from the crowd to his own Olympian height of contemplation, Chinook sat in a corner and looked down upon all others. There was no curiosity in his eye, neither was there remorse, but only a calm seeing of mortality to which he was linked rather by the accident of flesh than by the weakness of kind. His eye was the color of the sea when storm clouds are piled above still water, and from that eye came neither question nor answer. Nothing approached him, either dog or man. No matter how the tug pitched against the gale, tumbling men and animals about in confusion on the housed deck, nothing rolled near Chinook. Men shrank from him; the bravest of the "inside" dogs, fierce as wolves and like wolves in their power, dared not blunder close to him. Yet it was more might of spirit than of body that impressed them. So still was he that he looked sometimes like an image rather than flesh and blood, a colossal image such as might have served the Egyptians for the worship of Anubis, the dog god.

He was of that enormous breed called the Porcupine River or Mackenzie husky — the finest of all freighters and the biggest. They will turn out an average of a hundred and sixty pounds for a well selected team, but Chinook was larger still, with a tawny robe over his neck and shoulders that gave him the regal dignity of a lion. He had a forearm as big as a man's, and one paw lay across the other in an almost human crossing of hands.

Nothing could attract the attention of Chinook, except the movements of his master, Andrew Steen, who sat beside him. But Steen moved hardly at all. He kept one foot braced against a cleat on the deck, and so managed to support himself with ease, no matter how the tug bucked at the waves that were pitching down the narrow Lynn Canal with the wind leaning behind their shoulders. As Chinook was among dogs, so was he among men, lofty and lordly, with danger in his dark face and contempt in his eye, or cold indifference.

Andrew Steen was no chechako, but a sourdough who had already holed up one winter in Alaska and now was returning, presumably to hunt for gold, but in reality to taste the rigors of that stern land again. He was between thirty and thirty-five, perhaps closer to the former age, though a

8

narrow beard and a close-cropped mustache added a little to his apparent years. A picture of this man would have shown a handsome face, but those who glanced at him openly or stared in secret thought nothing of good looks, so impressed were they by his solemnity and a sinister suggestion of force and craft in him. Half a dozen innocent chechakos had attempted to get information about the white wilderness from this veteran, but he answered — "Yes." — and — "No." — or at last silenced them with the weight of his eye.

It was no wonder that people, no matter where they reeled and stumbled on that unhappy voyage over the hundred miles from Juneau to Dyea, took care not to lurch against this monster. So he and his dog were left in peace, with a semicircle free before them.

Yet the deck was packed. Bedrolls, dogs, men, baggage of all sorts had been wedged upon the narrow deck; many, both dogs and men, were seasick and lay prostrate, groaning miserably, while the blackness seized their eyes and the whirling took their brains.

There were men of all nations. There were tall, rawboned Scandinavians, cool-eyed Englishmen, sleek Poles with

9

little heads and vast shoulders, Americans, Negroes, Chinese, one tiny Japanese, Frenchmen, Canadians, a Sicilian, smiling wanly in spite of seasickness, and, in a corner, two square-faced Germans, looking as like one another as two peas, for, in fact, they were twin brothers who had come across the world from a little Rhine town to try their fortune in the Northland.

The dogs were as various as the men. It seemed incredible that human beings could be so foolish in their choice of animals for traction in a region of bitter cold. At least half of the total number were short-haired, including a waddling bulldog, strong as a fort but almost as slow, a slender greyhound, whom the first thrust of winter would stab to the vitals, and several mongrels of indefinite breed, their softness of paw, as it were, showing in their eyes. There were other animals that would be of use — a Newfoundland, a whole team of half-breed St. Bernards, some Chesapeake Bay dogs, a little undersize for freighting, but wonderfully tough and enduring. Yet among the long-haired animals there was actually a little Chow and a Spitz hardly able to pull the weight of a real freighter's harness! Someone had brought five goats, that would either pull a sleigh or else would furnish a delightful repast for those with strong jaws. But one felt that the animals on that crowded deck could tell almost as many stories of interest as the men who owned them.

The northwester did not ease away but swung a point higher in the north so as to cuff them back more effectively. It leaped at them more fiercely. The heads of the waves smashed against the deck-housings with thunder and exploded so high in the air that sometimes the tug disappeared and looked like a mere eruption of steam to any eye on shore.

It was only a hundred miles from Juneau to Dyea up the narrow canal, but already they had been laboring bitterly for twenty hours, and they were not yet on the land. To deepen their griefs, snow began to fall, and sleet, while low-riding clouds turned the middle of the day as dark as evening.

Exhaustion, nausea, hunger, the increasing bucking of the ship, gradually had worn down the nerves of man and beast. Half a dozen dog fights were in constant progress, and the weary owners sometimes let the antagonists half fight it out, before they interfered. Men snarled at one another very much as did the dogs, and, if no blows were struck, it was not for the lack of black

11

looks and insulting words.

The waves now became so steep that the captain of the tug altered his course, taking the crests under his port bow and so quartering them. This new motion was more easy, but it had a wild pitch up to the crest and a stagger in the trough that made some of the men collapse on the deck and lie like the dead, with glassy eyes and yellow-green faces.

Some of the dogs felt it more, too, and especially the bulldog. He had kept his composure tolerably well, for a bulldog really is the best natured of animals. Perhaps the reason is that every one of them feels like a rather fat Alexander the Great, and they do not pick fights with others because they are profoundly convinced that they always will win. A bulldog is like a man afraid of the power of his own punch.

This one was a brindled monster who had remained at the side of the seasick Frenchman who owned him until a lurch of the tug sent the knee of the master into the ribs of his honor. The bulldog did not snap. He did not even grunt. But he licked his nose and went in search of trouble.

Through a forest of staggering legs he went. At one side he saw the five goats and regarded them with a momentary interest, but then passed on, scanning canine faces with a grim intentness until in the corner he saw Chinook. That sight pleased every fiber of his mighty body. It made the rolling muscles of his shoulders grow tense with anticipatory delight and his lower jaw thrust out a fraction of an inch, as though already his teeth were lodged and locked in flesh.

A heave of the ship almost made him lose his footing, then he went straight to his mark, without haste. Under the very shadow of the throne, as it were, he paused. The hair along his muscular back rose like bristles. A growl rumbled deeply in him.

At this, Chinook allowed his glance to wander upward toward his master, and his eye crossed that of the man. That was all, and apparently it was all that was needed, for without apparent haste, with inescapable swiftness, the monster slid from his place, his teeth flashed with the sidewise fling of his head, and the brindle bulldog fell to the deck. He did not stir again. He was dead, as though a sure hand had struck him with a sword, and the next sway of the tug skidded the poor fellow limply away into a corner.

Chinook, having delivered the stroke, almost before the enemy fell, had slipped back into his own place, as a gun recoils after shooting, and settled into his former position, with paws crossed and eyes dull. His red tongue licked the still redder drops from his lips, and then all was still.

The Frenchman who owned the dog was informed of the catastrophe by a bystander, but he merely groaned in the throes of sea-sickness. No other man stirred to make comment, except for a big young man with sandy hair, from the farther side of the deck, who rose and came closer. Before the seated owner of Chinook he paused.

"You oughta keep a muzzle on that killer," he said.

Steen looked up with one flash of aston-ishment, but then his eyes grew dull and dark again. He said nothing in reply.

"You hear me?" said the sandy-haired man. "I'm talkin' to you, doctor!"

Steen yawned, but he did not look up a second time.

At this the hand of the stranger swung out, pointing. "Don't you . . . ," he began.

At the movement of his hand, Chinook slid forward again, like dark lightning, his lip curled back from the glitter of his teeth. But the hand of the stranger was not with-drawn, neither did he stir back from the leap of the huge dog. Instead, he turned his eye squarely upon the monster, and the sword

14

slash of Chinook's stroke, a blow that could hamstring a grown moose at one pass, was arrested in mid-air.

Chinook sank back into his corner, slowly, with one red-stained glance at his master to seek for instructions. Yet Steen did not stir.

"Don't you," went on the stranger, "understand that a dog like that could kill another dog as easy as a lion could?"

"Dogs," said Steen at last, "don't interest me much. Dogs and fools!"

He nodded to give his remark point, while the tug heeled suddenly, and the stranger staggered a little. It was a forty percent cant of the deck, yet he steadied himself at once, handling his bulk with wonderful grace and ease. Of this, Andrew Steen took note, and of the long arms that dangled forward, the big hands, widened by labor.

Suddenly, Steen smiled. He waited, expectant, and heard the other saying in perfect calm: "That's for me, is it?"

"It's a thing I've said," answered Steen. "I dunno who it'll fit. I dunno that I care very much. Don't you like the sound of it?"

The stranger laughed. And in the putting back of his head, he showed the great standing chords of his neck, together with a fighting jaw, short and wide at the point.

"My name's Joe Harney," he said. "Who are you?"

"Steen," said the latter.

"Stand up, Steen," said Harney. "Stand up here like a good boy and tell these folks all around that you're a skunk!"

Chapter Two

The Fight

The tug here literally stood upon its nose. The prostrate seasick skidded here and there with groans. Baggage tumbled about, and bedrolls shot from one lodging point to another. But all who had heard the last remark of Harney forgot the reeling of the ship, and forgot their own illness. Even the sick sat up, suddenly, and paid no heed to the whirling of their brains as they fastened their eager attention upon the two big men.

Steen waited until every eye was upon him, then he moved as the great dog had moved before him, rising with swift grace, striking with irresistible might to begin and end the battle with a single blow. The will to break bones was in his hand and in his savage heart, but the sandy head of Harney dropped to the side, the arm shot over his shoulder like the walking beam of a huge engine, and the next instant he was hammering blows against the body of Steen.

It was like hitting a barrel tightly filled and ribbed with massive whalebone. He heard Steen grunt, then upon him fell such a grip as he never had dreamed of. Steen had caught him around the head with a solid lock, and now he pressed the bone of his right forearm along the temple of Harney until darkness and red pain blurred the mind of the younger man.

He struggled. The grip was strong as a vise and held while the ship heeled violently and flung them both across the deck. People scrambled from their path with a cheer. Head over heels they tumbled, and behind them came Chinook, his great fangs bared, ready, as it seemed, to slash Harney to the bone, but withheld from that purpose by a singular barrier, such as that which had prevented him in the first place from attacking the man. Wild with fury and with eagerness to help his master, still he could not make his teeth sink into the flesh of Harney, but like a tawny lion he glided after the two with the taste of battle in his mouth.

Harney, hurtling across the deck with the headlock still clamped upon him, crashed against the side of the deck housing. The shock nearly stunned him, but it left him free to stumble to his feet and see big Steen rising in turn, bewildered, drunk with the blow he had received against the ship's side, and actually staggering with his back turned to his enemy.

"This way!" bellowed Harney. "I've only begun on you, with your strangle holds and all. I'm gonna break your heart, Steen."

The other turned and saw Harney laughing with the pure joy of strife. He saw a blue eye aflame, fierce as the eye of a charging bull, and Steen's brain was cleared by the shock of that sight. He saw Harney rush, strove to side-step, and was crushed to the deck with a mighty left-hander.

He, Steen, was down! In all his days it never had happened to him before. Never in his boyhood and never in his youth or his manhood had another laid him on his back as he was laid now. The punch had landed flush upon his jaw, and the leverage of the bone snapped the shock into his brain. He was numbed by it. Only vaguely he realized that he lay upon his back, and that all those who stood by were yelling with joy over his fall. For he was the stranger, the outlier, the man sufficient unto himself, and, therefore, they hated him. In one glance they felt the darkness of his heart and wished him all evil.

Yet it was no crowd that had pulled him down as a pack of dogs pull down a timber wolf. One man had felled him, and the horror and the mystery of it lifted him to his knee. There he hung for a moment, staring up at Harney, while his head cleared. In the distance, someone was counting like a referee in a ring, swinging one hand up and down and shouting the numbers above the roar of the sea, the labor of the machinery, the confused shouting of the excited watchers.

"Five . . . six . . . seven. . . ."

Yonder was Harney looking flushed with joy, not of the knockdown, but of the battle that had been and the battle that was about to be, and laughing a little with irrepressible glee. There was no malice in the Irish heart of this boy, but Steen, looking up, knew that for once he was matched.

In fierce disdain, he rose and moved at the other with the lurch of the ship behind him. No sudden sally could win this fight, he now knew, but his was no clumsy strength; it was an educated skill, carefully watched, cherished, improved from time to time whenever he could find a man big enough or drunk enough to stand up to him. So he moved in at Harney with gliding steps, feinted for the head with the left, and smashed at the body with the right.

The guard of Harney was lifted by the feint. The right went solidly home upon his ribs, and he felt as though a horse had kicked him. His heart seemed to burst with the terrific pressure. His hands lowered, and, instantly, long, driving punches shot at his head. He rolled the blows off. He could breathe again, and, as he breathed, he stepped in and smote upward, a short punch that was an explosion of nerve energy. It clipped Steen fairly beneath the chin, and Harney stepped back to let the man fall. In all his days that stroke had never failed him. It had been his *coup de grâce* in school, where the wild youngsters of the range wrangled and fought through three winter months each year; it had taken him through the furious brawls of the lumber camps and emptied many a Canuck's hand of the lifted knife; it had been like a shaft of lightning in his defense in the cow camps, at the rodeos. Guns were good, but this was better, quicker, and did not need a coroner's inquest after the blow had been struck.

So he stepped back to see the inevitable fall of Steen. The head of the man jerked back until the neck showed with the skin stretched to bursting. Then it snapped forward, and Steen's knees loosened, wavering beneath his weight, his arms fell — and suddenly he was driving at Harney with hammer strokes of either hand.

No matter how those who watched desired the fall of the dark-faced man, this exhibition of wonderful courage, of still more wonderful animal power, brought out a yell that tore their throats. Harney himself went backward before the storm, amazed, uncertain. The shifts and the tricks learned in a thousand fights saved him, but every blow that glanced from his body or his head might have been the finishing stroke, he knew.

Then beneath his feet the deck pitched like a broncho, flinging him against the side of the housing. It was bad luck, nothing else, but the shock stunned him to a momentary helplessness. In that dreadful moment he heard the shouting of men who yelled: "Steen, Steen, give him time!"

But he saw the great dog, Chinook, standing braced to the heeling of the ship, his red tongue hanging out and his eyes mere slits of fire. As the dog, so the master, he suddenly was sure. Then Steen was at him. Even his half-paralyzed nerves warned him in time to avoid partially the first blow, but the force of the glancing stroke thrust him against the side of the ship again, where an overhand swing hammered on his jaw and slammed his head back against a beam of the housing.

All his body turned to water. Through darkness he slid to the deck, slumping back against the housing, and dreamed in that instant that he was asleep, and that a demon with great grinning white teeth was before him. The horror roused him to see Chinook, whose muzzle was inches from his throat, a muzzle that slavered with terrible desire.

"Six . . . seven . . . ," shouted the voice of the self-appointed timekeeper.

Then shame stood up like a giant in the heart of Harney. He, too, never had been beaten down. Even now he felt that luck had smitten him down more than the hand of Steen.

"Eight . . . nine . . . ," yelled the timekeeper.

Harney lurched upward. He felt sure that his knees would not endure the burden of his weight, but by miracle they sustained him. He dived under a reaching fist that looked to him like a battering-ram capable of crumbling walls of stone, and locked his arms around the body of Steen. Mightily that body writhed and heaved to tear itself away and so deliver the finishing stroke.

They were screaming and grunting and yelling for it now — all these bystanders. They had wanted victory for Harney, at first, to be sure, but now it did not matter, so long as there was a chance to see victory completed, whoever the victor. For it was more than an ordinary fist fight, as the dullest eye could comprehend. Here were two never matched before, two giants made of whalebone, sinew, and India rubber, as it seemed, who delivered such blows as might have crushed the bones of ordinary mortals, but enduring those strokes they still fought on until at last it seemed that the decision must be reached. Sandy-haired Joe Harney must go down, and down surely he must have fallen, as Steen, tearing himself loose at last, poised his fist for the finishing stroke. For that stroke the crowd yelled with a savage joy.

Then fate acted, as it seemed. The tug had been bucking the waves like a tough-headed bull all the hundred miles from Juneau, but now a flat-sided monster pitched up before her so suddenly that the steersman could not swerve to meet it. It roared against the stout little ship, and with its massive head smashed the housing on the port bow just behind the two fighters.

There was a splintering of timbers, a rush of ice-cold water, and instantly the whole forward end of the ship was a mass of tumbling men, dogs, baggage, and scrambling goats. In that whirlpool, down went both the champions. The savage shouting of the spectators turned into groans, yelps of fear. There was a snarling of dogs, a noisy cursing of men as the wave gushed back along the decks until it struck a bulkhead. From that it recoiled in great part, and with the downward heave of the ship, it plunged back toward the hole from which it came. Men and dogs had scampered to the sides of the deck, away from this menace, so that the leap of water caught nothing more important than baggage, which it whirled along in its rush.

Harney, still half dazed, watched it lunge down the deck. Then he saw that one large object tumbled in the wave that was not baggage, but the form of a man, a tall, massive form. . . .

Now Chinook leaped into the water and set his teeth in the coat of his master, for it was Steen who lay there. In his fall he must have been stunned, and now he lay there like a sack, borne helplessly along in the rush of the water. Even the weight and the braced feet of Chinook could not hold him, and straight toward the gaping hole he tumbled. Outside of it were the angry hands of the sea, from which he never could be recovered.

Chapter Three

Mush!

Now every spot of face, head, and body where the blows of Steen had fallen cried out to Harney to let the man go. If one had to be taken, surely there could not be found a man more worthy to go than this somber-eyed fellow. But the next instant, Harney was rushing forward. He felt the grip of the water tugging at his knees. At the same moment the force of the wave tore the cloth from the teeth of Chinook, and the great dog instinctively leaped aside to keep from being carried overboard.

Just before them was the raw-edged hole, the wind screaming through it, the wild face of ocean beyond, as Harney leaned and secured a grip inside the collar of Steen's coat. With his free hand and right leg he grasped a beam at the side of the aperture, then Steen slid through with the recoiling wave, and all that burden of the huge body, the heavy clothes and boots, the gun belted at his thigh, dropped with a jerk. The wrench of it threatened to snap the shoulder sinews. His finger slipped, grinding away the skin of the tips, but then they held again, while electric currents of pain sprang into the brain of Harney and seared it. He strove to lift that mass. But he was powerless for the moment.

The tug lifted on a crest, then dropped with a crash into the trough, while a blinding, stinging shower of spray smothered and whipped the rescuer. However, the lift of the water along the side of the boat half floated the dead weight of the senseless man, and Harney could drag it up to the edge of the gap.

More he could not have done with one hand, but Chinook was there, growling terribly deep in his throat, and instantly his teeth were in the shoulder of his master's coat. With all the might of his great body he dragged back. Suddenly it was an easy thing to lift the bulk of Steen and draw him to safety through the hole, then, staggering, to pull him far to the side of the deck. There were plenty to help, then.

Harney retired to hunt for his own baggage in the piles that were scattered here and there about the deck, while others revived Steen. His baggage he found luckily. There were others raving and raging because of their losses, but even these were quickly forgotten now.

Suddenly the water had grown calm.

Through the hole in the housing they could see floating pieces of ice, then a beach, and a wretched cluster of houses a mile away. That was Dyea, now dim behind the flutter of falling snow. A miserable gate, but one to a promised land that made all the miseries of the trip north seem as nothing, or the money that had been spent, or the bitter weather and hardships that lay ahead. Somewhere in this Northland there was gold, and for that gold they must venture everything.

The fight, the rescue, the recovery of big Steen were as nothing. For now the tug anchored; a lighter was pulled alongside, everything piled aboard it, and the smaller boat was warped inshore. In the crowd of men and baggage on the lighter was Steen, among the rest. Although he now seemed perfectly recovered, except for a bandage around his head, he paid no attention to Harney. Not a word, not a glance was given by the big fellow to those around him, but all his attention was concentrated forward on that bleak coast.

He could not fail, it seemed to Harney. If there were treasures in the Yukon, Steen would find them and bring back in his mighty hands enough for the building of palaces. Yet there was no light in the face of the man as he stared toward the land. The same cynical or indifferent gloom continually possessed him, even when the lighter moored at the wharf before the trading post and they actually stood upon the Northland, that thing which had been a dream.

Harney had no time to regard the big fellow any longer. He was busy as most of the others were in preparing his sled, spreading the canvas sheet, then heaping the load upon it, keeping his eye out to see how others were doing, for this was a strange country and a strange set of conditions to him.

A shadow fell upon him as he finished piling on the last article.

"Peel it all off!" said a deep voice behind him.

He looked up and saw Steen, with the great Chinook at heel.

Harney did not pause to question, he obeyed, and at once Steen commenced rebuilding the pack.

He made only one remark: "You wanta keep the heaviest part a third from the front end. The dogs can give it a better lift, that way. So can you in the straps." So he said, weaving the long lashropes from either end across and across the load.

Harney stood by with silent attention.

"You're a chechako. You don't know this game?"

"I'm green at it," admitted Harney.

"Dogs?"

"No."

"Money to buy 'em?"

He waved his hand at some Indians who had come out of the shacks near the Heron & Wilson trading post; every one of them had a dog of some sort with him, sometimes more than one. They were animals of all sorts and sizes, mostly starvation poor, but the chechakos who had just arrived were buying them up at any price.

"No money to buy anything," said Harney cheerfully.

"Then pull your sled over behind mine," commanded Steen, pointing, and he walked away.

Obediently, Harney drew his sled behind the one that had been designated, and waited there, while Steen greeted a half-breed coming up with a string of six dogs. They were big malemutes of the right husky kind — thick shouldered, with plenty of bone and the treacherous eyes of wolves.

"You grease-eating, flat-faced pup," said Steen calmly to the man, "you've starved my dogs. I've more than half a mind to break your head."

The other broke into an excited harangue. He had fed the dogs every day. But, mysteriously, they would not stay fat. A curse must have been put upon them. They had been bewitched.

"I left you money to feed them," said Steen. "You gambled it away. Don't try to lie to me! Here. Help me hitch them up."

The other began to work at once, as though eager to undo his original fault. Harney saw the harnesses arranged with speed. There were little leather collars, somewhat like horse collars, though lighter in every way, and without hames. To the collars the traces were directly fastened, being held in place by a back and belly band, the traces running on past the dog to the rear and fastening a little behind his hips. Five dogs were arranged in a string in this fashion, the traces of the last one fastening to a small whiffletree at the front of the sled. But the sixth, or sled dog, was independently fastened to the same whiffletree, for reasons which Harney was to learn.

It was a good team, all in all, and much the most complete of any that appeared upon the beach that day, for the others were apt to be "outside" dogs with little chance of weathering even a single trip to the Yukon, and many men, like Harney, had no dogs at all. They were already tugging away at their straps and hauling the heavy sleds through the thin, slushy snow along the beach. There most of them picked out a place to camp, preparatory for the long journey into the interior.

"If you come with me," said Steen to Harney, "you start now. I'm making time."

"I'm ready to start," answered Harney, a little dubiously, for he was not sure that he wished to be alone with Steen for an entire trip. "But if you're after time . . . well, that's a heavy sled."

"That team," said Steen, "could pull two more sleds the like of these. Lash your front tie-rope onto the end of my sled. Here, I'll show you the way to do it." He finished the work in a moment. Then he stood back and surveyed his outfit. "You want Circle City, I guess?" he said.

"Yes. I'm headed that way."

"We'll make the whole trip together, then," said Steen. "That is, if you're a man that'll work your share. Otherwise, I finish, and you can get on by hand and foot."

"I've never backed down from a job yet," answered Harney.

"You never have yet?" asked Steen, surveying the other with a gloomy eye. "You don't know what work is. Nobody does that ain't been up here." Then he turned to the team. "Hai!" he called. "Mush!"

Chinook stiffened his traces in the lead, but the other members of the team were demoralized by long idleness, perhaps depressed by poor feeding. At any rate, not one of them leaned into its collar.

"They've gone soft," commented Steen. "They've softened up. The paws, too!" He leaned and felt the pads of a wincing wolf dog. Then he stepped back and cracked his long dog whip. "Hai, mush! Mush on you!"

Chinook struck his collar with the force of a horse, then turned his head and glanced back at the disordered team.

"He'll police 'em," commented Steen under his breath.

Chinook did not wait for instruction. He whirled in a short circle and fell upon the third dog behind him, that had lain down unconcernedly in the snow. The danger was seen before it struck, but there was no escape for the wretched malemute. The teeth of Chinook flashed, and he turned back to his position, licking blood from his lips.

"Now you'll see a change," said Steen.

He called once more, and this time every dog of the seven moved together. The sled runners grated a little against the snow, then both sleds started onward together.

Still, Harney walked with his eye turned back. For he felt that it was neither right nor safe for him to accompany one who had been an enemy, and who seemed capable of any act of violence. Yet he told himself that this was too much of a blessing to be dreamed of, this opportunity to have dogs pull in his supplies. He had heard enough of the dreary slowness of the hand-pulled sled in Alaska.

So he faced forward, and started up the bank of the Dyea River with the sense that one life was dead behind him, and a new one was about to begin. But had he been able to guess some of its phases, he would have turned about at that moment and asked for passage back upon the tug.

Chapter Four

Driver Down, Dog Up!

Children at the door of fairyland could not have been more eager, more expectant, more frightened than were the men on the beach as the long train of dogs and sleds went past them. Harney never could forget the picture of one bald-headed man of fifty, his hat in his hand, looking out to sea against the bitterness of the wind with the expression of one who dreamed and knew not why he was there. He saw youngsters, laughing at the cold, at the pressure of the wind, at the misfortunes and accidents that happened to themselves and to others. He saw grim-faced men making methodical preparations for their camp, and others walking idly around, observing the workers, great contentment on their faces, as though already they were millionaires.

Then, floundering somewhat on his snowshoes, for he was unfamiliar with them, he looked ahead at the tall form of Steen, breaking trail through the soft surface snow for the team. There was something about the set of the man's head and the swing of his shoulders that made Harney think of incalculable perils and difficulties ahead. He had Steen to take him through. But what of those others back there on the beach, so recklessly confident?

He shrugged his wide shoulders and settled down to the serious work of mastering the art of snowshoeing, studying carefully the manner in which Steen raised his feet and put them down again.

They were passing up the side of the Dyea River now, a narrow stretch of level ground on each bank, beyond which great rocky mountains sprang up, skirted with timber about their feet. So for a few easy miles they went, and then found the first great difficulties before them.

The mountain wall split and through the split came the Dyea River, roaring in cascades. But above it, many feet in some places, was a sheeting of ice, formed at a time of much higher water. The sun, the occasional dashing of the water, thawed and broke out the ice in places, so that only here and there was it stretched in a solid sheet from wall to wall, and the sled had to be dragged close to the rocks, with the ice sometimes trembling and groaning beneath its weight.

With snowshoes off now, it needed the

full force of both strong men, and all the labors of Chinook and his teammates to bring the load up the rough steps of ice until, at last, the cañon turned into a deep hollow, Sheep Camp, surrounded by a circle of lofty mountains that presented an unbroken wall, except for a single deep notch, famous over the world by the name of the Chilkoot Pass.

It was easier going, descending into Sheep Camp, so named from the hunters of the mountain sheep who camped there. But many others had temporary camps at the same place. From Dyea men came with a hundred or a hundred and fifty pounds, cached it here, and returned to the beach to get another installment of their stores. So the entire weight eventually was collected, and the passage of the Chilkoot was begun, a rise so steep that it looked to Harney, when he first saw it, like a sheer face of snow.

Even now it was stretched from top to bottom with dark spots of men and animals climbing up the precipitous trail from the bottom, or perhaps descending again to get another portion of their pack and carry it up. At the foot of the pass, a well-discernible trail led to the camp itself, a wretched scattering of tents, lean-tos, and shacks toward the center of the valley floor. Even from this distance, never had Harney observed a scene of such confusion. A house on moving day would have been orderly in comparison. It was more like a cattle stampede, or a battlefield. Men were flinging headlong north, and suddenly he threw up his hands and shouted.

Steen looked back.

"Only glad that I'm here, that's all," said Harney. "Let's get on! Can we climb up the trail tonight?"

Steen turned and smiled a little. "It's five miles from that camp to the trail, and Chilkoot is twelve hundred feet high," he said. "You can make up your mind for yourself, partner!"

He spoke in a manner more affable than that which he had used at any other time during their acquaintance, so that a slight outpouring of emotion occurred in Harney, and he wondered if, after all, he and this dark-faced giant were destined to become good friends. Stranger things had happened in the world.

Steen had stopped where the down slope began. Therefore, it was easy to start the sled on, and they went at a good pace downward, with big Steen now straddling the tug rope and bearing back with a good deal of weight upon the gee pole when the slope of the descent became too great and the sled threatened to slide forward upon the dogs.

It seemed a position of great danger to Harney who watched with a scowl, wondering when the same sort of work might be demanded of him. For, at any instant, the sled might heel on a patch of glassy snow and shoot forward impelled by a lurch of the team, and, if the feet of the driver were knocked from under him, he might well go down in a common ruin of sleds and entangled, fighting dogs. He grimaced as he thought of this, but then concentrated on studying the skillful methods of Steen as he worked the team down the slippery and treacherous grade.

The snowshoes, too, gave Harney infinite difficulty, for sometimes the snow surface was soft, and now and again it was harshly crusted over with stiff ice on which the shoes skidded wildly. Twice he tumbled head over heels. But these matters were nothing to a champion rough-and-tumble fighter. He came to the bottom of the slope with reddened face and smiling lips, delighted with this Northland and its rough ways.

At the bottom, Steen stopped the team again and looked back once more to his companion. "Did you watch that?" he asked.

"Yeah. I watched it."

"You'll take the easy little slope that we come to, Harney. So keep your eyes open. Hello!"

He pointed back, and Harney turned as well. Down the slope above them, and following closely on the trail they had followed, came another team of six dogs with a single sled behind it, the driver like Steen straddling the tug rope, and handling the gee pole. Three of the dogs had been unsnapped and tethered behind the sled, and the remaining three were bringing it down at a sufficiently smart clip. In fact, it lurched at times over iced places at a rate that made the feet of the driver twinkle to keep from being run down.

"Hello!" said Steen again, coming back to Harney. "Look at that second dog."

"He's a hard worker," said Harney.

For the dog was always tugging straight ahead, his tongue lolled out. Even in the distance he seemed fighting to get quickly to the end of the trail.

"He's a hard worker," repeated Steen. "Yeah. He's mad, I guess."

"Mad?" said Harney.

"He looks it. When they pull straight away, like a whip was over 'em all the time, pawing at the snow to get ahead, then mostly they're mad, you can take it."

"Look here," said Harney. "A mad dog . . . why, when they bite you. . . ."

"Not up here. Never heard of a man getting hydrophobia from the bite of a mad dog."

"But a mad dog that would be apt to turn loose and slash you any minute would. . . ."

"I've heard of a gent havin' his throat cut by one of 'em," replied Steen carelessly. "But mostly they're free workers, and you're glad to have 'em in the team."

"Not even muzzled?"

"When they get pretty bad, you can muzzle 'em, but they don't breathe as good with a muzzle over 'em. There's something queer about that outfit," he added, a moment later.

"How come?"

"That's an old-timer," said Steen. "That sled's loaded the way that it should be, and he knows how to drive, too. But they's something wrong."

"I don't see where, except that he's coming pretty fast."

"Too fast. He's light. He's mighty light. He's as light as a kid," said Steen.

"He's small enough to be a boy," remarked Harney.

"He's small enough to be a boy," agreed Steen. "But who'd trust a kid with a sled and a load and six dogs even this far toward Chilkoot?"

The sled now struck the last sharp descent, veering off toward the left from the trail that Steen had followed.

"Light! Mighty light," said Steen again. "No force on the gee pole."

Down skidded the sled, with the undersized driver bracing his legs against the drive of the weight behind him. So he came safely to the bottom of the slope, where the dog that Steen had called mad, finding that the teammate before him had come within range, instantly sank tooth in him. The leader whirled around. The sled dog was involved. All three became a whirling tangle of raging, snarling brutes.

Harney, with an exclamation, started to give help.

"Stay where you are!" snarled Steen. "If he's gonna work a mad dog, let's see if he knows his business. It ain't our fault . . . it's his own, if he's in trouble."

Harney submitted reluctantly, not that he felt Steen was morally right, but, as a new man in a new world, he thought that he should in all matters obey the dictates of the veterans. So he drew back, gloomily, and watched the other driver work.

The latter went swiftly about his task in a business-like manner. With the heavy butt of his whip he beat off the leader and the sled dog. The brute that Steen had called mad, however, cowered an instant with belly to snow, then leaped with a flash of teeth.

"He's got it!" said Steen with a voice of infinite satisfaction.

The dog struck — the arm of the driver receiving the blow, as it seemed to Harney — yet the man neither shouted, nor cursed, nor swung the bludgeon of the whip handle on the dangerous brute. Instead, he received the stroke without moving.

"He knows his business!" exclaimed Steen in admiration. "That's the only way. If you make a fast move when they go for you, they're apt to tear you to bits, and they've got the jaw power to do it. He's an old sourdough. Maybe withered up, maybe seventy. But he knows this part of the world, all right!"

The driver was now methodically straightening out the tangled dog harness, the excited animal standing patiently, with lolling tongue, when without warning he turned and struck again. The driver went down, and the beast was instantly on top!

Chapter Five

Kate Winslow

What that meant, Harney could conceive by a glance at the big leader that worked for Steen. For the entire team, which the other traveler was handling, seemed to be composed of Mackenzie huskies — huge, brawny, with the bite of a wolf, and the weight of a full-grown man. One rip would be enough to open a man's throat from ear to ear. Suppose that Chinook, for instance, were to get down any man, no matter how formidable, to say nothing of a frantic brute in the grip of a convulsion.

He reached for his revolver instantly, watching with fascinated eyes as the stranger thrust the whip handle into the mouth of the big dog, then, in the struggle, dog and driver tumbled head over heels. He could not risk a shot at that distance, so he ran forward, with Steen close behind him, now no longer protesting against interference, only exclaiming as he went: "He knows his business! Cool fellow, that driver! Never seen a cooler! Why don't he knife the brute, or sink a chunk of lead into him?"

He might not have a gun, however. So they reached the confusion of man and dog and whirling snow with Harney a step in the lead. He saw the driver down again, still beating the whip handle into the gaping mouth of the dog. A small man, a youth, almost a child. It struck him with amazement. For the face was pink and white, big, dark eyes stared up at the furious mask of the wolf dog, and about the mouth and chin there was that delicacy which appears in the face of a woman, or a young child. Even inside the thick mittens the hand of the stranger was absurdly small.

These things he saw with keen eyes as he came up. Perhaps it was the sense of difference between his own mighty hands and those of the fallen driver that made him drop his revolver into the snow and lunge at the husky with no better weapon than his fingers. That was a famous grip, however. In more than one camp, before fame cramped his style, he had won fat wagers by tearing packs of cards. All the confidence that others felt in the power of their shoulders, their hips, was placed by Harney in his iron grasp.

The weight of his lunge knocked the slavering husky upside down, then, as it sprang up at him, the thumbs of his hands crunched down into the windpipe. It was like holding a maniac. The red tongue lolled out. The white teeth, like curved, deadly knives, gnashed at his arms and tore the fur. The froth flew. But, above all, the eyes were terrible, red-stained, frightful, with the greed to kill.

For half a minute, Harney struggled as he never had struggled before, except when in the vast arms of Steen. It was not only a matter of controlling the head of the beast, but the legs were beating up against him savagely. But the convulsion passed as the throttling continued. The red tongue grew purplish. The mask of the dog swelled with congested blood. Suddenly he was still.

"One more ten seconds and he'll go where all good dogs go, stranger," said Harney. "Do you want me to keep my grip?"

"Oh, poor boy," said the gentle, panting voice of a woman beside him.

He turned his head in amazement. Slight, indeed, for a man. Light, as Steen well had said, even for a youth. But it was a woman who was encased in the thick parka!

Remembering that expert steering of the sled, that coolness in battling with the great dog, Harney was overwhelmed. Gaping, he watched her stroke the head of the quivering brute.

"Poor boy," she said. "So good, so strong, and such a worker. How can I bear to see him die? No, no. Let him go, please!"

Harney raised bewildered eyes to the face of Steen. But that dark man's eye was entirely occupied in brooding with a sort of bitter contempt upon the face of the girl. His nostrils flared and his lip was curled as Harney had seen him look at that moment when he was flattened against the housing of the deck, helpless before the rush of the mighty Steen.

There was no word to be had from Steen, and, therefore, Harney relaxed his grip, slowly, and straightened. He found that his knees shook a little beneath his weight, and sagged still more when he found his revolver and stooped to pick it up. There had been more shock in this brief horror than he had imagined.

He heard Steen say, in a voice that sounded far away: "That's it. You better keep that on him now."

She had fastened a muzzle around the head and face of the dog that had rolled over on its belly and was beginning to draw rasping breaths once more.

Then she stood up and regarded the animal critically. "I've only two better ones," she said.

Steen said, as harshly as before: "He ought to last you up the Chilkoot, all right."

"He'll be worthwhile for a couple of days on the other side, too," she suggested. "I give him three more days, maybe."

"Did he draw blood when he knifed you?"

She touched her arm. "Just a bit. Hardly worth a bandage, I suppose."

"All right," said Steen. "Is it the real Alaska hydrophobia?"

"I suppose so," she answered. "He's been out, but he's an inside dog."

She was as calm as ice, discussing this matter which meant for her life, or a horrible death, frenzy, convulsions. Then she took the three dogs from behind the sled and fastened them in their places in front. The leader was a specially fine fellow, almost as huge as Chinook, black as night, and stockinged all around with white which made his feet seem to disappear into the snow.

"That's a dog," commented Steen.

"He's a dog," she agreed, "in spots. But there's a lot of wolf in him, too. If it comes to a short pinch on grubstakes, he's as likely to eat me as I am to eat him."

At this grim jest of her own, she tilted back her head in the parka and laughed musically, while the blood of Harney was flecked with cold.

She mystified him completely. Certainly she was not a man, yet she was different from any woman he ever had met or conceived of meeting.

She came to him now and stood before him with an eye as straight and level as any man's. She could hardly be more than four or five inches above five feet, so that Harney towered a foot above her, and she had to tilt back her head to look up at him. Yet almost at once he ceased to be conscious of her size, of her delicate beauty, of everything except the straightness of those fearless eyes, and the calm voice, rather husky and low pitched.

"My arms were getting pretty tired," she said to him. "In another second he would have had me, so I want to thank you, partly for my own sake and partly for the husky. I don't suppose there's another man in Alaska that would have used his hands for that job . . . the rest would have whanged him over the head or sunk a bullet through him." She glanced down and laughed again. "But there aren't many others that have your hands, are there?"

Harney looked down at them, where they dangled stupidly. He could not find a word to answer.

"My name is Kate Winslow," she said,

and held out her hand that he accepted with a mutter that he was called Harney.

"And your big friend?"

"He's Steen."

She shook hands with Steen also, a light touch almost lost in the muffling of the mitten.

"You're going clear in?" asked Steen.

"Circle City, I suppose," she said.

Harney stared at Steen as though he might find the answer in the face of his companion, but Steen looked at nothing but the girl, steadily, grimly as before.

"You'll get there," he said. "You're light enough to skim the surface where we'd break through."

"I'll get there, I think," she said. "I hope so, anyway. Are you bound the same way?"

"The same trail."

"I'll be seeing you later, then," she stated, and, with that, she waved to them and turned back to her team.

A word from her sent them lunging into their collars, the muzzled dog scratching furiously to get a better grip upon the snow. And so the sled started with popping noises of the snow that had begun to freeze to the runners, and presently was sliding forward at a seven-mile clip, the girl running lightly beside them with her hand upon the gee pole.

"Well?" asked Harney, turning suddenly back on Steen.

But Steen was staring fixedly after the girl, his face darkened by a scowl.

"What would you say?" insisted Harney. "Nineteen? Twenty? Twenty-one?"

Steen turned his back with a shrug and started on for the sled.

"I dunno that this is a very lucky day," was all he would say, and it was an answer that threw the simple mind of Harney into confusion again, striving to get at the bottom of the other's thought.

That, however, was a dark well into which he could not look deeply, for the shadows formed too thickly in front of his eyes, and what it was that went on at the bottom of Steen's soul he could not even remotely guess. He was inclined to make all dark and grim about his conceptions of this strange fellow, and, yet again, he thought that Steen was perhaps redeemed by small touches of kindness and friendship with which their relations had been softened.

He looked up from these thoughts, suddenly startled by the white mountains about him. They rushed into his mind like a thing unseen before. All was new. A new world, a new condition, a new people, where one found such men as Steen, such women as Kate Winslow.

Sheep Camp was closer. He could hear the voices coming clearly through the cold air, and yet beneath this variety of sounds it seemed to Harney that he could distinguish an uncertain murmur, like the groaning of a man in pain who never drew breath in his agony of complaint. This was a startling suggestion that immediately disappeared from his hearing at least, though it remained engraved in his mind during all his stay in the white North. It was such a sound as one hears from the wind on a winter night. He could not help but feel that it was a prophecy.

Chapter Six

Trails to Tagish

Promptly the next morning they broke camp and began the labor of carrying their packs up the side of the Chilkoot. Fifty pounds was a load for many a man in making that climb a quarter of a mile into the air, on steps cut in the hard snow, but Harney and his partner, like pack horses, took up vast loads, humped on their backs.

To Steen, no work was good, except hard work, swiftly and heavily undertaken. Therefore, he labored as three men now, as always. But to Harney there was an added incentive in toiling up the slope in that he wished with a curious desire to find again Kate Winslow. But she had gone on. The very afternoon of her arrival at Sheep Camp she had hired men to carry her outfit to the top of the pass, and had gone skidding down to Crater Lake beyond. Near there she must have camped in the dusk of the day, alone, with the wind whooping and screaming around her.

Alone in this country! It seemed to Harney, as he examined his thoughts about her, that he was not led on by any romantic emotion concerning her, but rather that he was impelled by sheer curiosity, as at some strange phenomenon by which scientists would be intrigued. The mad dog was still with her. The other five were as wild as wolves, except that great black leader. Even he, perhaps, had more beauty and intelligence than gentleness. But there she was over the rim of the pass, committed to the great white North, with only her small hands to wrestle with problems that had beaten many a strong man to the ground.

Bowed beneath his pack, as he labored up the slope of the Chilkoot, he named these things to himself, and then remembered what Steen had said. She was light enough to skim over surface through which men would break. There seemed a mysterious significance to this. And he named all that he had seen and heard of her, quietly, feature by feature, to himself. He saw again her delicacy, her strangely impersonal beauty, the straightness of her look, her courage, like the courage of more than a man. It was that, he told himself, which made the vast difference. In other women, one felt femininity, but she was like a detached spirit, gazing at danger and estimating it with the uttermost calm.

It came to him, as he remembered, that there had been no tremor in her after she had escaped from the great husky, but rather she had been as one who has seen something upon a stage on which she did not step. Her voice had been steady as she talked to him. She had seemed to pity, in a way, the dog that nearly had killed her an instant before.

Yet there was something more than masculine cruelty in her attitude. There were three more days of work to be squeezed from the sick dog, and the three days she would have without fail, if they could be gained. After that, she would stand aside and shoot the brute, then slowly, laboriously, drag him from his place in the team, and leave his bulk to be covered by the snow, or devoured by the prowling wolves. Even his own heart, nerved by many encounters and stiff with strength, recoiled from such cold-blooded calculation. Yet he felt that it was redeemed by her bravery.

Had they not been near, she must have died, killed by a dog. Aye, perhaps devoured by the hungry team! Yet this chance did not daunt her, and she went cheerfully on across the Chilkoot, where her trail must be followed in loneliness.

She was all contrast, all contradiction.

There was the most fragile beauty, and that delicate contour of lips and chin, like those of a child. But, in addition, there was the straight look, the impersonal and detached air. Even for her very life, she had thanked him as another girl might have thanked him for a pleasant lunch or a gay ride.

So he toiled upward on the Chilkoot, wondering when they might overtake her trail, if ever. And stood at last on the summit, regardless of the cold inland wind that cut at him, and staring down across Crater Lake at the indefinite beyond. There lay gold, there lay the hopes of the hundreds of thousands, who were crowding behind him and before, but it seemed to Harney that there was nothing of importance, really, except this girl and the solution of her personality.

The climbing of the Chilkoot was a small thing, part of a dream. At last they were over. They had made the roller-coaster voyage down to Crater Lake, they had embarked for the inland. Day by day, he learned important details. He learned how to make camp, how, above all, to cook. He learned how to make bread by scooping a hole and building a fire in it, while sourdough was allowed to rise between two gold pans. Then, ashes and dirt were taken out, the pans inserted, then covered with the heated ashes and sand. In an hour or so one could produce in this manner bread, covered with a thick, golden crust. He learned how to cut lean meat into thin strips and how to dry them on a rack with a smoky fire burning to keep the flies away. When the meat was jerked, it was black, hard as board, but wonderfully nourishing for its weight and capable of being carried in the pocket like crackers. So he learned the ways of the Northland from Steen, learned more by demonstration than by words, for a day would go by and Steen would never speak.

They were bending on toward Lake Tagish, where they would begin the navigation of the Yukon — quickly, if they could buy a boat, after some weeks if they had to whipsaw one out of round logs, building out of green timber as heavy as lead, as cranky as a sick ship with which to tempt the rapids beyond the lakes.

These things Steen had explained, and Harney braced himself to meet the struggle ahead. Now and again, they passed other people on the trail, for all the teams seemed to go more slowly than their own, struggling forward courageously through the snow, but falling constantly behind the pace as the malemutes and big Chinook ate up the miles.

Chinook was not a dog. He was a human being, full of wiles, full of courage and wisdom. The rest of the team, all new to him, he soon subdued, and there was not a husky, no matter how powerful, that did not shrink when the eyes of the leader fell upon him. Not one that had not tasted the tooth of the leader before the trail was two days old.

Steen the great dog obeyed, but Harney seemed to be a perpetual problem to him. He would spend hours lying at the feet of Harney, looking up into his face with the fixed stare that only a dog knows how to use, letting his glance waver away the instant the eye of the man fell upon him, but bringing it back the next moment once more to resurvey the stranger. One would have thought that Harney was a new landscape, never learned, that his face was an unmapped world, to see the fashion in which the dog was never tired of perusing him, feature by feature.

It was his way to lie at a little distance and then begin to wriggle closer and closer, snake-like, catching instants when the eye of the man was not upon him. Until, at last, he lay just under the feet of Harney and looked earnestly up into his face, as though asking a question to which he never could gain a complete answer.

When the team was unhitched, the big fellow used to wander behind Harney, stealing along through the woods and prowling after the man as though he were game to be stalked and surprised. If Harney turned, the wolf dog leaped behind a tree, timorous as though a rifle had been pointed at him. If he went straight forward, Chinook gradually consumed the distance behind and came up until his muzzle was at the lifting heels of Harney.

Apparently, he was studying this stranger as a child would study a new book. When Harney spoke, it was a familiar sight to see the leader jump up and stand with one forefoot poised, as though ready either for flight or to attack.

"He's afraid of you," said Steen in explanation. "And that makes him want to cut your throat. Watch yourself at night, Harney, or he'll sneak up and do the job for you, I say."

Harney could believe it. For the courage and the strength and the ferocity of Chinook were things to see, but hardly to believe. Not as a dog he prowled through the woods, but as a wolf, a wild beast of prey. It was a thing that could keep Harney employed for minutes at a time, to slip behind a

tree and from the edge of it view the pro-
ceedings of Chinook, prowling through the
wilderness, soft as a fox and terrible as a
lion.

It was an object lesson to see the big
fellow glide over the snow with no more
sound than the pressure of down upon the
crystals, to see him drift among the
shadows, silently as the shadows themselves, creeping from tree to tree upon the
trail of the man who himself was hunting
Chinook.

They had many a silent and rather horrible laugh at this sport, the man springing
out behind the dog and shouting, while Chinook spun about, teeth bared and ready for
a stroke. Or, again, Chinook would spring
suddenly into the path of Harney,
crouched, prepared to leap, with malicious
pleasure glistening in his eyes as he surprised the man and made him stumble
backward.

This grim game went on constantly between them. Sometimes it seemed to
Harney that the dog waited merely for a
good opportunity to flesh his fangs in him;
sometimes he thought that the big leader
really enjoyed the play as a game. But he
never could be sure, and, whenever Chinook was near, he had a hand ready for a

weapon and a sudden blow.

There was a similarity, he was sure, between the master and the dog. There was the same silence, the same craft, the same great size and silken grace. First of all, he had noticed it on the tug, but now it was confirmed in his mind over and over again as he watched the ways of the two from day to day.

They had a subtle means of communication also, as it seemed. A flick of the master's eye was enough to make the wolf dog move with hesitation, and then with a leap. A wave of the hand was as good as a spoken sentence. And Harney was soon familiar with the sight of Chinook rushing away with his head thrown over his shoulder, looking back for the last directions from the eye of the man. There was no other animal like the great leader; equally so, there was no other man like Steen, who ruled the dog from a distance by the sheer weight of his eye.

So they labored on through the wilderness of darkness of forest and whiteness of snow, until they came to a near distance from Lake Tagish. And, on that day, it happened that they were talking together about Kate.

"There seem," said Harney, "to be as many trails to Tagish as there is hairs to your head. But, still, I wouldn't be a lot sur-prised if we found Kate Winslow again on the way."

To which Steen answered with an upward throwing of his head that was a character-istic gesture of pride and disdain: "I hope we never lay eyes on her again. There's no luck in her, Harney. No luck in her for us."

Chapter Seven

A Pretty Job

They twice passed stragglers, in each instance men who were bowed against the harness straps, pulling their own sled without the help of dogs. These they dropped behind them at several miles an hour, pursued by envious glances, for the team was growing stronger and faster every day, their blood enriched by the game they devoured. For a number of times the rifles of the men were successful.

So they came on a sound of rifles one day, the noise of explosions coming with a peculiar loudness across the snows. There was no wind. Voices welled up as though through water when they halted the sled and spoke of the shots they were hearing.

"Somebody's shooting at a target," said Harney.

"Then the target's shooting back," answered Steen.

Harney listened. It was true that there was a difference in the explosions, some seeming farther away, and one gun speaking nearer.

"We'll go take a look," suggested Harney.

"Why?" said Steen. "Any business that has to be talked over with guns is private business. I ain't an eavesdropper."

"It sounds like half a dozen against one," said Harney.

"Fifty to one, maybe. What do we care? They don't bother us on our trail."

"Look at Chinook," said Harney. "He votes with me."

Chinook had swung toward the side and was pricking his ears at the noise of firing.

"You keep on along the trail," suggested Harney, picking up his rifle. "I'll sashay over yonder and see what's what."

"I don't like it," confessed big Steen, "but if you want to go, I'll have to go with you."

He called to the team, jerked on the gee pole, and they were off up a slight slope that continued gently climbing on their right. For a half hour they continued in this manner, the dogs tugging steadily in their collars, with a light creaking of the traces, while all the noise had ended before them. Then it began again, under their very noses, as it were.

They halted the team at the top of the rise. Below them was a hill face turned fairly to the north, all its front encased with ice that glittered like glass in the morning light.

From a nook in its central base a solitary marksman fired from time to time and was answered by the rifles of half a dozen men scattered in a semicircle among some low hummocks. The six were plainly in view; the quarry, however, was hidden from sight behind a heap of stones that had fallen to the foot of the hill.

"Six to one," said Harney. "The dogs!"

"They may be wolves, not dogs," said Steen, nevertheless, picking up his rifle. "We'll see how they like the game." And grasping his gun he fired into the air.

The answer was an instant bustling among the six. They rose and skulked with great speed off to the left, one behind the other, in a close file, running low and dodging from side to side as though they expected that the two might draw a bead of them at any moment.

"Indians," said Steen.

"How can you tell?"

"By the way they run, by the way they use their snowshoes. They've got some other red-skinned murderer holed up there, and now they'll never forget their grudge ag'in' us for spoiling their little party. Well, we'll go in and see what he looks like." He went on, accordingly.

They left the dog team behind them on

65

the top of the rise and went down, rifles in readiness, and rounded the heap of rocks at the bottom of the icy cliff.

There they saw three dogs dead on the ice, three more lying crouched close against the rocks, and one of these was the big black-and-white leader of Kate Winslow. She herself was busy drawing taut the lashing on her sled. She paused to welcome them.

"Thanks for dropping by," she said. "They got three out of seven, and I suppose they soon would have mopped me up. I was getting ready a small pack. I intended to make a break as soon as it got to be dusk, but you've saved me the trouble of that."

"What started these Indians after you?" asked Steen.

"I don't know. They were hungry, I guess. They rushed me on the trail, just after I'd started moving this morning, but I managed to get away."

"You got away? When they rushed you?" asked Steen.

"There were eight of 'em," she nodded at him. "I let out a whoop and whanged a couple with this." She pulled out a .32 revolver, small, nickel plated, but with the handle fitted neatly to her hand.

"You killed two out of the eight and got away?"

"Oh, no, I didn't kill 'em! One got it through the leg, and the other was scratched somewhere around the right shoulder. They still were far enough away, so that I didn't need to shoot to kill." Her face darkened a trifle as she waved to the hummocks that had given the red men shelter. "I managed to get down here before one of the dogs went down. Then they began potting. You can bet that I wanted to kill them off then. But they were sly as foxes. I trimmed the cap of one of them, though. And you should have heard him howl."

The darkness disappeared from her face, and she began to laugh. Steen had taken the lashings from her and was making fast the load on the sled.

"They got three of the dogs . . . that's hard luck," said Harney.

"Luck?" said the girl. "Well, all the luck was my way, or they would have had my scalp long ago. We'd better get out of here before they come back and trap the three of us."

She began to hook up the dogs, Harney helping, while she said to Steen: "How did your trail happen to pass this way?"

"Why," he answered, "it didn't, but we heard the guns."

"Well," she said, "there are a lot that

wouldn't be curious about gunfire when they're trekking north."

"I wasn't," answered Steen. "But Harney had to have a look. He helps the under-dogs."

He said it with a subdued sneer that made his partner uncomfortable. But the girl, at this, had turned about and stared straight at big Harney.

"Steen wouldn't be eavesdroppin'," said Harney in modest explanation. "But I'm more curious."

"Yes," she answered. "I guess you are."

Not a word of thanks to him, but only that direct, searching stare that troubled him more than the eye of any man could have done.

The sled was prepared now, the dogs in line, and with Steen at the gee pole they broke the frozen runners loose and started the load up the hill.

Presently they gained the low crest, where Steen's team was waiting, and the dogs howled like wolves at the sight of one another. Steen silenced them with a roar and went wordlessly to his own sled.

"Look here," said Harney to the girl, "Indians up here don't hunt down the whites, do they? How come that they should've picked you out?"

"Why, I was alone," she answered. "And, besides, I looked pretty small to 'em, I guess." She waved: "Thanks, partners. Maybe I'll see you again at Tagish. You're heading that way?"

Steen merely grunted, but Harney broke in: "You'd tackle the trail alone again? Before we've sunk those Indians? Why, they're hangin' around now, waitin' for another chance at you, most likely."

"They've burned their fingers once," she said, "and I guess they won't bother again."

"Everything's a chance up here," growled Steen. "Them that don't want to take the chances shouldn't ever come here."

Harney flushed at this brutally blunt speech, but the girl did not seem to be disturbed. She looked upon Steen with the same open and untroubled eye, while she nodded at him.

"Of course, that's right," she agreed. "I'm up here not to be helped . . . I'm up here to drive my dogs to Circle City, and I think I'll get through."

But Harney could not let it go at this. In a sense, he was tormented by the position into which Steen had thrust him by the last rude remark. But, on the other hand, he was determined that the girl must not go on by herself through dangers the face of which he so recently had been able to see.

So he broke out: "Look here, Steen don't mean what you think. Of course, we're going to see you through to Lake Tagish!"

At this, before she could answer, Steen burst out, with a dark face: "If you want to take her, cut your sled loose from mine. I'm going on!"

Angry blood rushed to the brain of Harney. "I'll cut my sled loose glad and willing," he spit, and stepped forward to do so.

The laughter of the girl stopped him. "Who'll be our chaperon, then?"

Harney turned with a gloomy brow, when he was relieved to hear Steen saying: "Well, we'll go together. Mush on, and we'll ride herd behind you."

"My trail's to Tagish," she answered. "If you want to go my way, all right." And with that she gave the word to her dogs, the big leader laid into his collar, and off she went, the dogs trotting on the down slope.

It must have been that she was traveling with a very light pack. For, though Steen's team was more than sufficient for the two sleds they were drawing, yet they found it difficult to keep up with the pace that she set. She, unwearingly, went ahead with short, quick steps.

"Light, light!" said Steen once. "She

70

don't break the surface. She skims along. Give her wings and she could fly. Oh, she could fly, all right!"

With this, he laughed loudly, while Harney strove to penetrate the meaning of that laughter and of the odd words that the other had used. It seemed plain that Steen had no use for the girl, that there was something about her which actually irritated him. At this Harney could not but wonder. For her beauty, her courage, her loneliness, the danger through which she had just passed, would have appealed, he thought, to a man of ice.

However, Steen did not speak of her again until they had entered the dark of the woods around Lake Tagish. Then, as they paused after toiling up a grade, with the girl a dim picture a hundred yards ahead, Steen said: "Now we've started, we'll have to stick with her. With six Indians to carry on our shoulders. That'll be a pretty load to pack clear to Circle City!"

"What do you mean?" asked Harney.

Steen answered brutally: "Can't you see that they never would have tackled her, if they hadn't been hired for the job? Somebody wants to keep her away from Circle City, and we've got the job of seein' her through."

Chapter Eight

Chinook Snarls

Deep sounds of thunder, crashings, and single reports, like the explosions of great cannon, rolled ahead of them through the woods, and Steen explained it briefly. "The ice is breaking up. It's going out," he said. Even the voice of Steen rang with enthusiasm as he spoke.

They came on through the woods until the gleam of the lake was before them, and, as they halted at Steen's signal of a raised arm, close to the point where the girl had stopped, they could hear the moan and shudder of a saw grinding through green wood. Staring to the left, Harney made out a platform, a shadowy form above it and another beneath, laboring a long saw through a log from end to end.

"There goes a mill," said Steen gloomily. "That's what we start at tomorrow, old son. She knows her business. Watch her work!"

It was Kate Winslow to whom he referred now.

She was rapidly undoing her sled pack

and taking out the light duck of a small tent, that she next began to string between two trees. Their own outfit they set up not fifty steps away, and though they had two pair of strong hands, yet hers was snugged down with guy ropes before they had finished, and her axe was ringing in the woods as she cut wood for the stove and boughs to lay inside the tent.

"Where does she get her strength?" asked Harney, amazed by her dexterity and speed.

"She's got brains in her hands," answered Steen.

There was dry kindling in the stove, brought on from the last camp, and this was now lighted and fed with the driest wood they could find. Steen tended the stove and started the bacon frying; outside, Harney was building a fire under the kettle that would cook the food for the dogs. When both were ablaze, the men returned to the tent to pull off their heavy footgear and drag on, instead, socks made of caribou-hide with the hair turned inside for dryness and warmth. The footwear of the day hung drying from the ridge line inside the tent. For there is nothing more important than the feet in snow travel. One hand can do the work, but a bad foot is ruin or death. So their first care ever was the soaked footgear.

The caribou socks were strong enough and warm enough for the camp usage.

When Harney came inside, he found Steen with the flour sack open, mixing in it the flapjack with salt, baking powder, and water poured into a hole made in the flour surface. It followed the bacon into the pan to soak up the thick bacon fat, then beans followed to thaw and fry, with tea the last of the supper dishes. It was food that even a sailor might have found hard going, but the knife-like cold stimulates appetites in the Northland.

While this cookery was in progress, Harney tried again to talk to Steen about the girl. He said in his direct and simple way: "Steen, what's wrong with the girl? I ain't seen anything bad about her. She's cool. Yes! But she's got everything else that you could ask. No yellow streak in her, and she's not hard on the eyes."

Steen turned, his face flushed by the heat of the stove. "You'll find out before the finish," he said. "You'll wish that you'd met up with the old Nick himself before you run into her pretty face up here, son. Mark what I tell you!"

"I'm marking it," said Harney. "I'm asking you for reasons."

"Oh, hang reasons," answered the other.

"What have reasons got to do with women, anyway?"

He would talk no more about it, while Harney, obsessed with troubled thoughts, swallowed his supper rapidly and did not press the question. Something, he felt, was wrong. He himself felt a difference between Kate Winslow and other women he had known, but what the difference was he could not place. A certain indifference, perhaps, was the main thing.

He fed the dogs, who had regained their appetites by the rest at the end of the day's work. They ate wolfishly, tails hanging low, backs humped, bellies heaving. When they had ended their rations, unappeased and furious hunger still blazed in their eyes.

He left them behind him and, attended only by the shadowy presence of Chinook, walked across to the girl's tent. The stove glowed faintly inside it. The fire for the dogs' food glared before the flap. The keen, sweet fragrance of boiling tea drifted through the air. The heart of the man swelled, and only slowly subsided.

"Hello!" he called.

The flap parted instantly.

"Hello!" she said. "Come in and have a smoke."

He entered.

She had arranged everything with comfort, in spite of the haste with which she had worked. She had laid a deep layer of boughs upon the floor and unrolled her sleeping sack above this. The air of the tent already was warm and sweet with the smell of the tea. Her footgear hung from the ridge line, close above the heat of the stove, that was not the usual pair of collapsed five-gallon tins, but a rather larger and more elaborate structure made, as it seemed to him, of thin aluminum and kept very bright and shining by her care.

All things about her were neat. A little writing portfolio of red leather lay open upon the sleeping sack, with the ends of paper and envelopes visible in stacks. A sewing kit was spread out nearby for repairs to be undertaken later.

She seated him on the bed and gave him a cup filled with steaming tea, black and powerful.

"How's everything?" she asked.

"Why, all well," he answered.

"I mean, Little Sunshine," she went on, pointing in the direction of their tent.

He grinned as he understood her to mean Steen. "He's the same, I guess. But I wanted to tell you. Steen's got a hard crust. He's all right, deep down."

"To you," she answered. "Because you kept the sea from eating him. But I'm not making trouble between you. He's all right. You find 'em that way up North, sometimes. Even the wind's enough to thicken your skin. I don't mind Steen."

He told her that he was glad of that, staring at her while he spoke. The question that would not down came at last to his lips and sounded foolishly loud and booming in the small tent.

"What's brought you up here to make a trip like this alone?"

She looked him fairly in the face and, as always, when once her gaze was fixed upon him, he found her eyes less big, less soft, less blue than they had been before.

"Health," she replied.

"Health?" he echoed stupidly.

"Yes," she said. "You take weak nerves as far North as this, and they soon get strong again."

"Health," he said again. "I would've thought . . . that you'd never seen a sick day in your life!"

"Would you?" murmured she, still watching his face. "Well, I hope to be strong enough by the time I reach Circle City. Strong enough to travel back again."

She did not laugh as she spoke, but he

knew that she was mocking him, and that knowledge did not fill him with anger. Instead, he was embarrassed. Twice, at least, he had been of some service to her, and it seemed that she might speak to him as something more than a stranger. He would have found some answer but, at that moment, the flap of the tent moved aside.

"Here's someone looking for you," said the girl.

It was Chinook's wolfish face and furry ears that looked in upon them. His eyes glowed, and his tongue lolled out at the smell of recent cookery and the feeling of the warmth.

"He's sent him to watch you, I guess," suggested Kate Winslow.

"I don't know how to make him out," said Harney. "Whether he's getting fond of me, or wants to cut my throat."

"He's a grand dog," she replied. "Has he a will of his own?"

"Aye, he has a will of his own."

"Well, we'll see," she said. "Chinook! Come here!"

Chinook, instead, lowered his head and crouched.

"Oh, he has a will of his own, well enough," said the girl.

She laughed, but her laughter, musical

though it was, passed coldly along the veins of Harney.

"He don't like you. But I guess he don't like anybody," he said.

"I'll try to make him," she answered. "Chinook, come here! Look me in the eye like a brave dog, and come in at once!"

Chinook, to the bewilderment of Harney, actually glided into the tent, but he came upon his belly, wriggling low across the snow.

"Look out," he warned the girl. "He wants to jump, I think. I'd better grab him."

"Don't touch him," she whispered. "Don't touch him. You see. I'll make him kiss my hand."

He looked at her in increasing wonder, and increasing dread. Her face had grown tense, with slightly compressed lips and with eyes that blazed at the dog.

"Come, Chinook, come!"

She stripped the glove from her hand and held it out, dainty as the hand of an infant, as Harney thought again, and wondered at the axe strokes that he had heard ringing in the woods.

The wolf dog snarled aloud, but, with his mane bristling until he looked more leonine than ever, he dragged himself forward and forward.

"Here, here!" she said urgently. "Chinook! Do you hear me?"

Suddenly he rose between them, his powerful shoulders braced against Harney's knees, thrusting the man back, while he faced the girl with lips writhed back from the big white fangs.

"Ah, see, see," said the girl. "He's saving you from me, I think. He's saving you from me." She laughed again, a pulse of sound almost too soft to be heard and without a trace of mirth in her eyes. For they still blazed with that same uncanny, hypnotic light at Chinook. "Now, boy! Now! Come here!" she commanded.

The whole body of Chinook shook, then his teeth clipped the air with that same sword stroke that had killed many a strong dog with a single blow. It was almost as inescapable as the stroke of a snake, and yet the girl was able to snatch her hand away in time, while Harney gripped Chinook by the mane and dragged him back.

"Get out, you murdering dog!" he commanded, and swung his hand toward the tent flap.

But Chinook, who was as sensitive to commands as any human, merely sank at his feet, and, keeping his head turned toward the girl, silently he snarled his green-eyed hate.

Chapter Nine

A Man, a Dog, a Girl

As for the girl, she sank back a little, supporting herself on a hand and arm that, as Harney thought, trembled a little. She seemed pale and suddenly very tired. Was it only his imagination that traced a film of purple shadow beneath her eyes?

"He has . . . a will of his own," she murmured. "He has a will of his own."

"He's a dangerous beast," said Harney quickly. "He's been trailin' me around like a panther. Confound him, if he ain't always with me."

"Because he loves you," said the girl. "That's the reason of it." She sat up, as though struck suddenly by a startling idea. "That's what's happened. Why didn't I think of that before?" She, then, made a brief, impulsive gesture. "If you weren't near," she continued, "then maybe I could have brought him to time. I think I could."

She looked earnestly into the face of Chinook, nodding, but the dog snarled again and, rising on his haunches, pressed close and hard against the legs of Harney, and faced her with the same utter hate.

"How did you do it?" she asked.

"I don't know. I never paid much attention to him," said Harney.

"Petted him?"

"No."

"He was hurt, then, and you helped to take care of him?"

"No. Never."

At this, she lifted her eyes suddenly to his face. "What did you do, then?"

"I don't know. I can't make it out . . . if he's fond of me, the way that you say."

"We'll prove that, too," she said. "Just now he hates me worse than he'd hate a wild wolf or a lynx. He feels that way about me. Now see if you can make him sit still while I touch him." She approached with extended hand.

"Don't do it!" Harney begged. "I tell you that . . . he'll take your arm off. He could chop your hand off at the wrist!"

"I know, but you try to keep him from it."

"Please keep back!"

"He will slash me, if you don't try to handle him. No, not with your hands" — as Harney grasped the neck of the dog — "but with your voice. Try that."

"Steady, boy!" said Harney hastily. "Steady, and sit still!"

Chinook, tipping up his head a little, flashed a glance into the face of the man, then quickly pointed back at the woman.

"Here, Chinook!" called Harney.

The wolfish snarl rumbled and rose high in the throat of the big fellow, then broke suddenly into the whine of a dog in torment of pain and grief. He pressed back as far as he could against Harney, and, behold, as the man spoke to him, Chinook put out a protesting paw and tried to thrust the girl away.

"Wonderful," she said beneath her breath.

But her amazement was nothing compared with that of the man. He looked at her tense face, her pale beauty, her hypnotically intent eyes, and then down at the great massive fighting head of Chinook. He could not doubt, now, what she had said — that in some mysterious fashion there had been roused in Chinook a devotion to this new master. And, in the same unexplainable manner, the dog had conceived a deadly hatred of the girl. For his own sake, for the sake of the man, he shuddered and bristled as she moved her hand slowly closer. Twice his head jerked convulsively, the fangs bared to strike, and twice the hurried, commanding voice of Harney stopped him until at last, trembling all over, his eyes winked hard shut, and he allowed the hand of the girl to fall upon him and rest unharmed for an instant.

At once, she stepped back. Her gaze was no longer for the dog but for Harney, as though she were seeing him for the first time and in a new light.

"He's yours," she said. "And he's a treasure. And you don't know how you did it?"

"It beats me," he confessed simply. "I don't foller the ways of his brain. Do you?"

She did not answer, so intent was her study of him. At length, she murmured: "Some have to hunt for their luck, and some stumble on it, I suppose. I'm . . . I'm going to get out of this stuffy place."

She pulled the hood of the parka over her head and stepped outside the tent, with Harney following her, bewildered and ill at ease. The forest was still. There was not wind enough to push to either side the thin column of smoke that lifted from above the fire in front of the tent, but it streamed far up, above the tops of the black trees, and made a faint figure pointing against the stars. All were in sight. Not a cloud gloomed between the horizons, but the broad sweep of brightness rose from the trees of the east and descended to the trees of the west in an unbroken splendor.

To these the girl looked up, and he could hear her breathing deeply.

"That's better," he heard her say to herself.

A hand fell lightly upon his arm.

"I felt giddy a moment ago," she said. "Those stoves . . . they eat the oxygen out of the air."

"Of course, they do," he said, though he knew that this was no explanation.

"Well . . . it's all right now."

"I'd better go on back to my tent, then."

"Yes."

"Good night."

"Good night, Harney."

He had turned away from her and made a few steps, when Chinook whirled about at his heels with a growl. As he looked back, he saw the girl running after him. A word made Chinook leap aside, and she came close to Harney, slipping her arm under his.

"Don't go yet."

"Why," he stated, "of course, I'll stay till you want me to go."

"We'll walk up and down for a moment," she suggested. "I'm nervous. I don't know why."

Nervous, to be sure! As they walked, she paused now and again like one stopped by weakness, or a sudden thought, but ever and again a tremor passed up his arm from her body, and once or twice she caught his arm close to her, like one clinging desperately to a support.

For a full half hour they walked through the gathering iciness of the night air until she spoke for the first time during that strange promenade, turning, and pointing toward Chinook.

"I know what you think," she said.

"About what?"

"About me. You think that Chinook's right, and that he's discovered something wicked in me. You think that?"

"No. What's the brain of a dog good for?"

"Good for? Why, a dog can begin thinking where people leave off, I sometimes believe." She paused, leaving him unable to speak, before she went on: "What is in your mind about me? Will you tell me that?"

"A lot of doubts . . . and a terrible lot of surprises," he confessed in his usual straightforward manner. "I dunno that I make you out at all."

"Am I as bad as all that?"

"It ain't a question of badness, d'you see? It's a question of something else. It's a question of not understanding. That's all."

She made another pause, and he saw her head nod in agreement.

"Yes," she said, "that's a terrible thing. Not to understand. Not to be able to see. I realized that, tonight. When I tried to understand you, I mean."

"Me?" said Harney, fairly staggered. "Why, there ain't a thing about me that's hard to understand."

"No?" she murmured, with a little rising inclination of mockery in her voice.

"Why, not a thing," he affirmed. "I'm about the most simple fellow you ever could meet. Ah," he went on, "maybe I foller the drift that's in your mind. You mean because Chinook seems to've cottoned to me a little? Why, I don't understand that any more than you do. It just happened, d'you see?"

"Nothing just happens," she answered thoughtfully. "Nothing in the world just happens. Look at him now."

She paused short, and Chinook, wincing down to the snow, showed her the dim flash of his bared teeth by the starlight.

She laughed at him, a soft flutter of sound that seemed absurdly childish to Harney.

"If you weren't here," she said, "Chinook would take himself for a wolf, and me for a veal. How he hates me." Then she tipped her head back and looked up to Harney.

"But he doesn't hate you, and yet I've never struck him or called him names."

He grappled at the difficulty.

"You tried to make him do something," he said, fumbling for a key to the mystery. "Just by looking and talking soft . . . maybe that was what got him scared of you. I dunno. I don't understand."

"But you didn't try. Only suddenly he was following you at heel. He was loving you, and you didn't guess. But still you say that you're a simple man?"

"Why," said Harney, "there was never a strange thing in my life. It's always been simple things with me. Never nothing much has happened."

"I wonder," she mused. "I'd like to hear a little about you. D'you mind talking?"

"Well," he said pointedly, "I'd say one thing, I didn't come up here for my health. I had pretty good nerves before I started, even."

She laughed, confessing the hit. "All right," she said. "I admit that's probably true. It was gold that brought you, of course."

"Gold? Well, I dunno. The fact is that a fellow wants to turn corners."

"What do you mean by that?"

"Well, the street that you're walkin' on

ain't likely to seem the best one in town. And around the corner. . . ."

"Not to get rich?"

"No, not that. I figger that most of the gents that come up here go back lame and poorer than when they came. Or else they've been through misery, and they try to buy relief when they get back, and the rates is kind of high."

They laughed together.

"But to get your hands filled with a man-sized job. That's one pretty good thing."

Chapter Ten

An Uneventful Life!

"Perhaps I understand that," she said. "A man's size job . . . fill your hands? Well! You came up here for the fun of it, is another way of putting it?"

"Well, maybe so. But I want to talk more about you than me. I'm a common kind of a fellow. I've never done anything interesting. But you. . . ." He hesitated. "There ain't anybody else like you, of course."

"Hum," she said. "Well, just let me hear about some of the unimportant things, then?"

"About me? About my life?" he said.

"Yes. How many times have you been in jail?"

"Hello! How'd you guess that?"

"I didn't," she said, with laughter. "I simply hit out in the dark."

"Well," he murmured, "that's a funny thing. The first time was just a pair of Mexicans, but the sheriff, he was a reform sheriff. I mean, the old women and the Sunday-school folks had elected him."

"I see. But what about the two Mexicans?"

"They was a pair of lit-up, fancy, no account, high-steppin' gents from the wrong side of the Rio Grande," he explained. "The kind that's always lookin' for trouble. When they hit our town, they stumbled onto me, and there was a little trouble, so the sheriff, he come and put me in jail."

"There was a little trouble. What kind of trouble?"

"Shootin' trouble, nacherally," said Harney. "One of 'em come behind me, and one from the side."

"With guns?"

"Yeah, with guns. The second time that I got in jail was. . . ."

"But I want to hear more about the first time. One came behind you with a gun. But he missed?"

"No, but my shoulder blade turned that bullet, and the second one bounced off my skull, but it knocked me down. I had to shoot 'em from the floor. And you take bullets anglin' up, they're apt to hurt. So that was why I got in jail, before the judge heard the rights of the thing."

"Were they both hurt?"

"Yes. They was both hurt."

"They lied about it, I suppose?"

"Why, the fact is that they wasn't able to lie afterward. Both of them bein' dead, as you might say."

"You killed them both?"

"Yes. I killed them both. The second feller, I was kind of sorry for, because, after he dropped, he come at me with a knife, crawlin'. I didn't want to kill that *hombre,* so I just tapped him over the head with the barrel of my Colt. But the trouble was that he had a pretty thin skull. The gun barrel, it just seemed to sort of sink right in."

"I see." She was not horrified. Her voice was still gently musical as she urged him on. "But you got out of the jail?"

"Yeah. The judge, he was a pretty good sort of an *hombre.* He understood how things go with high-steppin' Mexicans. He turned me loose. And the sheriff, he went and took a vacation."

"Well, wasn't that pretty exciting?"

"That? Why, you see how it was. The sheriff was kind of scary, and he didn't trust me much, but I wouldn't have hurt him."

"I mean, the fight was exciting."

"It didn't last long. About two seconds, maybe, while I was falling and getting out the guns. That was exciting. But you can't live on remembering things that only lasted two seconds, I guess?"

He appealed to her serious judgment, and she nodded.

"I suppose you can't. The second time, then?"

"Well, that was a kind of a sad thing. That was down in Chihuahua. There was a friend of mine by name of Giveney with his tongue hangin' out, as you might say, for a game of poker. This here Giveney, he was an amusin' gent, but crooked at cards and a professional. So finally I says that I'll play. We start blackjack. If he crooked me, I told him it would be a fight, I warned him beforehand. That's the one thing that makes me feel better about it." He sighed.

"And there was a fight?" said the girl.

"Well, sir, he pulled an ace off the bottom of the pack along about the end of the first hour, with me a measly hundred in. It wasn't the money he'd lost, but just the old habit is the way that I've figgered ever since. But I seen him pull the ace. 'Fill your hand,' says I to him. He filled his hand, and I pulled the trigger, and the next morning, there I was in a Mexican hoosegow, headed for a rope."

"Good heavens, did you kill him?"

"It was so close," said Harney, apologetically. "The fact was that I wouldn't have wanted to hurt him, but he was pretty fast with a gun, and I didn't have a chance to think about pickin' the easy spots. It sure was a terrible shock to me, though, to see Giveney sinkin' back in his chair with his mouth open and the eyes starin' wide in his face."

"Horrible!" said the girl.

"How horrible, you'd never guess. But he lived long enough to say that I done right. But that made me feel worse than ever. That sort of rides me at nights, I gotta say."

"And there you were in jail," she broke in. "For the second time, and to be hung? Was there a good judge in Chihuahua also?"

"Why, as a matter of fact, there wasn't. So I had to bust out of the jail and get a hoss. . . ."

"How did you break out?"

"Why, I just reached through the bars and got a keeper and took the keys out of his pocket and unlocked the door. It was about noon, when most of the Mexicans was sleepin'. So I got away, all right. It was a mighty fine pinto that I found, and he carried me pretty till I got across the border."

"Was that exciting, or just dull?"

"It was sort of exciting," admitted Harney, "till I realized that it was noon, and the rest of them was sleeping."

"Another dull day," she said. "But, at least, you were twice in jail."

"Well, more times than that. The third

94

time, there was three Canucks up in a lumber camp. The three of them and me, we was out on a job together, and, along about noon, we got to quarreling, and the whole three of the skunks turned loose on me. And I didn't have no gun." He paused and shook his head at the thought.

"That was careless," she remarked.

"Yeah. It sure was, considering that they was Canucks. I ought to've known better, I must say." He sighed at the thought of such negligence.

"And what happened? Did they have guns?"

"Only two of 'em. The third one had a knife. I had to knock one of 'em down, while the knifer was sinkin' the steel into me. But it turned on the shoulder bone. After havin' the gun, of course, it was easy, and I shouldn't have shot to kill, but the fact was that that there knife hurt like sixty when it grinded ag'in' the bone. And so I just turned loose, not thinkin', as you might say."

"Ah, yes," she agreed. "And what happened?"

"One of 'em sure had a tough skull, and he lived. . . ."

"Ah, I'm glad that only two were killed."

"Yeah," said Harney. "The third gent lived for pretty nigh ten days. It was wonderful the way that he lasted."

"What a comfort to you," she said.

"Speakin' personal," he explained, "Canucks don't interest me much. But they jailed me on account of that."

"But why, when the others had attacked you?"

"Well, they said that nobody could've done what I said had happened. They called me a liar, to put it short. It made me mad to hear the way they talked."

"And then?"

"They got me convicted, all right, but just at the end down comes a pardon."

"Was that exciting?"

"What?"

"Why, the fight, the trial, the conviction, and the pardon?"

"The trouble with the fight was that them Canucks couldn't handle guns. The trial would've been all right except for the lawyer gents, who talked a lot, very tiresome. It spoiled all the days of the trial, I'd say. The layout of grub was pretty bad, too. I was glad to get that pardon before I got indigestion."

"I understand. That's six men dead and three times in jail. Well, I suppose life has been pretty dull for you."

"The fourth time was just for breakin' the

peace. I mean, I felt kind of foolish and coltish and full of life. Y'understand? Shouldn't talk like this to a woman, but the fact is that I got pied. I mean, I had too much red-eye and made some noise."

"Shouting?"

"Why, it appears like I took a misliking to a bartender in a place, and I throwed him out, and, when he comes back with friends, I throwed him and the friends out, too, which caused a lot of breakin' of glass, which made the noise, and disturbed the peace, and got me in jail."

"I see. That's four times. I'm very glad no men were killed, though."

"Well, there was one that time," he corrected her. "It was a lad by name of Martínez, when he fractured his skull ag'in' the wall. After I'd hit him, I mean. Then he died."

"Was nothing done about that?"

"Why, no, because it turned out that this Martínez had done a murder just previous, and, when they went through his room after his death, they found the stuff he'd stolen, and the judge, he give me a compliment and turned me loose. Very lucky for me, because they fed on rice and molasses, mostly, in that jail, and I never cottoned to rice."

"Four times. No more?"

"The fifth time and the sixth time was both on account of fights that was picked with me by other gents that I didn't bother none. Considerin' that I paid the funeral expenses complete, the judge both times let me go with a caution, as they call it."

"Two more men!" she exclaimed.

"There was two, on one of them parties," he remembered.

"And that was all?"

"Yes, sir. Only six times in jail!"

Chapter Eleven

She's Different

At this, she laughed again, and suddenly it appeared to him that he might have been ridiculous. Her viewpoint leaped into his mind, and he stopped short with a groan.

"Maybe that sounds like a lot of times," said Harney. "Maybe it is. But what I mean is that nothing serious happened any of those times."

"You mean that you got out alive?"

"Never went up to the pen."

"So you came up hunting for blizzards for playmates?"

"Why, I dunno that I'd put it that strong."

"But besides getting into and out of jail, what have you done?"

"Well, what everybody does along the range. Nothing new. Punched cows, a good deal. Did a little prospecting, after I'd had a few spells in the mines . . . spent a few seasons runnin' wild hosses, too . . . and had a whirl at lumbering, of course."

"The wild horses. They were pretty exciting, I guess."

"There was some money in 'em."

"You caught so many?"

"The catching wasn't so good. Other gents done that, but we gentled the ones we caught. You take most of those wild caught mustangs and they're never much more pleasant to deal with than a tangle of snakes full of poison. Wild caught mustang's idea of the right sort of a day would make a dog-gone African lion feel like a retired banker. You couldn't get no price for 'em. So we worked out a way of gentling them."

"Who did?"

"Mostly me."

"How did you do it?" she asked, with an almost breathless interest.

He wondered at her restrained excitement, but went on: "By learnin' their language."

"Horse talk?" she chuckled.

"I mean, you know how it is. Mostly, you take a look at a hoss and hate him, because he's actin' up. But he's mean because he's scared. Would you like to be tied to a snubbin' post and have a grizzly bear come and strap a saddle on your back, and then get into the saddle and rake your stomach with his claws? No, I guess that you wouldn't. No more would I! No more does the hoss like men. He's snortin' and jerkin' back, and he gets a fool look in his eye. Like the look that most men get when a gun is held under their nose. 'Fool hoss,' you call him. But he ain't a fool. He's only scared. And when I learned that, it wasn't hard to get those hosses to eat out of your hand. I didn't fight 'em. I talked to 'em, like they was in school. I tamed scores of 'em, and we got a good price."

"You tamed them," she repeated, as if she had heard a marvel. "Tell me. Did you talk to Chinook, too?"

"To him? Why, I hardly spoke a word."

"Have you tamed other dogs?"

"Not a one. They was all tame dogs that I met up with, until I landed in this part of the world."

"You never tried your hand even with a puppy, when you were young?"

"No, I never tried."

"I don't understand," she murmured. "Unless it's hypnosis."

"I'm no hypnotizer."

"And people, too?"

"What about 'em?"

"You've had a fight with Steen one day, and the next day you've turned him into your friend."

"That was by accident. By which I mean, he didn't want to slide into the ocean that day. And nacherally, every time he sees me, he thinks of dyin' on dry land, which is more to his likin'.'"

"I see that you can't help talking small about yourself," she commented. "But I'm mightily interested. Tell me . . . did a horse ever kick you?"

"Well, I dunno that it ever did."

"Did a horse ever throw you?"

"No, I been pretty lucky, that way."

"Yet you've broken wild horses?"

"I used to ride 'em with talk, a lot of the time. I got them used to me, and then it was easy."

"Did a dog ever bite you?"

"No. I guess not ever." He laughed in his turn. "I feel like I was in court ag'in, and about to get thirty days!"

She paid no heed to this interruption, but went on: "When you were fighting Steen on the tug. . . ."

"Yes?"

"What was Chinook doing?"

"Chinook? He was sliding around the floor at the heels of his master, ready to slice into me if ever I did any harm."

"Didn't you knock big Steen actually flat?"

"Yeah. I actually got in a lucky punch."

"And did the dog jump at you, then?"

"He come for me, but changed his mind. I guess he seen that his boss would get up pretty soon."

She shook her head. "Do you know why he didn't leap at your throat?"

"Chinook? No, I dunno, except for the reason I told you. Or maybe Steen gave him word to keep off, and I didn't hear it."

"Chinook couldn't touch you, that was all."

"I'm not as fast as all that. And Steen had me slowed up to a stop toward the end. Besides, Chinook can move as fast as a cat, in spite of his weight."

"Of course, he can move fast. I didn't mean that he couldn't catch you, but that he couldn't persuade himself to tackle you."

"Well, that might be. He's a real sport, is old Chinook, and wouldn't play two ag'in' one, likely."

"Is that the way you explain it?"

"Why, how else?"

"How else, indeed?" she murmured. "I wish I could tell. How else!"

"Is it something important?"

"Important?" she cried at him, facing him almost angrily. "Of course, it's important. Call him here."

Harney made a gesture, and the great wolf

dog sprang in front of him, staring up at his face.

"You don't even have to speak to him!" Kate exclaimed. "Keep him there while I say good night."

"I wouldn't bother him ag'in."

She paid no attention, but went straight forward to the dog, and Chinook remained where he was, crouching, showing his teeth, but held in his place by the cautionary finger that Harney had raised.

So she leaned a little above him and took the huge head between her hands.

Then Harney heard her say: "I'd rather be able to make a slave of such a dog than to find a ton of gold under the snow. He belongs to you, body and soul. He belongs to you."

He was amazed by the seriousness with which she spoke, but he answered: "I've talked up a good deal about myself. Ain't it time that you should tell me something about you?"

"There's only one important thing," she stated. "I'm mighty cold and have to go back to the tent. Good night, Joe Harney!"

She hurried off to her tent and disappeared inside it, while Harney looked vaguely after her, then started back toward his own.

The fire had almost died down, but by the last red glow of it he saw the high-shouldered bulk of the sled dog rise from the snow like a ghost and fling itself across his path. Instantly, the tawny shadow of Chinook hurtled between. Stiff-legged, with bristling mane, he stood above the other husky, and the sled dog, as though ashamed, slunk down into its sleeping place once more.

Harney watched with interest, wondering what the girl would have thought if she could have seen this quick little byplay. He was himself disturbed by the innuendoes and the questions of Kate Winslow, but he could not put them together. It was only plain to him that she regarded something about him as a mystery. About him! Simple Joe Harney. He chuckled at the thought as he entered the tent and found his partner, by the light of a pine torch, mending patiently and skillfully a torn mukluk.

"Well," growled Steen, without raising his head, "did you tell her everything you know?"

The calm good nature of Harney was strained to the breaking point by this unnecessary rudeness. But he controlled his voice as he answered: "Why d'you do it, Steen? What's the use always starting trouble?

Have I been stepping on your toes or anything?"

Steen rolled back his big head and looked up. "Don't you understand yet?" he barked.

"What?"

"The girl, I mean."

"I don't understand her," answered Harney. "Dog-gone me if I understand anything about her!" He added, after meeting the searching eye of the other for a moment: "Do you?"

"I know this," said Steen sternly. "Before you're through with her, she'll make you sicker than malaria and typhoid fever and rheumatism, all together!"

"I don't believe it," replied Harney, with a rising anger in his throat. "You don't like her. Well, everybody can't be liked by everyone. But, the way I look at her, she's got other people beat because she's different. That's all I have to say."

"Aye!" sneered Steen, "she's different, all right. You can lay your last penny that she's different. You'll travel around the world and never meet another like her."

He added something else in a mutter that Harney could not decipher immediately, but it sounded as though Steen said: "A Gila monster's different, too. But that ain't any reason for making a house pet out of him, is it?"

However, it appeared that Steen had not expected the words to be heard. Harney did not reply, but went straightway to bed. There he lay awake for a long time after the torch had been extinguished, trying to fit together his whirl of impressions of Chinook, of Kate Winslow, of Steen's cruel comments. Finally he slept, but in the dark something cold touched his face, and, when he stirred his hand, it was licked by a rough tongue.

Chinook stood over him, but, as though reassured, the great dog now silently left the tent, and his new master fell asleep again.

Chapter Twelve

Ship Ahoy!

They were up early, with the saw already groaning in the woods about them, and as soon as breakfast was over they set about selecting a proper place near the edge of the lake, so that they could erect their platform and begin the long agony of cutting timbers out of round green logs. But early as their start was, the girl was already away from her tent. They looked in for her on their way.

"Well, she's taken herself off our hands," said Steen with satisfaction. "But no matter what else she can do, I dunno how she can handle the weight of one of them long saws."

"She'll hire some gents to build for her," said Harney. "Hey, listen to that!"

They had come into a thick growth of woods, through which Chinook glided with his usual silent stride, when up went a wild babel of screeches and howls and shrieks that curdled the blood.

"Sounds like half a dozen dogs pullin' the tails of catamounts and gettin' their noses scratched," observed Harney. "Let's go look."

They broke through into a small clearing at the farther side of which appeared the platform for sawing timbers, and near it a travel-worn and time-stained little tent, out of which the occupant was crawling at that moment. He was a man with a tremendous brush of red beard thrusting out in front of his face, and he shouted with dismay as he saw what had happened.

In the center of the clearing stood Chinook, and all the trees about the clearing fairly blossomed with cats that clambered up and down the trunks, clawed their way along the branches, or lay stretched out at safe heights, looking down with green eyes of rage and fear, and lashing their sides with their tails. They made no noise now, except for the distinct sound of their claws in the bark of the trees.

"Call off your dog!" said the red-bearded man. "He's scared my whole scow-load of cats into the trees, and it'll take me a month to get 'em caged up ag'in! Here, kitty, kitty! Look at 'em! Every hair standin' on end. Confound 'em, I've been feedin' 'em slick all this way to the water, and now they've had a thousand pound of dried fish scared out of 'em. Take that dog away, and then help me climb these trees!"

He began to swear with enormous earnestness as he surveyed the damage that had been done.

"Partner," laughed Harney, "what on earth are you gonna do with these cats?"

"I'm gonna take 'em to Circle City," said the other. "If they ain't worth an ounce apiece, then it ain't true that the town's ate up with rats. They's enough rats in any Yukon town to turn the snow brown."

"It's true," said Steen. "They ate my grub last summer till I was near starved."

"Sure," said the man of the red beard. "A Yukon rat can eat twice his weight. Everybody knows that!"

"Yukon rats have fires in their stomachs, and they gotta keep them burning or die," agreed Steen. "So you're taking a whole scow-load to the Circle?"

"Sure I am," replied the other. "I'm doin' two good turns . . . one for them that I took the cats from, and one for them that I'm deliverin' them to. They ain't no disease worse'n too many of 'em, and they ain't no sickness worse than not havin' 'em at all."

"For every one of these here cats," said Steen, "there's gonna be about fifty dogs standin' waitin'. They ain't nothin' that a husky will swaller quicker'n a cat. Cats' claws only sort of tickle their palate."

However, he and Harney called off Chinook and then helped the red beard to gather the scowload of cats together once more by climbing the trees, or by coaxing them down. Finally, an exhibition of raw chopped fish brought every last one of them scampering out of the trees and back into the power of their owner — so that at last he was to take down the river the strangest cargo the Yukon ever saw.

But Steen and Harney went on to the edge of the lake and saw that the ice, indeed, had gone out from Lake Tagish, so that the big sheet of water lay rosy in the dawn of the day. Along the shore, they saw three scows in the building, the planks being fitted on over the rude frame of the boats, and already there was a sound of hammering. But what seemed to the two watchers, staring enviously, the most beautiful of pictures, was one complete boat with her thick mast up, and the low square sail set upon it and bellying and tugging in the wind, that now went out into the lake from her anchorage.

"They're free! They're started," said Harney bitterly. "They'll be down in the fun with the last of the ice, I guess."

"I wonder why they're pulling over toward the shore?" asked Steen.

"It's a trial voyage, maybe. There don't seem to be no cargo much aboard her."

There was a sweep forward and another aft for handling the clumsy craft, but in spite of her big belly and blunt entrance she seemed to Harney both a swift and noble ship compared to the boat that he and Steen would be able to construct with unskilled hands. Furthermore, that ship was ready at this moment to start for the Yukon, for gold, for the great adventure.

The wind favored her. She came with a curling bow-wave on either side and a deep ripple in her wake. When she came closer, running up along the shore, they could see that she was decked over, fore and aft, a feature that would mean much strength and some comfort for her crew.

"Where is her crew?" asked Harney, seeing no one except a solitary steersman.

"Blanketed behind that sail, most likely," suggested Steen. "They've done a good job, makin' her! Hey! Are they gonna run her ashore?"

For here the boat made a sudden swerve and stood in for the beach. The square sail was let go by the run, and hung flapping and trailing toward the water, while a voice hailed them cheerfully from the steersman: "Stand by, Joe! Stand by, Steen, and catch this rope!"

It was Kate Winslow who was bringing

the boat up to them, the headway being sufficient to waft it in, gently, while she ran forward and threw a line to Steen.

"You might walk her up shore a little," said the girl. "We could be a shade closer to our camps, I guess."

Even Steen was startled out of his usual calm. "Where'd you get it?" he asked.

"Out of my pocket," she answered crisply, and she would say no more, but stood back to wait until Steen and Harney, working together, had drawn the craft inshore. Then she jumped on the gunwale and lightly down to a rock, thence to another, and so to the beach.

She stood beside them, nodding at the boat. "What d'you think, boys?" she asked them in her matter-of-fact way. "Is it good enough for the trip?"

"It'll do fine," said Steen. "You can't do much tacking with any of these scows, they're so green and crank, but that's one of the best. It'll get you down the river in grand style. Where's your crew?"

"I've got a couple of good men," she said.

"Know the river?"

"One of 'em does, pretty well."

"That's what you want," advised Steen, enviously eyeing the craft. "They need to know where the pinches are likely to come.

Why didn't they help you bring the craft in?"

"They did," said she, gravely. "They caught the line for me." She turned to Steen with a slight chuckle. "If you're feeling kinder about me," she said, "I thought the boat might cheer you up a little."

Steen instinctively rubbed his hands together. "That would take a lot of the ache out of my shoulders," he assured her. "Well, is it a go?"

"I could be the crew and sleep in the forecastle," she said. "You two would be officers and take the after cabin."

Harney stared at her, open-mouthed, and she noticed the look.

"See how he's staring," she observed. "He doesn't realize that we're too far north for chaperons."

Harney recovered himself with a little grunt of embarrassment and flushed.

"It's a go with me," said Harney. "We'll save weeks . . . we'll get there with the first. How much do we pay?"

She waved her hand with a brief gesture.

"No pay for you . . . no price for the boat. That's fair, I guess. I invest the capital, you do the work, and there's plenty of work to take her down."

Steen laughed out of sheer pleasure. The

darkness of his manner toward her now was completely dissolved, and he clapped Harney heavily over the shoulder.

"Maybe we've found our luck, after all," he said. "Come on, Harney, and we'll start shifting our stuff."

They trudged away to the camp. Snow was beginning to fall as the sky had become overcast. Soon it was a smothering thickness, furring the dark branches of the evergreens and wavering down through every gap in the woods so that one could see hardly an arm's length in front of one's face. Through this windless mist of white they labored, carrying sleds and all their camp equipment in several loads down to the edge of the water, where the boat had turned into a white ship. It was slippery and wet work, getting the goods out to the scow at its moorings, but they dared not bring her in farther toward dry land for fear of lodging her on the beach with the weight of the cargo they put aboard, for though all three were traveling starvation light, still the burden of nine dogs and three camp outfits, no matter how small, was sure to tell on such a small scow.

According to agreement, they stowed their dunnage aft, and then went to the girl's camp. She was not in the tent, when they went to call for her; they got no answer, the air seeming altogether too thick with snow to let the sound pass through.

So they looked at one another, frowning, and Harney plunged back into the tent for some clue to her mysterious disappearance. There was nothing to be seen except the open portfolio upon her sleeping bag, and one sheet of a letter, crossed by two worn lines of folding. He picked it up, merely because there was nothing else that met his eye, but, when he turned it over and glanced at the contents, he was frozen in his place.

Chapter Thirteen

A Letter Unfinished

It was not that he was a natural eaves-dropper, but that, having seen the first words, he could not take his eyes from the ones that followed. In a man's bold hand, the letter ran:

Dear Kate:
Everything that you ask I have to refuse, and the reason is simply that, I no longer can trust you!

That was the sentence which gripped the attention of big Harney and held him in suspense, until the reasons were solved. The letter ran on:

Only in one respect you may have what you want — and that is in regard to the money. Heaven knows that I don't want to make your life as poor physically as I'm afraid it is now poor spiritually. You shall have enough money to give you comfort, so that at least no one shall be able

to say that the lack of funds has forced you into wrong ways of life.

What those ways are apt to be, what they already have been, I hardly can make myself think, even with perfect evidence placed before me, which eyes and ears cannot doubt. But the old love of you persists in a measure, against my better judgment and against my will. There are moments when a sense of your dearness overmasters me, and then I sit with my head in my hands and wonder why I should have needed such a lesson as your coming into my life has given me!

But, whatever your sins have been and may be in the future, at least I feel that I may indulge myself in the luxury of being far removed from them. Even so the knowledge must eventually seep into my world, no matter how remote, for you were made to wreck the lives of good men. The coldness and the selfish calculation which appear in your manner, your face, are only seasoning for the bait, as it appears, and a touch of sin seems to make beauty more beautiful. So I assume that you cannot help making victim after victim, like the poor creatures who were said to throw themselves under the car of Juggernaut. And eventually some echo of their misery will reach to my ears!

Let it be from a great distance, however. That is the one mercy which I ask of life and of you.

As for the tenderness that I poured out on you so long, when you were the center of the world to me and when the house or garden were empty without you, I don't expect a harvest home. That is gone, thrown away.

Unless, perhaps, as time goes on, I am able to tell myself that there are two Kates, the one I loved, who was worthy of my love; and the one who now lives, sneers at the world with a cold heart, betrays all love, gentleness, and sweetness that comes in her way, and puts poison into the veins of the poor sick world.

However, the time has not yet come, and meanwhile the love that I once felt for you is now merely giving greater pain to all my thoughts of you. You see that I cannot say that I forgive you. I have tried to bring myself to it, but a writhing bitterness takes hold of me that I cannot master.

I have looked back over this letter. And there is no doubt that it is too cruel to be written even to you, considering the sacred bond that still, I suppose, ties us together, but I. . . .

That page of the letter ended here, and, as Harney mechanically turned it and then looked hungrily at the portfolio, he heard the voice of Steen behind him.

"That makes it all pretty clear, eh?"

"I dunno," groaned Harney.

"Her husband's in Circle City begging this wildcat to keep away from him. That's clear, ain't it?"

"I suppose it is. Husband?"

"Well . . . 'sacred bond'?"

"That's right. And the one thing that poor gent wants is not to have to be caught in the same noose that pulled them together once before."

Harney put down the letter exactly as he had found it and turned a sick face to his companion.

"What's the matter?" asked Steen. "You act as though you never could've guessed that there was dynamite in that package. Didn't I tell you that she was poison?"

"You told me," muttered Harney. "I sort of thought something myself. But . . . what a letter! From a man that once was married to her."

"Those are the ones that see the truth . . . the husbands, I mean."

"But, bein' married to her, no matter what she did, murder, poison, lying, stealing, anything. . . ."

"How could he give her up, you mean?"

"That's what I mean."

"Because she's pretty, you poor loon?"

"Aye, pretty," said Harney. "Beautiful, Steen. I can see her as exact as paint right here in the air before my eyes."

"You've got it," said Steen, with a penetrating scowl fastened upon the face of his companion.

But Harney did not hear the remark. He laid a hand upon the arm of Steen. "I can make her voice sound up in my ears, man, as plain as the ticking of a clock and better to hear than doves talkin' downstream in the afternoon. I can think her voice right into my mind and hear the ringin' of the words."

"You've got it," said Steen, with the same bitter sneer of contempt and understanding.

"And how," went on Harney, "could a man that had her for his wife, and her face to see every day, and her voice to listen to . . . how could a man like that write that kind of a letter?"

"You couldn't? I could! Except that I wouldn't have been able to rip off the hide as well as he's done. There's a good man . . . and a patient man. Loved her for years, you see."

"Yeah. He must've married her young."

"Older than her. That ain't the way that a young man would write a letter. Not so old-fashioned as that. There he was, all those years pouring out his heart, and her kicking it up and down the street. I tell you, there ain't any soul in her, Joe!"

His voice rose in denunciation so fierce that Harney blinked at his companion. "I dunno anything about women," he admitted. "But you seen from the first that she was no good."

"I seen it. Sure! She looked like just one thing to me, the minute I seen her pretty face. Trouble. Trouble!"

"She's brave," enumerated Harney, "strong, quick, pretty good natured, and . . . she's got a fine laugh, a fine-soundin' laugh, Steen. That's sort of out of the heart, wouldn't you say?"

"You talk like a child," declared the other.

"Do I?" asked Harney sadly. "Still, there she is, alone, bucking the snow . . . even men wouldn't have wanted to try that alone. But she did it. Mad dog jumps her. She don't bat an eye. Murdering swine surround her and begin pot-shooting at her. Well, she comes out of that leaving dead dogs behind her, and as cheerful as May in California."

"Strange, ain't she?"

"Aye, strange, there's no denyin' that. There's no harm in that, either. It takes all kinds of people to make up a. . . ."

"Shut up, Harney. It makes me kind of sick to hear you talk this way. Lemme tell you. Strange women are no good. The good ones live the regular way. They stay at home . . . they have children . . . they raise 'em . . . they make peace around a house . . . they don't look over the fence too often . . . and between the front gate and the barn is far enough for them to keep all of their thinking inside. Take a woman that's outside of that, and they's something wrong about her."

Harney groaned. "Aye, maybe you're right. But still. . . ."

"I ain't gonna argue with you. She's poisoned you already, because she's given you a chance to go ahead and fight a mad dog for her and get shot by Indians. But look at that letter. There's her husband that's come up here to the end of the world to get shut of news about her goings on. Gives her all the money she wants. Lets her carry on the way that she pleases. Only asks that she stay away from him. And what happens? Why, she's so damned mean that nothin' pleases her except to come a-sashayin' all the way up here and ruin his life for him a second time! Oh, she's a beauty, she is!" He finished with a snarl.

"You think she's as hard as nails?"

"I know she is."

"But when she read that letter over again, she had to run out of the tent and take the air in the woods. That looks like it hurt her. And . . . and she's comin' up here to find that husband of hers and say that she was wrong, maybe, in the past. But she wants to make things right, now. She's come up here to beg him to forgive her and. . . ."

"Man, man," broke in Steen. "Think of that frosty eye of hers. Then you try to imagine her askin' anybody's pardon! Besides, she didn't go out into the woods for air, after readin' that letter. She sat here and laughed about it . . . and, while she was laughin', she looked up, and she seen that somebody had come for her."

"Hold on, Steen!" gasped big Harney.

"Little Joe, you got no eyes. You got no eyes at all!"

"Eyes for what? What you seen?" Harney looked wildly around.

"Look there. Ain't her footgear hangin' there on the line over the stove?"

"Well, what about that?"

"Would she've stepped out into the snow and stayed away this long in caribou slippers, d'you think?"

"I'm blind . . . I'm blind! Then . . . they've come and got her here, under our noses?"

"They've come and got her," said Steen, with grim satisfaction.

"Where away, then? Where would they have taken her? Steen, Steen, we've gotta find her trail!"

He lurched from the tent. The snow waved in his face like the wide, soft wing of a moth. The day was smothered by it; the trees were like ghosts behind this dense veil.

"Find a trail with this snow comin' down?" asked Steen. "Chinook couldn't do it himself. Besides, what could two of us do, when they's likely to be six of them?"

"Damn the numbers, if I get a chance to use my hands," said Harney, breathing hard. "Steen, you're smart . . . you have ideas . . . give me an idea what to do, will you?"

"Help me finish loadin' the boat, that's all, and then sit down aboard and thank our stars that she's been put out of our way, and that we'll never have to weigh down our eyes with lookin' at her again!"

Chapter Fourteen

With Chinook to Lead

To poor Harney it appeared indubitable truth that Steen was speaking, and yet his soul revolted at the thought of sitting with folded hands while the girl was carried away. And he told himself as well, that no human being ever had been more frightfully condemned than was beautiful Kate Winslow by the letter that they had read. For out of the words of the letter he was able to make for himself a picture of the writer — grave, troubled, honest, affectionate. Only those who have tenderness in their hearts are able to be thoroughly cruel, and such was the cruelty of the letter, Harney felt. Besides — it would have needed far less than the denunciations in the writing to convince him that the girl had all the evil qualities that were there attributed to her. He had sensed the same failings from the first moment that he had met her. She was ice — dangerous ice.

He looked at Steen with desperation, but finally he exclaimed: "Ah, man, are you gonna stand to see her go to death?"

"I'd help her on the way," replied Steen.

"Then I'll go alone," declared Harney.

"Go where?"

"I don't know . . . but I'll try to find the trail."

"When it's blind with this snow?"

"Where's Chinook?" groaned Harney.

"He hated her," said Steen. "He wouldn't follow a step on her trail."

"Unless he thought that we were hunting her."

At this, Steen laughed aloud. "Well, try Chinook," he said. "Even with him, you never could make it through to her. She's got too long a start on us."

From the ridge line, Harney took the mukluks of the girl and showed them to Chinook, who crouched snarling in his own wicked, high-pitched whine.

"Dogs, they know people, you bet," said Steen in his gloomy way. "Look at Chinook," he insisted. "That's the kind of a mirror for you to see the girl by."

Harney merely caught up his rifle, and straightway he issued from the tent. Before him went Chinook, backing through the soft snow as though he were trying to read the mind of the new master. Then, apparently realizing what was wanted, he scoured away through the snow, using his nose like the tip of a plow. In this manner he cut in a circle around the tent, but eventually stiffened on one spot with a howl that shrieked in the ear of Harney with a sense of all disaster. He thought that he recognized the hunting call of a wolf to his pack as he starts upon a trail. At any rate, Chinook in an instant disappeared.

Harney floundered with haste as he pushed forward, anxious to get close to the sign before the snow smothered it again. But though he hastened, the deep holes which the feet of Chinook had made were filled or drifted across before he reached the spot. He tried to maintain the general direction in which the great dog had gone, but he shook his head with a groan when he came almost at once to an impenetrable thicket.

He turned to the right along this, then recollected that there was no better way of becoming dangerously lost than by changing direction blindly in woods. So he halted. Above him, the sky was close down and of a purplish gray, with the pure white of the great flakes streaking out of it softly. They wavered down like wings through the stirless air, and with innumerable pale, cold hands they touched the face of Harney. Confusion grew up in his mind. It was like standing in the horizon; it was like entering the blue of the sky, or in some other way coming to the end of sense experience, so strange was it to see the air crowded by the white falling of the snow.

A shadow wavered toward him through the white twilight of that strange atmosphere, and he saw that it was Chinook, who immediately turned again, and this time went off at such a moderate pace that Harney had no difficulty in following. He increased his speed. The labor of crossing the trails to Tagish Lake had made him fairly expert in the use of the snowshoes, and he had the great advantage of a long stride as against the handicap of crushing weight. So he went on with huge steps, the snow puffing like dust before the strokes of the snowshoes, the rifle swinging in his hand after the fashion of Alpine regiments on a forced march.

It was the strangest moment of his life. He felt that now, in relating his experiences, he would not be able to say that his years had given him nothing but dullness, for they had given him this contact with Kate Winslow, which had sweetness and poison commingled like life and death.

Still there was no breath of wind. The blind limit of his horizon lay never more than a stride or so in front, and he could see the flakes, from the corner of his eye, whirling over his shoulder like dead leaves that follow a running boy. And that made him see again the street of the village of his boyhood, the smoke of Saturday mornings in the fall of the year, when yards were raked and leaf piles burned, and when the racings and fightings up and down the street were followed by flurries of the leaves again. So the white flakes whirled in soundless motion over his broad shoulder; and he quickened his pace, moving with a longer and a more powerful stroke than before, like a big, capable machine. He kept it up for hours.

In front of him, Chinook appeared and disappeared. Sometimes he faded from view, to come back into the picture again a moment later. Once he stood fast until Harney was almost upon him, allowing the man to see his red-stained eyes, gleaming with incredible ferocity. It was almost as if the great beast were luring the man farther and farther, not on a trail, but merely to corner and slay him in a remote part of the wilderness.

They passed through a great waste in which nothing loomed through the snow storm, but after this the tall, dark shadows of trees came faintly on the eye of Harney and disappeared again like forms of the mind rather than images of fact.

Then he stumbled and found that he had tripped on a furrow, such as that heaped by the turning of sleds. He dropped to his knees to study the sign. There were blurred marks of snowshoes on either side. Another in the center, where the driver was walking, or else forging ahead to break trail for the team.

Now the fall of snow was so much lighter that he could even distinguish the distinct footmarks of the dogs, and found them eight in all. A long team, with three sleds behind it, and three men to guard it all. He stopped short and actually looked back over his shoulder, so great was his desire at this moment for the companionship of Steen. But, then, Steen was in the right, and he, Harney, was in the wrong. For the woman was totally a creature of evil, and it was only a curse to save her from whatever unlucky fate now had taken her.

Doubtless it was her own husband who had sent out to remove her from the northern trail, a thing that would be accomplished gently, mercifully, and so the matter ended unless she strove again to come onto the northern road. So thought big Harney, yet cursing as he looked back through the whirling snow, and then forward to the darkening way.

The light of the day had fallen into a dull twilight. The woods thickened. The trees were not lofty, but stood shoulder to shoulder, in many places. They gave the odd effect of heads looking out over a wall and staring at Harney from either side of his way, since the falling snow and the gathering dark piled up an additional duskiness close to the ground. Higher up, the heads of the trees appeared against the sky.

Steen! He needed Steen. With that great warrior beside him, he would not have given the battle two thoughts, but now there were three against one. And against one who was no expert on snowshoes, half helpless in this freezing new environment.

He went on, more rapidly than ever, feeling that he must thrust himself boldly and instantly forward upon his fate, or otherwise his courage would congeal and be incapable of motion. A shadow drifted among the trees. Chinook, doubtless, gone off to take a separate line, now that his companion had visible signs to follow and did not need a lantern to light him on the way. Harney was glad of that flanking form, for if the fight became hand-to-hand conflict, then well might the dog become the decisive factor.

And again he stopped short, struck

heavily by a thought. He should not be here. Even now he should turn his back and go toward the camp and the boat on the edge of Lake Tagish.

He knew that he could not pause long, but with the surety of a dropped stone he must fall to his doom. So he started once again, with a sudden lunge, when from the trees at his left that same shadow stepped forth. Chinook risen on his rear feet? No, not Chinook at all, but a man with a rifle coming to the shoulder.

While Harney was making sure of this with a slow, numb brain, his own weapon was stiffly carried beneath his elbow, and it was not until he saw the flash of the fire at the mouth of the gun and heard the clang of the report that he was ready for action.

He had felt the very breath of the bullet in his face as he himself fired hip-high, a trick that he had learned in his boyhood and never forgotten. Snap shots with a revolver are more simple, more expected, but snap shots with a rifle usually are a different matter.

The other began to stagger to the side, like a man slipping down an icy incline. Then he turned and fell face down into the snow.

By this time, Harney was close upon him

and found a very sick Indian, a tough and withered fellow of at least sixty. The bullet had gone through his body, and though it had not touched heart or lungs to judge by the bleeding, still there seemed little chance of the old man living.

But Harney said to him: "You speak English? I come back here to find you, if I win."

The old fellow parted his lips with a grin that showed a few yellow fangs remaining.

"All right," he said, singing out the words in the most amazingly cheerful manner, "I stay and wait here for you, brother."

Harney backed away, half expecting that he would be followed by a bullet from behind, but the wounded man, having braced his back on a fallen log close by him, now was busily loading a pipe and looked about him upon the darkening woods with the utmost indifference.

It was good, thought Harney, to see any human face death in this attitude. He wished that he had asked the fallen man something about his two companions, but speed was now more important than information, probably. He thrust forward eagerly along the trail, running hard, for the noise of the rifles was sure to have alarmed the drivers of the sleds.

Chapter Fifteen

Enter and Exit Scar-face

As Harney ran forward, the surrounding air suddenly was shaken into tumult as if by the beating of great white wings that hurtled about him. It was the coming of the wind that lifted the snow away, whirling the sky clear except for the thin gray clouds that stretched across the zenith. But it was like issuing from a room of darkness and stepping into the open. For, suddenly, Harney could see well before him. The trees were clear before his eyes, the branches set off with level streaks of white, sometimes all the foliage powdered with faintly glimmering crystals.

Before him went Chinook, now swiftly where the wind had scoured the newly fallen snow away, now shouldering through a drift that flew to dust under the impact.

A swale dipped at the feet of Harney. Beyond it, he saw the three sleds streaking away into the obscurity of the trees. He could not even get the rifle to his shoulder before the procession vanished — straining dogs and two men running, and on the first sled what looked to him like the dim outline of a prone form. It was Kate Winslow, he told himself, and he lurched forward down the slope at full speed.

Halfway down, he tripped on a projection of the lower, encrusted snow, and rolled head over heels. The rifle had disappeared when he came to his feet, but he did not stop to hunt for it, since there was another weapon beneath his parka. He took it out and rejoiced in the feel of it, for he was at home with a Colt. Moreover, the loss of the rifle lightened him, and he was making good time through the brush and woods when a tremendous snarling and barking broke out just before him, then the voices of men shouting in rage and alarm. So he came out from cover onto the strangest sight he ever had seen.

Chinook, single-handed, had fallen upon the team of eight dogs, backed by two men. Already he had laid the leader dead, with widely gaping throat and white chest fur all splashed with crimson. Now, as he dodged away, two rifles played at him, but it was like shooting at a will-o'-the-wisp, as he cut in again, not toward the shelter of the trees, but straight at the next dog of the team. This was a high-shouldered Mackenzie husky that, not a whit dismayed by the leader's fall, presented a steady front to the invader.

It was a vain courage. He went down with a howl under the charge of Chinook. Harney saw the deadly white flash of the teeth as the big fellow struck. The husky rolled sprawling, and Chinook was away on the farther side, with rifle bullets and curses raining about him.

It seemed to Harney that, as Chinook dodged, he turned his head a little to look at his companion, and the man responded. He was already drawing his bead, in fact, on the first of the men, who was dressed in a strange covering of clothes and furs with a sort of turban about his head.

He had seen Harney the instant before and jerked his smoking rifle about for a shot at the new enemy just as the big man fired. It was as though the other had been struck on the head with a club. He simply folded up in the snow as if driven into a hole in the ground. His companion sprang away among the trees, with a bullet singing after him.

He disappeared with a yelp like that of a dog surprised by an overtaking stone, dodging off into the shadows of the woods as the bullet nipped him. Chinook already was at his heels, but the whistle of Harney made him circle back.

In fact, there seemed no need to pursue the wounded man. For something in his manner of running proclaimed one bent to get to a distance as fast as possible. Besides, even if death itself had been pointing a rifle at him from the dark shrubs beside the sled, Harney would scarcely have heeded, for he was bent on the shrouded form that lay upon the first sled. A tarpaulin and a ragged fur robe that were fastened over it he tore or cut away, and looked down into the face of Kate Winslow, now white and still. Her cheek was cold to his touch. There seemed no rise or fall of her breast in breathing. The knees of big Harney were unstrung beneath him so that he dropped upon the crusted snow and leaned over her.

If it were death, it had not marred her, but left about the eyes a delicate purple shadow that lay upon the lips likewise. Yet it seemed to Harney that the evil of her life appeared even now — as though the long black lashes were drooped to cover a thought in her eyes, as though the smile were a faint one of mockery. Now a strong gust of wind pressed the cheek flap of her parka against her face and that caressing touch turned the heart of Harney cold, for all the radiance of life and vigor and fresh youth that he had seen shining from her, like a light through translucent flesh, was now turned to stone. He leaned closer above her, reverently, with an aching heart. Then, wondering how so much wrong could have been locked up in a body so lovely, he kissed the pale lips, so cold that a thrill of sorrow passed into his very soul.

"I love you," said Harney. "Good or bad, I love you."

He gathered the whole heap, girl and wrappings, into his arms, drawing her close to his breast, yearning over her.

"Between this here and the day I die," he muttered, "there'll be no other woman in my life. Good or bad, I'm gonna keep the thought of you inside of my arms and inside of my heart, like a wife." It was like a miracle. To Harney, it was as though the piercing force of the grief and the joy that he felt for her had sent the electric thrill of life back into her body — for he felt a faint tremor, then saw the lips part.

Harney looked up to the face of the sky, as men will do when gratitude overflows in their hearts. He looked up, and as he did so, he heard the most intangible of whispers saying: "Dearest . . . dearest. . . ."

Harney laid her back in her first position in haste. If there was happiness in this miracle of returning life, there was stabbing pain in the thought that her word and her love were for some other man. He of Circle

City, doubtless, to whom she was drawn back partly to torment him, partly for love. So, in the moment of seeing life restored to her, he saw her snatched away from him by a greater distance than miles could measure. In that bitter moment, he almost wished that death actually had come to her, for now it meant that she could walk on through life, scattering troubles on either hand until at last the years began to write on her face, and all the sins of her nature appeared in her eyes. He was not the first man, in this manner, to turn from reality and prefer a dream. Yet with a half-sad and a half-delighted wonder he watched the color daintily stain her face, redden in her lips, and give back the glow of mortal beauty.

Chinook came softly beside him then. The big dog had been sitting on his haunches, keeping watch over the team that backed up in a helpless mass around the sled dog, showed their teeth in silence, looked with awe from the dead leader to the lolling tongue and the grinning mask of the conqueror.

Now he left the watch of the dogs and returned to the side of Harney, where he softly stole forward and thrust his muzzle toward the face of the girl. Never was there movement more stealthy, more snake-like in deadliness, so that Harney caught the big fellow by the scruff of his neck and pulled him back. Chinook, as though taken utterly by surprise while stalking prey, flashed his head about. The long fangs settled over the wrist of Harney, but they did not sink home. Instead, Chinook overwhelmed with guilt, slid away, his tail between his legs, at the very moment when the girl sat up.

Wildly she looked around her, at the low gray sky, at the trees, black as iron, at the uneasy tangle of the dogs, at the dead leader, at the Indian's body, hunched in the snow. Last of all, her glance fastened on Harney. He saw her eyes widen, her hand caught suddenly to her lips. Something, at least, she could remember out of her semiconsciousness, and it brought blood into his face.

"I thought you were dead," he muttered. "You'd only fainted, I guess. Did they hurt you?"

She stood up and stepped from the sled, balancing with some difficulty. "There were three of them," she said, and waited in question.

"One was a rear guard," said Harney. "He's back yonder. One of 'em ran off. I guess he won't come back in a hurry. The third gent had no luck."

He went to the man and looked down at the most repulsive face he ever had seen. The dark copper of the skin had been slashed across each cheek and puckered by old scars. On the upper lip was a thin bristling of hairs that made a grisly imitation of a mustache.

"It's Scar-face," she said. "They've been pretty thorough to get me, Joe. Even Scar-face! They've risked even that."

She was perfectly calm as she faced him. She seemed to feel no horror at the nearness of the dead man or the repulsiveness of his face, but merely a quiet curiosity and surprise, so that all at once this strange adventure became almost commonplace, something that could have happened at any time or spot.

"You didn't see him before?" asked Harney.

"Not when they caught me. They stifled me in a rug and tied me on the sled in the woods. But Scar-face . . . yes, I've seen him before."

A strong suggestion of distaste came into her voice, but that was all. She uttered no explanation.

Then she added: "Do we take this team back?"

"Yes," he said.

"If you want to take Scar-face into the woods," she added, "I'll straighten out the team. Chinook I can't handle. But the rest I'll line out."

He turned from her without a word, wonder stricken at her coolness, but saying again to himself that innocence and virtue never could have accompanied such nerves as these. She was like a man in poise and ease in this crisis. For it was not as if the danger were ended. Between them and the camp a score of hunters might be searching for them even now, and after the camp itself was gained, what security could they expect?

He left her working over the dogs, her voice ringing crisp and hard as she talked to them. For his own part, he dragged the dead Indian, Scar-face, into the woods, and there briefly went through his effects. There was nothing on him worthy of note except for a specially long and sharp knife, an old-style .44, and a money belt containing at least a pound in dust. That gold he left untouched. He could guess that it was blood money, and he shrank from making it his own.

Chapter Sixteen

Little Joe

He left Scar-face lying face up in the snow. There was no way of burying the body with any ease. Then he went back to find that the husky team had been lined out by the girl. Only Chinook was left out of the harness. He sat at a distance, still lolling his tongue and panting, until his eyes almost disappeared among wrinkles. Kate Winslow was finishing the re-roping of the pack on the front sled, working with rapid hands, but now she stepped back and waved to Harney.

"Are we ready?" she called.

"Don't you want Chinook in there in the lead?" Harney asked.

"Could you put him in?"

"Why, I can try."

"Go on, then," she answered. "He'll give us another mile an hour. He can pull like a horse."

He turned rather doubtfully to the big dog, but Chinook came at the first wave of his hand and stepped willingly into the traces that had been taken from the body of the dead leader. The dogs in the rear shrank back a little as Chinook turned his head and laughed at them.

"Look," said the girl, marveling. "He wants to work for you."

"He did a turn for you, too," said Harney shortly. "He tackled that whole team, and stopped the sled till I came up. He killed the leader, you see."

"And Chinook made the trail out through that snow smother, I suppose?"

"Yes, he made the trail out."

"How did you give him my scent?"

"With your mukluks."

She closed her eyes in thought, and then nodded. "He was hunting for my blood, Joe. What a fiend he is!"

Did she say it with fear and horror? If so, laughter came bubbling immediately afterward. But Harney turned to the gee pole with a grim face. He could not understand her. Her very gaiety was a barrier between them; her casual good nature and her reckless disregard of danger seemed all unwomanly, impossible to him.

So he labored at the pole and shouted as the team started with a lurch, and Chinook began to swing the sled, with the sled dog pulling out at right angles.

Kate Winslow, too, was adding her weight on the gee side of the second sled, and so in a broad circle they turned and doubled back up the trail that already had been broken by the kidnappers. They traveled fast, so that even Harney was troubled to keep the pace, and often was hanging on the pole as he floundered through the snow.

Yet the girl kept effortlessly beside him. As Steen had said, she floated over the surface, where strong men broke through. Besides, she had an uncanny skill in her management of the snowshoes. He was able to wonder at it, but he could not imitate her motions.

So they moved back along the trail, with all the dogs working hard, especially Chinook and the big Mackenzie husky that he had tumbled in the snow with a gashed shoulder.

"And Steen?" asked the girl suddenly.

He turned toward her, floundering in his step. "Steen?"

"He wouldn't come to help?"

"Steen?" Harney hesitated, for his mind was filled with uncertainty. After all, if he had let the girl go, she would have been snatched out of his life by the three Indians to remain only a beautiful and dubious tale in the future, and finally as thin as any illusion of childhood. But as things stood now, he had seen her dead, as it were, and had watched life reborn in her face as if his longing for her had reawakened it. The sight of that miracle would never leave him now. Either from death or from some other horror he had saved her, and, seeing that this was the case, the life of his giving became doubly dear to him. She was irrevocably lodged in his mind. There could be no other woman from this day to the end. And Steen's harsh counsel would have saved him from that surety. So he hesitated for an instant, then shielded the other man.

"Steen had to stay. We couldn't go off, both of us, and leave the boat, and all the other things. Couldn't very well do that, you see."

She drifted on beside him, wonderfully light and at ease, though he breathed hard with the work.

"I know what Steen thought," she answered carelessly. "I can almost hear what he would say. There's our wood before us."

Time had gone swiftly in this struggle homeward through the snow.

She went on cheerfully: "We've brought home another outfit. That ought to make Steen happy, even if it's not as good as his own sled. D'you think that will make him happier?"

He looked askance at her, suspecting

mockery, and surprised to find only a real trouble in her face. "Steen's all right. He just has a grouchy way about him," suggested Harney.

She called out, and the dogs stopped, and hung panting against their collars.

"I want to say something more about you," she said, facing Harney. "I've been wondering how to put it all the way home. And I can't. I'm tongue-tied. All I can say is that this is the third time."

"Why," he mumbled, "that's nothing. What anybody would do. Don't you think about it."

She nodded considerably. "I'll think about it, right enough. I'll never forget," she said. Then she added: "What has Steen been telling you to make you look at me as though I were a criminal? What have I done? What has he told you?"

"Steen?" he asked vacantly. Then he remembered another thing that, in all honor, he must tell her about.

"I gotta say this," he put it bluntly. "When we looked for you, and you didn't answer when we hollered . . . then we went into your tent. . . ."

"Naturally," she said.

"And on top of the bed sack there was a letter lying open. . . ."

She started, but said nothing.

"I picked the letter up . . . ," continued Harney.

"Did you expect to find me in a sheet of paper?" she cried.

"I didn't know. I was worried," stammered Harney, trying to face her, but finding that his eyes lifted from her angry eyes to the trees beyond. "I just picked it up, and after the first couple of words, I couldn't stop."

"You read on to the end of it?" she exclaimed.

"I done that. I was wrong, I know. But I had to tell you. You had to know that I'd . . . listened in at the door, you might say. Your husband up in Circle City that you're going after, I suppose we ought to keep you from getting there. Steen wouldn't want to help you. That's to explain what Steen thinks. You oughta know."

He blundered this out miserably, his face very flushed, and his eye uneasy. But when, at last, he looked down into her face, it was pale and stiff with anger. All that he had guessed from Steen's talk, all that he had feared from the perusal of the letter, now seemed to him visibly imprinted in the flaring nostrils and in the fierce eyes of the girl, so that he actually swayed back a little

150

and recoiled from her, as though from the danger of some superior power.

She did not speak, however. She seemed to realize that the sight of her fury and her disdain must in themselves be more than any words of hers. She made only a brief little gesture for him to go on, and Harney turned back to the team and shouted.

The way from that point to the camp was short, indeed, but it seemed to him almost as long as all the journey before. For with every step that he made, he felt more of her scorn than if she had been speaking it with a voice of thunder.

But, at last, the trees cleared. On each side they heard the shudder and screech of the long saws that were ripping planks out of the green logs. Far away, axes were ringing, the blithest of all woodland sounds, and then, near at hand, a treetop swayed, shaking out a white shower of snow, then fell with a crash that made the ground quiver beneath them.

They were very close to the camp now. On the left hand they could see the boat, turned into a white ship, and on the right the narrow opening among the trees where the camp of the girl stood.

As big Harney strode ahead, bowed as though facing a wind, filled with hot shame and shivering with guilt, the girl ran up beside him again.

The wind had now fallen, and they could hear the panting of the dogs, and the sound of the sled runners in the snow, like the noise of a fiercely indrawn breath. The girl touched Harney's arm, so that he turned to her in alarm.

She had been thinking of words that could be used adequately to express her opinion of him, no doubt, but as he turned to her, he was amazed to see that she was smiling up to him.

"I'll tell you what, Little Joe," she said, "you've done enough for me to read any letter that I ever got. You've read it now . . . you know all about me . . . and you're welcome."

Harney sighed as he watched her.

"But, oh," said the girl, "after you knew what I was . . . what I am . . . how could you waste the time to go out after me . . . and to follow three men who would have cut your throat without thinking?"

He would have answered, but there was again in her smile a touch of the mockery that so often baffled him, so that now he simply lowered his head and faced straight forward, until the team came up to the girl's tent, and there halted.

Big Steen came out from the flap of the shelter and stood before them with legs braced far apart. He looked, as always, something more than other men. It was not mere size — for Harney himself was scarcely an inch shorter than the dark-faced man — but something in the bearing of Steen impressed the mind and seemed to actually fill the eye.

He said not a word to the girl, but exclaimed in his deep, rumbling voice: "Seven new dogs and three sleds . . . we can use that stuff. It'll bring a price in Circle City." Then he stalked off toward the boat.

"But I won't bring a price in Circle City," said the girl. She interrupted further: "There's no use in me, except to make the load heavier!"

Harney did not reply; he could not find the words.

Chapter Seventeen

Request for the Truth

They started to work, at once, to strike the tent of the girl and load her belongings on board the scow. It was a busy time, with Harney exhausted by his long march, but setting his teeth to endure still more fatigue. He took everything as it was brought and stowed it forward, where she had chosen her quarters. Steen, in the meantime, was shifting the weightier packs and bringing up the sleds, while the girl handled the dogs fearlessly, getting them out onto the rocks and making them run up one of the sleds, that had been arranged as a gangplank, sometimes stinging them with a whip to force them to the last spring aboard.

In this manner they worked with Chinook gone from sight among the woods, but that was no point with the big dog. Generally, he was out of view, except when he was stealthily following big Harney, like a ghost. But he could be summoned with a whistle such as Steen knew how to send shrieking among the trees.

They had gone back, Steen and the girl, to

get the last of the dogs, one of the Indian huskies, that cowered in the snow and showed its teeth at the white men, yet dared not run away from the long-lashed whip, only circling half in fear and half in defiance around them.

She broke out suddenly: "Steen!"

"Ladyship?" he sneered, without looking at her.

"It's not easy," she protested. "You might endeavor to make it a little simpler for me when I try to talk to you."

"Fire away," he said, stalking toward the dog.

"I'll talk when you face me."

"Bah," he said.

"Are you afraid to?"

He whirled about. "What nonsense is this?" he demanded.

"Afraid to talk to me, afraid to face me, Steen? Is that the trouble with you?"

He came up close to her and looked down at her from his height, seeming enormous in his furs. "You're out of your head," he declared. "What sort of lingo is this?"

"I'll tell you why. You hate me, and you hate me because you're afraid of me. That's the main reason."

"I'm afraid, am I?" he retorted. "And how come that I'm afraid of you?"

"Ah, how can I tell that?" she asked him. "But all the while you've been skulking and scowling like a boy that has been whipped!"

"Whipped?" he echoed, flinging up his great head.

"Whipped," she asserted, and deliberately nodded.

"Listen," said Steen. "Maybe I know what's in the back of your mind. I'm afraid of you, because I'm afraid that I'll lose my head about your pretty face. Is that it?"

"I'm not as vain as that," she replied without heat.

"Afraid of bein' near you, because I might get dizzy and take a tumble," he went on growling. "Why, my girl, if you had ten faces instead of one, they wouldn't be enough to upset Steen. You can lay your money on that fact!"

"Why should I want to upset you?" she asked. "I want only a fair chance to be civil to you, and have you civil to me. That's all I care about!"

"It's a lie," said Steen heavily.

She started. The whip leaped in her hand, so that the husky sprang far away. Then the lash fell and lay in a long, slender streak of darkness along the ground.

"I have to take that," she replied. "I'm not

a man, to stand against you, and you know it!"

"Go back to get Harney," he urged her. "Harney'll fight for you. Get Harney and urge him at me. You won't have to work hard. He'll fight for you, and he fights pretty good, at that."

She shook her head. "I won't do that. You know I won't do that. You want to misunderstand everything I say."

"Then why d'you try to talk to me?" snarled Steen.

"Because we've got a long trip ahead of us. . . ."

"Aye, a long trip!" he exclaimed.

"And all along on that trip you'll be a thundercloud and make things miserable. I thought that we could make an agreement like sensible people . . . that we'd try to be reasonably pleasant. Merely decently pleasant."

"Rot!" said Steen.

"You don't understand," she replied. "I won't force myself in your way. I won't hunt up conversational corners. But simply for the sake of taking away some of the friction. That's what I mean, and you ought to be willing to make some effort."

"I know what you mean," said Steen, "but I don't like the idea. My advice to you is, keep away from me. Gimme elbow room. Don't crowd me. Don't talk to me. That's all. And I'll do the same for you. If I have to look at you, I'll look through you. You do the same by me, and we'll be even." He made an impatient gesture with both hands.

"It's a hard and selfish attitude," she said. "You'll make the whole trip down the Yukon a perfect misery trail, and you know it. Steen, Steen, won't you think it over again?"

"I've done my thinking about you, young woman."

"Whatever you think, I won't deny it," said the girl, actual pleading coming into the voice. "But whatever I may have been and whatever I may be in the future, there's no good reason why we can't act like three friends going down the river. Otherwise, every day will be like a murder."

He stared fixedly. "Every day'll be like a murder, anyway."

"Why, Steen?"

"I'll have to stand by and watch you poison Joe Harney."

"Poison him?"

"Ah, I don't want to talk to you no more," he exclaimed in sudden disgust.

"I don't know what you mean, Steen," she said with emotion. "If you'll only try to explain what's in the back of your mind, then I might be able to. . . ."

"You couldn't change yourself," said Steen gloomily. "You couldn't help but smile at him, now and then, and sort of pat him with your eyes, and melt once in a while. You couldn't help but do that, and what's poor Joe Harney that he could stand up to you?"

She put her hands together with an expression of childish distress. "Say that over again," she begged.

"There you go," sneered Steen, "melting at me, and soft eyeing me. As if I could be bothered! But Harney's different. They's no casing of ten winters of ice around him. You could thaw him out every day and make spring and summer and winter of him. He's soft. And you found it out, and turned him into putty."

She folded her arms and stood on tiptoe to answer. "I've never tried to flirt with him," she insisted.

"Aw, I know," said the other wearily. "But the fact is that you've just been kind to him, eh? It don't take flirting to turn a Joe Harney into a fool. He's got the shoulders and the hands of a man, but he's got the head of a boy. He's never grown up. He ain't going to. Why, you know all that. You knew it the first look that you took at him."

"It's wrong! And he has a mind of his own," she declared.

"Bah!" he ejaculated. "It makes me tired to listen to you . . . and to watch you. As if I was one of the softies that could be handled in the same way? And now I've gotta stand by and watch Harney pulverized, till the poison gets so deep into him that he'll never get over it." He paused and then exclaimed with a sudden emphasis that came oddly and almost reverently from his lips: "Him . . . he's one of them that would love only one woman, and only her all of their days."

"There are no men left in the world like that," she replied.

"Ain't there? Watch him and see. You'll have a chance. You'll have a chance to see him trailin' around you and worshipping you, when the rest that have followed you are sick of seein' the meanness come out into your face, with the wrinkles, and the saggin' cheeks. You'll find Joe Harney still standin' outside of your door, worshippin'. He's that kind of a lad . . . heaven bless him!" His voice softened wonderfully toward the end.

"Why, Steen," said the girl, so moved that she paid no heed to his denunciation of her, "you love Harney, I see."

"Love him?" sneered Steen. "I don't love nobody. I'm sick of hearin' the word and talkin' about it. Calf stuff, moonshine, pine-tree flavorin', and the whole thing nothin' but air, thinner than that even. I don't love nobody. But," — he added in a threatening tone — "I want you to watch yourself with the boy. Get a little chilly. You could even frost up pretty bad now and then, and make him a little frightened. You hear me, Kate?"

"I hear you," she said sullenly.

"Because," he added slowly, "what a mighty pity it would be if one dark night, when we're in rapids, you was to lose your footing on the deck of the scow and fall overboard, and nobody was to hear you yell out as you hit the water? What a pity that would be, eh?"

His face was black with real danger, and she, realizing it, stepped back in haste from him.

"I think you'd do it. I think that you'd do it," she gasped.

"And why not?" he asked her. "Why not to polish you off, before you get to a place where you'll have more men than one to hurt at a time?"

"What do you think I am?" she asked, her voice trembling.

"I think nothing, but I know! I know all about you. Not. . . ."

"From the letter?"

"From my own sense of you, I tell you. There never was a time when I haven't seen through you. No face as pretty as yours ever come this far north without raising trouble. You've raised it already with Joe Harney. But, mind you, if you don't back up and go easy with him from now on, I'll do what I said. I'll wring your little neck and chuck you overboard. Now go get onto the boat while I catch this dog!"

She made no protest against orders or denunciations now, but drooped her head, and went obediently toward the scow.

Chapter Eighteen

Smooth Sailing

The wind favored them on their voyage across the lakes. It kept the square, clumsy sail stiffly bellying all the while, except when a huge thunderstorm overwhelmed them in the middle of Mud Lake, but then they went on again happily. Compared with the labor of the snow trail, this sailing was like traveling on the wings of heaven. Even Steen's dark face would brighten a little as he looked back to the bubbles showering up and breaking in the wake, or at the procession of the trees drifting down the banks, or the slower motion of the hills against the skyline.

Kate Winslow, too, was continually gay and laughing. Or else she trolled a spoon behind the boat and caught the big salmon trout. There were enough for the three humans, enough even to fill the maws of the dogs.

But no matter how pleased Harney might be with their progress down the river in that it brought him closer to the goal for which he had started, he was all the more troubled by the feeling that every mile toward Circle

City was a mile less in his companionship with the girl. And she, as though the beginning of the voyage ended her need of him and her respect for him, gave him hardly a glance. He did not and could not suspect that the conversation between her and Steen had altered her manner, and, therefore, he was shocked by her sudden and perfect indifference.

When he tried to help her land a huge trout that overtaxed even her wiry strength, she tossed over her shoulder: "I don't need your big hands, Harney. I'll land my own fish!"

There was no offense in the language, but something of a sneer in her manner of speaking that put a load on his heart. He avoided her for some time after that, and finally he could stand it no longer, but approached her again. Steen's eye was upon them, but he did not heed that.

"Look here, Kate," he said.

She was sitting on the gunwale of the port bow, watching the curl of the bow wave as the wind heeled the scow and made its green timbers groan together.

"Well?" she said. "What's up?"

"I was wondering," he answered, "what I'd done to step on your toes? You've been treating me pretty rough, Kate."

"Rough?"

"You know you have!" he exclaimed. "I haven't had a smile out of you since we climbed into the scow. Not one!"

"You talk as if we were in love the day before yesterday, partner," she answered him. "Don't be sentimental, Joe. You're too big to wear clothes of that kind, and, besides, we're too far north to be foolish."

This was decisive enough to check him, but not entirely to seal his mouth, and in an instant he broke out: "But I want to know what's happened that's made you so terribly silent? Damn me if something ain't come along and happened to you."

She made a quick little gesture that ended as she put back her head and laughed.

"That's like a man," she said. "They can't understand hints . . . they have to have the door locked."

Harney went hot with angry confusion. But he was almost more amazed than hurt, for it seemed incredible that any human creature should have been so grossly offensive to a friend, to say nothing of him to whom she owed her life twice.

A soft ruff of fur passed under his hand. It was Chinook, who had come up to stare at the girl and press back a little against Harney as though to get him away from danger. He had done it before, but never did it seem to Harney so significant as on this day.

"I suppose I've bothered you, Kate," he said with dignity. "I'm sorry about that. I won't get in your way again."

Even then she did not turn toward him, but continued to play the line and merely shrugged her shoulders in sign that she had heard and understood.

Harney retreated, blind with anger and with amazement. Only dimly he was aware of Steen at the steersman's sweep, looking up at the leech of the sail with the faintest of smiles. Besides, there was an instant diversion that kept him from trying to analyze that smile and its significance, for Steen's big sled dog at this point sprang at one of the captured huskies, and in a moment the deck of the scow was a writhing, twisting tangle of fighting dogs.

Chinook took charge of the situation at once. It did not need the bellow of Steen to tell him his duty, for he went down the careening deck in a bull-like charge. His snarl as he went in made the fighters wince apart. The blow of his shoulder toppled over the obstinate or the unruly. Even the new dogs did not resist his leadership, but huddled away under the gunwales, so that Chinook, for a time, promenaded up and down the deck, taking glory in his triumph.

Harney went back to take his turn at the sweep of the steering post. Chinook followed and lay down at his feet, licking his lips, for he had delivered one or two slashing cuts as he went through the mêlée.

Steen regarded them both with a philosophical eye. "The pair of you could get fat on trouble," was all he said, and then went forward to do something to the hoisting tackle of the sail.

It left Harney to brood. It seemed to the big man now that there was only one creature in all the world who really responded to him, and that was the huge dog, Chinook, for the great leader would turn his head and look up with his terrific grin of devotion whenever Harney looked gloomily down at him. It was a sad and yet a fierce solace to the man, and he darkly amused himself by vowing that the affection of such a mute beast as this was, after all, far more worthwhile than the most devoted love of that cold-hearted, that scheming beauty who sat by the gunwale and trolled the spoon behind the boat. He found himself taking deep breaths to rid his heart of pain, as they swept out of Mud Lake into Fifty Mile River.

Harder work began here. The sail could

only be used now and again as the wind particularly favored, and it was chiefly the work of the current that would take them from this point to Circle City. Too much current they would have at times. However, it was a relief to Harney to be employed. He could work out some of his emotion on the thick handle of the sweep.

Steen was the captain, directing how they should steer, where they should tie up at the bank for the night, how the camp should be made, and how much the dogs should be fed. Harney obeyed him implicitly, never raising a question, never debating an issue. For he had come to a point of almost absolute silence. The girl herself seemed to have commanded it upon the boat. Steen at no time had been talkative since the journey began, and, therefore, there was little or no conversation among the three of them. Shouted orders on the boat, muttered ones in the camp, were all that were heard, except when the girl broke out into song. She had a very sweet voice, with that strange husky fiber that made such an appeal to Harney, so that, he thought, he could have listened to it for endless hours. She sang a great deal, and one never could tell when the fancy would take her. Once, when an upriver gale threatened to crush the boat against the bank of the stream, big Harney heard her singing, half lost in the whistle of the wind, or drowned altogether. Or, again, in a whirling of snow she might break out into exultant music. Sometimes she talked to one of the dogs, for she had singled out two or three battle-scarred malemutes and Mackenzies to pet and spoil. She spoke to them with an absurd baby talk in a crooning or bubbling voice. It was this, as they camped one night, that gave Harney a sudden new insight into the nature of Steen.

The stove had heated their tent to such a point that they opened the flaps, and the light from the last embers of the fire over which the food for the dogs had been cooked gleamed in upon them and flushed the inside of the tent with the softest rose.

There was no stir of air that they could hear, except at times a far-off whisper among the trees, and so, very plainly, came the crunch of the girl's feet in the snow outside. She was in the habit of strolling off through the woods. The footsteps paused. They heard her call softly, heard plainly the rattle of a dog's ears as he rose from the snow and shook himself, then the voice of Kate Winslow breaking into that foolish, bubbling, childish talk, like a mother to a baby.

Involuntarily, a wide grin came upon Harney's lips. When he looked across at the dark, Egyptian face of Steen, he saw that the latter was smiling also, and that the keen eyes had softened wonderfully.

Then their glances met, and both chuckled foolishly, sheepishly.

"These here confounded women," said Harney under his breath.

"It's pretty far north," said Steen enigmatically, and slid into his sleeping sack.

It left Harney to ponder and to wonder if Steen's aversion to the girl had not dissolved in the course of the journey. For his own part, though she had locked the door against him, as she herself had said with wonderful and cold impertinence, and although he would take no step toward her for more amicable relations again, yet he knew that the first kind glance, the first pleasant smile from her would tear down the frail building of his pride and bring him to her feet once more.

This self-knowledge filled him with shame of his weaknesses, but the shame did not alter the truth. She haunted him, she filled his mind as a half-finished story fills the mind of a boy who cannot find the lost book. A dozen times a day he found himself fumbling in a haze to rediscover the lost thread of their friendship. It was her very coldness that, united with her beauty, made her so irresistible, he told himself. For the warmth of a man's own mind filled up the difference and kept supplying her with the quality that she lacked.

So he told himself, pondering the river on their next stage of the voyage down the Fifty Mile. It was a blind, hard day, with a thin drizzle of rain, thick as a fog, blowing softly in their faces, and Steen at the steering sweep as he generally was in critical moments. The girl, forward, had chosen this moment to break into a rollicking song — only danger seemed to make her gay, and there was danger enough in the blindness of their course on this day. Suddenly, Steen shouted: "Forward, there . . . be still!"

She stopped the song.

"Sharpen your ears, all of you," said Steen. "What mischief's coming up the river at us?"

Harney listened hard, and, gradually, out of the mist, he heard a wailing voice such as he never had listened to before in all his days.

Chapter Nineteen

Danger Comes Abreast

It was no voice of beast or man, he could be sure. It was a wail with an overtone of screeching in it and a depth like the moaning of the dead. It was a voice that contained many elements, all blended together, and yet fighting one against the other. He strained his eyes ahead, but yet he could make out nothing. The harder he stared, the thicker grew the rain fog.

So the voice came closer, rising in volume, but approaching them with wonderful slowness, certainly not with the speed of anything stemming the current, but rather as something they were overtaking. And presently he made out the low form of a scow on their left. It grew. The cry in the fog swept terribly close, piercing the ears. Then Harney saw the steersman at the sweep and another man amidships, busy with both hands.

The loud voice of Steen boomed: "What the devil have you got aboard there?"

Back came a sadly droning answer: "Cats!"

Harney leaned against the gunwale with a roar of laughter. The mystery dissolved that instant — and cats remained! It was their old companion of Lake Tagish, now taking his queer outfit down the river for sale. Now that Harney had the clue, he could dissolve the cry into frantic meowing, spitting, growling, screechings of rage and of pain.

The scow itself was crank and clumsy and too broad in the beam for its length, which explained the slowness of the craft and the fact that they were overtaking it.

The boatman now thundered above the clamor: "They're all tied up in knots, chawin' and scratchin'. I hope they chaw their own eyes out! The outbeatin'est lot of critters that you ever did see. Here I am, takin' 'em where they'll find rat meat cheaper'n potatoes are at home, and they can't wait. Cannibals is what they are, and ingrates! I hope the dogs catch 'em as fast as I sell 'em. Dog food is all they're good for, and good for nothin' but strong-stomached dogs, at that!"

They drifted past as the second man on the scow began to dip up buckets of water and scatter it in the hold of the scow. A great spitting and screeching ensued, and then a sudden blanket of silence fell over the river.

Shortly after this, the mist of rain ceased.

Under a sky of dull lead they drifted on until Harney saw that they were being overtaken rapidly by a small object in the middle of the current behind them. It developed into a lithe-bodied canoe with the hump of a small outfit under a dark tarpaulin in the center, and at the rear one man was paddling. The dip of the paddle and the dull silver flash of the blade fascinated Harney, as well as the easy rhythm of the shoulders as the stranger worked. He was paddling strongly, and yet with such a smooth grace that Harney picked him out at once to be an Indian. But he was wrong. As the paddler drew nearer, Harney discovered a lean face clothed in a short beard, deep-set, melancholy eyes, and a great expanse of forehead.

"How far to Miles Cañon?" hailed Steen in his booming voice.

The stranger did not answer, nor did he cease his paddling as he drew up abreast of the scow.

"Hello!" thundered Steen. "You, there! How far to Miles Cañon?"

Still the other returned no response, though he seemed to have heard. For he ceased his paddling, and actually retarded the canoe by dragging the paddle in the water. Now he swept the scow forward and aft, until his glance settled in the prow, where the girl was standing, and there it dwelt steadfastly.

"Confound you!" bellowed Steen. "Do you hear me, you . . . !"

The other replied with the dip of his paddle that shot him ahead of the bows, and he was soon well forward.

Steen, grasping the sweep in one hand, had actually picked up a rifle.

"I gotta mind to pump some lead into the head of that canoe!" he declared. "The low-down skunk! A white man, too!"

Harney did not reply, taking it for granted that Steen would attempt nothing so desperate. There was something else that interested him even more than rifle play at that moment, for as the stranger glided away, his paddle skimming the surface and then sinking deep, Kate Winslow sank, cowering down on the boarding that covered the bows and made a low forecastle there. By the sway of her head, he knew that she was close to fainting, and he joined her in an instant, kicking half a dozen dogs out of the way to reach her side.

She was deadly white, as he leaned above her. With vacant, despairing eyes she looked up to him, as though at a face she had never known. Then grief and fear welled up in her.

"Joe, Joe," she murmured. "He's found me. The Yukon will never take me alive to Circle City." She wrung her hands in a sudden ecstasy of great terror. Then she cried excitedly: "Raise the sail! We've got to overtake him. He was here in your hands. Why didn't you shoot then? Raise the sail! Raise the sail!"

"The wind's straight in our teeth," explained Harney.

"Ah, heaven help me," she groaned, as she saw the truth of what he had said. "Heaven help you both, as well . . . for you're with me, and he'll strike at all of us."

She covered her face with her hands, then sprang up and hurried aft where Steen remained at the steering sweep, huge and gloomy. He would not look at her, but stared steadily ahead down the river before them.

"Steen," she pleaded, "if there's any love of life in you, run ashore. Give up the boat. Take to the sleds, and we'll trek back. For if you go on . . . even a mile on . . . we're going to die! Do you hear me? Will you look at me? You . . . Harney . . . I . . . we'll die, we'll die!"

Steen parted his lips as though they were made of stiff metal. "This friend of yours, what's his moniker?" he asked. "What's his name, Kate?"

"He has twenty names," she replied. "But he's never done one good deed under any of them. He has twenty names, and a demon in him for every one."

"Tell me a few then."

"You'd never know them! You'd never know! Will you look at me? D'you think I'm talking nonsense, Steen? I tell you that I know him and what he can do!"

"You're plain hysterical," said Steen, after another pause. "I ain't a child. Neither is Harney. You can shoot straight yourself. You want me, serious, to beach the boat and turn back up the river?"

"Ah, I understand!" she cried, more desperately in earnest than before even. "Because there are two of you, you think that he'll be no danger to you. But, oh, Steen, try to believe me! I've never seen two braver men than you and Joe Harney, but it won't help you against him. You are wise, too, but not so wise as he is. Whatever you think of, he'll be able to fathom. Whatever you attempt, he'll forestall. Whatever you wish to try, he'll be before you. There's no trick he hasn't learned. There's nothing that he has not mastered in the way of inflicting pain and suffering on others."

"You're runnin' away with yourself," said Steen coldly. "He's a man. We're two men

. . . and a half, say. That's the other way of putting the thing."

She beat her hands together with childish impotence and more than childish anger, so that Harney was stirred, watching her. And his own blood was chilling as he listened to her who had faced the mad wolf dog, the guns of the Indians, abduction by them, with perfect calm and poise that was almost indifference. But now all that poise was thrown away. She was speaking half hysterically. The pupils of her eyes enlarged as though she were walking in the night, surrounded by half-seen horrors. She stammered and halted with terror in her speech, so that the face of the lone canoe man once more was painted before the eyes of Harney — the wide brow, and, above all, the dark and melancholy eyes.

"Haven't men tried to beat him before?" Kate now gasped at Steen. "Haven't they worked together in whole companies to catch him, to kill him? Haven't they tried poison, traps, as if he were some beast? And he is! He is! Like a cunning beast he senses everything that is dangerous about him. What other man in the world would have dared to come by as he did, calmly look me in the face, and then go on without hurry, while two rifles were ready to cover him?

But he knew, he knew!" She threw up her hands in the attitude of one who proclaims a marvel. "Oh, Steen, I tell you that even if you both had aimed at him, pointblank, you would have missed!"

She let her hands fall and remained stricken with fear, only half hoping, as she waited for the reply.

Steen slowly shook his head. "I never turned back on a trail," he said. "I never got the habit formed, and I ain't gonna start formin' it now."

He moved the steering sweep. Harney, glancing over the side, could see how much Steen had been shaken by the talk of the girl, which had absorbed him so that he had almost permitted the scow to run ashore.

Kate Winslow turned to Harney swiftly, holding out despairing hands of appeal, but he stood stupefied before her and made no sign.

"Then put me ashore by myself!" she cried. "That will free you from danger, and perhaps I can get away on the back trail. . . ."

"Well," said Steen, "you can follow your own way," and straight he turned the prow of the boat toward the land again.

Harney reached him with a stride and gripped the handle of the sweep.

"Sheer out into the river, partner," he said quietly. "We ain't gonna land her. It's the very thing that other gent would be lookin' for us to do. Sheer out into the water. I ain't gonna have her put on shore."

Wild anger leaped into the face of Steen. One hand released the oar and gripped into a huge fist, but he did not strike. Instead, his glance wavered, and suddenly he exclaimed in wonder: "Look, man! Look at that!"

Harney turned and scarcely kept back an exclamation in turn, for the girl had slipped to the boarding and was weeping silently, while before her stood the great Chinook — he who had always hated her so — licking the hands that were before her face.

Chapter Twenty

At Miles Cañon

Even Kate Winslow, then, could be as weak as other women, could weep like them, could slip half fainting to the ground at the mere sight of an enemy. Yet it was not a great comfort, for Harney began to suspect that she was right, and that he and Steen were fools beyond expression for persisting in their journey down the Yukon in this bull-headed manner, in spite of the dangers that already had sprung up around the path of the girl.

Now a six-knot current had them, and they swung down it between shores that rapidly glided behind them to a point where a number of scows were drawn up to the bank, and a small and confused camp had been made by many hands. Below the camp, the quarter-mile spread of the water gathered to a hundred feet, disappearing with an audible rush between lofty cliffs of stone.

"There's Miles Cañon. There's where our party starts," said Steen. "Look at the hump on the back of it! It's going to be a rough passage, boy."

In fact, the center of the current was piled up two or more yards higher than the sides, as the narrowed stream boiled back from the sides of the cliffs and heaped together in the middle. It veritably boiled, tossing up big, sudden waves in which it appeared that even a large boat could not have lived, far less a little crazy-built scow such as they were manning.

Steen decided that they had better go ashore at the camp to learn the latest news of conditions at the rapids, so the girl was sent forward to conceal herself beneath the forecastle top boarding, while the two men went ashore. Sheering into the quiet water under the bank, they soon had out mooring lines, fore and aft, and made their landing.

No one noticed them. The whole attention of the camp was focused, at that moment, upon the last man to start the perilous voyage through the rapids. He was pushing off now and alone. Two men had trouble enough in guiding a craft through the maëlstrom, but this undaunted fellow went at it single-handed and unabashed. He stood aft, handling the big sweep to work the prow out toward the center of the current, and somewhere in the boat he had a music box that was tinkling out a gay little ballad. He was a tall, slender man, giving back cheerful answers to the banter of the crowd.

"If it takes two men to get one boat through, how much will one man get?" asked a sardonic sourdough, remembering arithmetic days.

"Why, half a boat," said the boatman who was making this single-handed venture.

"You better throw away half before you start, then," suggested someone.

"Mister White Horse would rather take it from my hand," said the voyager.

"Yeah," laughed another. "That White Hoss is a hand-fed pet, all right."

"Here's luck to you, Limey!"

By which name, it appeared, that the traveler was an Englishman.

The tall boatman turned and waved his hand. "Thank you, Yank," he said. "I'm sure to find it."

"What does he mean by that?" murmured Harney to Steen.

The latter rewarded the question with one of his flashing glances of scorn.

"It don't take much thinking to figger that out. The poor gent is on his uppers. He's one of these here second sons of second sons most likely. England ain't big enough to give him a job, but out here talkin' back to the Yukon rapids, or stickin' natives in

Africa with their own spears, or puttin' a new polish on the South Pole with their handkerchiefs . . . that's where they feel mostly at home, I'd say!"

Harney nodded. "I've seen enough of 'em on the range," he said. "Some rotten, but mostly men. They never take no more than they give . . . from a cowboy to a sunfishin' bronc'. Hey, look at her go!"

The scow of the Englishman had now found the force of the current that took hold with a jerk that staggered the steerer.

"Look at him!" yelled someone. "He's never seen white water before, by the way he acts."

"He's righted her again," called another. "But he'll never get through."

"You're a liar," answered a third. "He's got luck, and here goes an empty to foller it!"

With that, he thrust off a scow with the aid of his partner, dashing knee-deep into the water to give the boat a final thrust.

"Why an empty boat?" asked Harney, as the current seized the scow in turn.

"It'll be caught below the rapids, and those gents will pack their stuff around on their backs. It takes longer, it costs you more trouble, but it gets you there sure. There he goes!"

The last words were in comment upon the Englishman, whose scow now had entered the mouth of the cañon. It was seen to pitch wildly, the steersman still erect, though wobbling like a loose-footed flagpole in a heavy wind.

An involuntary cheer burst from the throats of the watchers.

"Game! Dead game," muttered a tall man beside Harney. "Game, but a sure loser."

Harney stared at the point where the voyager had disappeared. His heart was beginning to rise at the thought of that perilous journey, and he smiled a little with set teeth. The empty scow, in the meantime, also had entered the mouth of the cañon, was seen to spin wildly, and then, straightening, it shot away from view like something flung from the hand of the water.

"A sure loser," continued the last commentator to Harney. "Nobody in the world is likely to get through the rapids with the water up like this. Nobody that ain't had experience. Nobody!"

"You're a pilot, eh?" said Steen.

"It ain't a job that I hanker for," declared the other. "But for fifty dollars. . . ."

"You're wasting time," Steen advised him. "I've been through before."

The face of the other fell, while Steen and

Harney wandered on through the groups, all of whom were now busied with their own affairs — making camp, arranging packs, restowing loads on the scows at the water's edge, or else taking out a portion to lighten the burden on the perilous journey. Those who did so, having gotten perhaps a half of their equipment through by boat, had to return and laboriously pack the rest of their goods around the rapids on their backs.

"Mule's work," said Steen. "Better be dead quick like a man than alive like a mule."

That seemed the opinion of at least half of the men who were gathered at this camp. They were preparing to make the voyage with a large portion of their packs. Many were trading off bulky articles for light ones, so as to diminish the draft of their scows before making the great attempt.

Steen, in the meantime, was going from man to man, collecting what information he could about the exact state of each of the rapids. They changed from year to year with the grinding down of the rocks and the strange appearance of new ones. They changed also with the amount of water that was flooding through the narrow gates. All agreed that the time was a dangerous one. That the poor Englishman had no chance, but that luck, of course, could accomplish anything.

"And if the Englishman has the luck of a Swede," said one, "he may come through."

"Why a Swede?"

"Why, there was a couple of 'em went out the other day, and they didn't know a boat from a can of sardines. They get into the cañon and go through pretty good, but they don't bear over far enough when they come to the whirlpool. It grabs 'em, and snakes 'em around fifty mile an hour. Every minute they was in danger of bein' eat up by the rocks. Rocks there that would bite a scow in two at one snap of their teeth. But for a couple of hours these Swedes was spinning like tops. Finally, they got dizzy, or something. Anyway, they gave up and lay down in their boat, and dog-gone my hide if the current didn't yank 'em right out of the pool and bring 'em down safe to the other end!"

Steen bought a pair of good axes from one who had a plentiful supply — ten dollars apiece for a dollar-and-a-half article, but considered a cheap price at that end of the world.

Carrying them back, he encountered Harney, who was listening to the sad tale of a man whose two partners had gone down the river with half their goods the week before. The Squaw Rapids had taken them and swallowed them. Now this lone survivor, making his last trip, intended to get his goods below the rapids on foot, and there he had bought a half-wrecked scow that must be repaired by another fortnight of bitter labor before he could resume his journey.

"Shall we camp here or run through?" asked Steen.

"Run through. Run through," said Harney. "Run through, man! He. . . ." He paused.

"Aye," agreed Steen soberly and without sarcasm. "That fellow may be here now, and ready to snag us. The faster we go, the less chance he's got of bothering us. Shall we cast off now and start?"

"Cast off," agreed Harney. "If she's willing."

"She!" exclaimed Steen. "Would you ask her opinion? Ask her for your life back, after somebody's knife has ripped it out of you! But don't ask her opinion. We're making this trip . . . she's added herself."

"It's her boat," suggested Harney.

"Her boat's been paid for. Suppose that her friend in the canoe had come by and found her alone on it . . . or with gents a little smaller sized?"

It was a pertinent comment that Harney interrupted by exclaiming: "There's a pair of fellows taking the wrong boat! They're actually taking off the mooring lines from our scow, Steen!"

It was a fact. Two men had loosened the mooring ropes on the scow and were now in the act of clambering aboard. One was white, one a half-breed or full Indian. The former tall and bulky, the latter squat, very active as he swarmed aboard and picked up the handle of the sweep.

"It's him," muttered Steen. "It's a pair of his men, and he's on our backs right now." He was charging as he gasped it out, and Harney was lurching along at his side.

Chapter Twenty-One

Rough Going

It all had happened too pat, too quickly on the heels of their meeting with the nemesis of Kate Winslow not to connect him with this sudden attack upon them. But Harney forgot the shadowy power that might be in the background. The present danger was too real and overwhelming. For his own part, he made straight for the stern of the boat, where the stocky fellow was thrusting the heel of the scow away from the shore, working with desperate energy. However, Harney would have reached the boat with ease, had it not been that a group of men before him, apparently scattering before his rush, really formed in a tangle. He crashed into one and went down heavily at the same time that he saw big Steen tripped so that he fell.

There was no accident here. They both had been blocked away, and some of the fear with which Kate Winslow had spoken of the mystery man now slid coldly into the heart of Harney. As he sprawled, two men toppled on him, cursing him for a blundering fool. But one of these ostensibly upset fellows instantly secured a half nelson with the force of an expert and the speed. Then the great heart of the fighter swelled in Harney. He broke that hold as though it had been secured with straw, heaved himself over, and came to his knees, only to be buried under a weight of men who shouted: "He's tryin' to murder Pat. Brain him!" Mighty hands grasped him. A strong arm jerked around his throat in that unbreakable hold which means the end of any rough-and-tumble fight, as a rule.

Yet Harney laughed through his teeth. Neither chance nor luck had made him the champion of so many lumber camps, so many bunkhouses on the range. This was the very atmosphere which he best knew. He stiffened, head thrown back, and kicked out with both feet, an effort that hurled one man from him and drove his head fairly into the face of the stranglehold artist.

In an instant he had tumbled free and rose in the midst of a dissolving group. There was only one danger — the rising gleam of steel as a Colt slid up in the hand of one of his assailants. But an empty hand is faster far than one loaded with a .45 — the fist of Harney clicked on the jaw of the man like rock on rock, and that barrier was down. He leaped on toward the boat, vaguely aware of

Steen rising from the heart of another struggling group and casting off men as if they were children. His real attention was on the boat, and the widening strip of water between it and the shore. There was still, he felt, a desperate last chance of leaping from the higher bank onto the boat, at the risk of broken legs if he struck the gunwale.

All was turmoil aboard. The dogs, frightened and howling and yelping, swirled here and there, while Kate Winslow had come up from the forecastle, rifle in hand. The tall man flung himself at her. Before she could bring the weapon to bear, it was snatched from her, exploding at the same time as the brute with clubbed fist struck her down into the heap of struggling dogs.

But Chinook, the man-killer, the king of dogs, where was he? He sat on the farther side of the boat, grinning broadly, his red tongue lolled out as though he tasted infinite delight in the battle. As big as a sitting man he looked, with his leonine ruff standing out around his massive neck. He had the power to end all this, but what was his interest in battles among mere humans?

Straight at the bank ran Harney, calculating his distance, making speed with all his might for the great effort. The man at the after sweep saw him coming. Still he thrust to widen the big gap until the last instant, then calmly loosed his hold upon the handle of the oar and drew a revolver. From the lip of the bank Harney leaped, hurling himself as high into the air as possible.

Every sense was so wonderfully sharpened at that moment that he was aware of the roaring of voices from the bank behind him, of the bright face of the water beneath him, as he seemed to hang at the height of his spring, or the tall man stumbling aft in haste with the rifle he had taken from Kate Winslow, and last and most important, the grin on the face of the Indian straight in line with his jump. It was not a smile of amusement, but the distorted grin of one who means to kill. Like a broad jumper, Harney kicked his legs in mid-air, felt the strange extra impulse as though delivered by the stroke of wings, and plunged downward. He buckled his knees up high to clear the gunwale. The leveled revolver spat in his face, though he felt no harm. Then his driving weight crunched on the body of the Indian, and they rolled together on the deck.

It was a heavy fall, even in spite of the break-shock which the body of the other had provided for him, for, as he spun across the deck, his head struck heavily against the timbers on the farther side, and then he found himself inert upon his back with a numbed body, although with a brain perfectly alert. He saw above him the sheeted gray of the sky with one lower cloud of a dazzling white blowing across it. Against that brilliant background, the second pirate strode. Good sense would have taught him to use the trigger and a bullet at such a time as this, but apparently his blood was hot for the shock of hand-to-hand conflict. The same brute in him that had made him strike down the girl as though she were a man, now made him sway the rifle aloft.

There it hung suspended for a fraction of an instant during which Harney strove to drag his senseless arms across his face to protect himself, but they would not move. The muscles jerked flaccidly and failed, but how wonderfully clear was his brain. For he could see the last detail not only of this man's face with its stub nose and flaring nostrils, its walrus-like mustache, its thick lips with big yellow teeth behind them, but also he saw the naked soul as well, degraded to the level of a beast, unsoftened by pity, remorse, or kindness, unhandled by civilization. With a strange calm, Harney looked up to that face, to the capable shoulders straining for the blow, to the rifle pitched high above, and the dazzling white of the cloud that framed this picture of horror.

Then, distinctly, he heard on the deck the scratching as of a dog working hard to get footing. He heard a snarl. Then the bulk of Chinook smote in from the side. At the head he struck. The sword-like flash of his teeth laid upon that unbeautiful face from temple to jaw, while his hard shoulder smote on the chest of the pirate. It was no light impact. It was a maneuver long practiced, and a hard-driven weight that had tumbled hundred-and-fifty-pound dogs head over heels as it now tumbled this human victim.

The man did not stagger. He was knocked from his feet, struck the gunwale knee-high, then toppled into the river with a cry that brought the life back into the nerves of Harney. Reeling to his feet, he staggered to the place where Chinook stood by the edge of the boat, his forefeet resting on the top of the gunwale, while with pricked ears he studied the course of his victim, now swimming toward the shore with a stain of crimson trailing behind him.

Big Steen was here at last. He had had to flounder out and catch the trailing end of a mooring line, by which he now was dragging himself on board.

"Behind you, Joe! Behind you!" screamed the voice of Kate from the waist of the boat.

He turned. The Indian had looked broken in every bone, lying heaped against the rail, but now he was scrambling to his feet.

"Chinook!" called Harney.

The big dog went for the fellow like a cat for a rat, but the Indian did not wait to receive the charge. Instead, he dove overboard into that icy water and then was seen swimming dog-fashion for the shore. Harney, with poised gun, waited, considered, and then did not shoot. Let them both go. They had been dangerous, but now they were a danger left far behind, since it was not likely that they would be able to overtake the scow if it succeeded in running the rapids. He housed the Colt again, turning to give Steen help onto the deck of the scow.

The big man came in a ravening fury, cursing the Yukon, all the humans on its waters, all the Northland, all traitors and murderers from one end of the world to the next. "They tripped me . . . me . . . Steen!" he cried to Harney, and turned with hands made into rending talons as he looked toward the confusion of spectators on the shore. "They had me down. One of 'em cracked me over the head. They were as thick as sardines in a can. I couldn't breathe for 'em. . . ." His head tilted back, remembering. That dark Egyptian face was lighted with savage pleasure.

"I smashed one face for 'em. It went in like an eggshell. I'll bet he swallowed half his teeth, because I sure knocked 'em down his throat! Then I got through, and here was the boat already out in the water. You were lucky, Harney. They didn't tackle you!"

"They tackled me," said Harney.

"They did? I was too busy to watch. How did you get loose?"

"Head work and foot work. I kicked one in the stomach and butted another in the face and managed to bust loose. I just made the deck on the jump."

"What smeared that black onto your face?"

"The little one. The one that's swimming there."

"Him?" said Steen. "Him? That ain't a man, old son. That's a dog, a mad dog. Wouldn't ever do to let him get to shore among men that he might bite." He snatched up the fallen rifle from the deck, but Harney struck the barrel aside.

"Let him go. He's behind us," he insisted. "We don't have to worry about what's behind us, but about what's in front. Besides, you'd be wastin' good ammunition."

"You're right," said Steen. "You're dead right. How's Kate?"

She was leaning against the gunwale on the farther side of the scow, looking steadfastly down the river.

"Was she hurt?" asked Steen, lowering his voice.

"She was knocked flat," said Harney, "but she's forgot that. She's thinking only about what's ahead of us."

"I guess you're right," nodded Steen. "She should've been a man. She should've been a man, because if she was, even her size wouldn't bother her none."

It was the first pleasant thing he had said of the girl, and Harney wondered a little, though he agreed with what Steen had said with all his heart. He went up to her now.

"Are you hurt, Kate?" he asked.

"Miles Cañon is running great guns," she answered, with hardly a glance at him. "You'd better get out the other sweep. No, I'm not hurt. Look at the waves, Joe . . . and get me the other sweep!"

Chapter Twenty-Two

A Desperate Decision

Now the crisis of the voyage was beginning. Steen left the rear sweep and went forward after the second one had been unshipped. This he fitted into place on the eight-foot outrigger. It was his duty to keep the forward end of the scow as nearly as possible on the crest of that wave which was heaped up in the middle of the cañon. The steersman at the after end merely labored to make the craft follow her nose. Sometimes, on larger craft, there were two sweeps mounted in the bows, but for a boat of this size one was considered enough, if the scow were lightly loaded. Swarming with dogs and with the weight from the packs of five sleds, they could not say that this little scow was actually lightly loaded, but Harney was willing to put all his trust in Steen.

He set his teeth as the noise of the water swelled with a booming and humming sound coming back from the mouth of Miles Cañon. But the girl, taking her post by the mast, which had not been unshipped, seemed to look forward to the passage with the keenest enjoyment. Once, actually, he saw her laugh, although the increasing noise drowned the sound of it. A little later he was sure that she was singing with head bent back in the pleasure of the danger and of her own song. She was alone in the world, he told himself. No other woman and no other man ever could understand that intricate nature, half natural as animals are natural, half sophisticated with an infinite world wisdom.

She had not spoken to him a single word about his recapture of the scow, or her rescue from all that she feared. It was as though the past had no interest for her, either its pleasure or its pain, but only the present and the future filled her attention. His reflections broke off short, however. For the mouth of the cañon seized them with converging currents, and the next moment they were leaping forward. It reminded Harney of the pitching of a horse, except that there was nothing to grip with the knees or the heels. They shot to the top of an undulation in the stream, then were jerked into the trough, darting instantly to a new crest.

Spray, cuffed up by the blunt prow, whipped after and stung his face. But staggering in his place, he worked ardently to do as Steen had taught him, and make her follow her nose, which Steen himself was keeping with wonderful accuracy in the center of the stream. They turned an angle. To the side was the whirlpool, edged with rocks like teeth, against which the water foamed with incredible speed. Steen thrust her nose well toward the opposite shore, Harney working hard to make her tail follow, but not quite succeeding. In the very center, he felt a sickening sensation of the boat sliding downhill into the grip of the circling pool. Then the main current snatched at them and jerked them half sidling down the stream again.

He saw the girl look back at him with a smile that made his heart jump, then she was staring ahead again. He could realize more clearly than ever that it was no more than a great game to her, the point of which was the nearness of their peril. This, while cold drops were starting out on him every moment.

They shot out of Miles Cañon into easier water, and presently the big teeth of Squaw Rapids were about them. Twice the boat struck, and once with such heaviness that Kate Winslow was almost flung from her grip on the mast. But in each instance fortune, or the skill of Steen, snatched them from the danger.

Dusk was gathering as they came down toward a mighty sound of roaring, and in the growing twilight Steen turned the head of the boat to the shore. A fire already twinkled there as it was kindled and broke into a broad, steady flare of light as they moored. It was the Englishman! He had come through in safety, in spite of all prophecies to the contrary. Half a dozen times, he said, he had had narrow squeaks.

"How many more of these jumping-off places are there in this blooming river?" he inquired. "And what's the blind beast that's roaring for meat, just ahead of me?"

"That's the White Horse," said Steen.

In the continual booming of the great rapids so near at hand, their voices sounded like noises in a dream. And dream-like appeared that shore with the heights behind, the darkness of mighty trees bringing night down more rapidly.

"What horse?" asked the Englishman.

Steen paused, with a smile that looked peculiarly grim by the firelight.

"The White Horse," he said. "The rapids that you hear over there. White because that's their color. Horse because the water runs like wild horses. Wild White Horses would be a better name than the other. You'll recognize the place when you see it."

"Good," said the Englishman. "I was always fond of horseflesh. You have a boy with you for the trip?"

He looked at Kate Winslow, half lost among the shadows, as she remained back from the firelight.

"Come up here, young fellow, and dry yourself by the fire. You're all sure to be wet after those rapids. It was worse than beaching a boat through a heavy surf."

She pointed to the side. "Thank you," she said. "But did someone run the rapids in that canoe?"

Their host had started as he heard the voice of a woman, but he controlled his surprise at once.

"Came down in a scow and was put off here," he replied. "Maybe he wants to do the White Horse, as you call it, in that shell of a boat?"

"He don't," said Steen. "No matter how crazy he may be, he don't want to do that! Indian, stranger?"

"As white as you or I. Gloomy-looking, and not a word out of him."

The girl turned abruptly to Harney. "Do you hear?" she whispered.

"I heard everything. What about it?"

"It's he!"

"Who?"

"It's that man who's haunting me, haunting all of us now! It's he who came down and was put off here. He's waiting to get the report from his men there above Miles Cañon. When that report comes, he'll start for us. D'you see, Joe? We can't camp here!"

The suggestion was sufficiently shocking. Harney drew Steen back and explained the idea of the girl, and Steen grunted like a startled horse when it feels the spur.

He went back to the Englishman.

"I think I know the fellow who owns that canoe," he said. "Can you gimme a better idea of him?"

"Why, a face easy to remember," said the Englishman. "Thin face, covered with a short beard, very wide forehead, and deep eyes. Set in deep under the forehead, I should say."

It was a description that could not be placed wrongly. It was undoubtedly their somber enemy, their man of mystery. The three stood silently, watching each others' faces by the firelight, as though they hoped to get inspiration from what they could read. They found none. A sort of weary despair had fallen upon them.

"It never ends," said the girl slowly. "It always keeps up. As long as he lives and I live, he'll never be off the trail. If I were generous," she added, with a sudden burst of emotion, "I'd throw myself into the mouth of the White Horse, and let it eat me. Because as long as I'm with you, he'll never stop! He's not a man. He's a ghost!"

Steen raised his hand. They had drawn back from earshot of the campfire, and the Englishman, readily taking the hint, did not follow them with questions, but merely began to brew tea.

"Talk sense," said Steen roughly to the girl. "Now, Harney, what idea you got around loose in your system?"

"We'll camp here," said Harney. "Camp here, and one of us keep guard, turn and turn about, all the night long. Chinook will help out, if there are strangers around, I guess."

"Stay here . . . and let him pick us up in his hand!" exclaimed the girl.

Steen brooded for a moment. Plainly he was the captain, and must decide. "We could get out the packs, take what we have to have, and the dogs. We could travel with them below the rough water, and let the rest of the stuff go."

"You couldn't take enough in one packload to keep from starving," she insisted. "And he'll send boats down the river, and with them he'll drop off scouts to hunt for us. In a day or two, they'll find us. They'll gather their friends with smoke signals. We'll be done for, all three, before a week's out. I know."

She said it with such perfect surety that it did not come into the mind of Harney to doubt her. Steen, also, was convinced, for he muttered: "Well, nobody could take the scow up the stream again."

"Nobody could," she answered.

"Then what's left?"

She was silent, staring at the ground. So were they, all three, for the question of Steen had answered itself in every mind. To stay here was to be taken into the hollow of his hand. To attempt to get down the river overland would be almost equally futile. The strength of this shadowy enchanter had been demonstrated too clearly against them, and they were willing to acknowledge their weakness. Their own courage, their own strength of hand, plus infinite luck, three times had baffled their enemy. But the fourth time was apt to be the end of the rope, and well they guessed it.

It was Steen who spoke again. "It's the White Horse then?"

"Now? At night?" asked Harney.

"Now . . . at night," echoed Steen grimly.

"What else is there?"

They could not speak in reply, and he went on heavily. "We'll have to make torches, and fix up the boat for the trip now. Harney, get some wood that'll burn to give us a light. You, Kate, build a fire. I'll bring out the stove. We'll eat something, and board up the scow across the mast so that we'll have half a chance of not swamping with the water we take aboard. Anybody got a better idea? No? Then start *pronto*. We'll be likely to need our time."

They did not question his decision. He had reduced the matter in the first place to one solitary point of escape, and now, half with determination and half with despair, they set about fulfilling his orders.

Chapter Twenty-Three

Riding White Horse

Working together, the thing was soon done. The men made from a number of loose boards, carried in the bottom of the scow, a hoarding braced against the mast, raising it several feet so that the sweep of the water dashed up by the bows might not come aft. They arranged it as strongly as possible to withstand the shock of driving water, and then came ashore where Kate was preparing food, and had finished it in readiness for them.

The Englishman had insisted that she use his ready-prepared fire, so that all went more rapidly. When he learned of their plan, he appeared to be enchanted. "Sporting," he called it, and a "jolly thought," and wondered if he should not pack up on board his craft and try to follow them. Steen briefly dissuaded him.

"One-to-ten chances like ours are all right," he said, "but who bets a thousand to win one iron man? You stay where you are. You'll need all the daylight you can find to-morrow."

A changing wind had polished every star in the sky, which would enable them to have at least a dim light on the journey. But as they finished their meal and the time came for the start, it seemed to Harney that the roar of the waters grew more and more threatening. As though a vast beast were stealing up on them, retreating, and then drawing closer again.

There was another uncomforting thought — that the man of the shadow might be somewhere near, peering out at them, stealing closer perhaps for a shot from the dark at Kate Winslow. All that might prevent his near approach was Chinook, prowling restlessly about the camp.

They were ready at last, Steen and Harney taking the last pull at their pipes, then rising to wave farewell to their host and stalking off to the scow, where the dogs greeted them with whimperings and growls, according to their individual natures. Now they were aboard, the mooring lines cast off, and the river began to take them. Slowly it urged them from the still water near the bank, but more and more strongly as the central theme of destruction involved them. Presently they saw a mist before them in a narrow mouth that gaped through the stone, a scant eight paces across.

The heart of Harney leaped as he watched it. It seemed like threading the eye of a needle to pass the scow through this narrow entrance, with the boiling of the water around them, but it was too late to turn now. A hundred oars could not have stemmed the sweep of the current. So they rapidly passed the lips of the cañon. It was like leaping into an icy cloud of white, filled with the shocks and the roarings of thunder, so thick was the spray that leaped above them, so bellowed the rocks as the river sprang at them and recoiled. They went with a dizzying speed.

The very first grip of the maëlstrom hurled them upward at an angle of forty-five degrees, then plunged them down with equal suddenness. They reeled, crashed broadside on a rock, and Harney prepared for death. But by grace there were no teeth in that rock face. It was polished smooth by the rubbing of the rapid water, and they glided off again onto the crest, with Steen making mighty use of his sweep at the prow. How any man could live through the dashings of the spray, the hammer strokes of great masses of upflung water, Harney could not tell. For it was rarely that he saw Steen other than as a fantastic shadow lost in the white and driving spume.

Sometimes, when the water lurched over the prow, it smote the hoardings with such force that almost all the way of the scow was lost and the spray exploded high in the air above them, putting out the stars. But yet the stars shone and gave Harney sight of what seemed inextricably entangled masses of white snakes that coiled and writhed in the hollow of the pass. Or again, as Steen in spite of himself allowed the craft to slide to the right off the crest of the current, Harney could understand why the place had taken its name. For, indeed, it was like the galloping of an endless chain of white horses with silver manes flying, with curved necks bowing up and down in their stride, with hoofs smiting on a hollow iron bridge so that the thunder jumped from rock to rock, and then rebellowed up to the lofty stars.

He lost all thought of all things. The nightmare seconds embraced and swallowed him, and he knew nothing of Steen, of the girl, of the dogs, of all the people in the world. Men have said that in such supreme moments of danger all their past flows before those about to die, but to Harney it was not true. He did not find a picture of his life rising before him, but, instead, he only knew that life itself was piercingly sweet, that it was about to slip from his hands, from the taste of his lips.

That thought made his arms steel to control the big-bladed sweep. Sometimes cross currents threatened to batter or jerk the handles out of his grip, but he maintained his hold and swept the entangled waters powerfully to keep the stern of the boat following as big Steen steered the prow. Sometimes, through the confusion of thunders, he could hear the dogs snarling in the pit of the boat as the icy water descended, drenching them, half filling the craft. That extra burden made the passage doubly difficult, giving the scow a greater drag against the sweeps, making it a lifeless and a leaden thing so far as the power of the arms of men were concerned, but a mere toy for the White Horse to toss and juggle.

That constant influx of water would have been fatal, if it had not been for Kate Winslow. With a collapsible bucket she worked unceasingly to bail the craft. If she could not decrease the amount of water on board, at least she could hold it level, unless the scow put her nose deliberately under a wave.

Let no one speak of waves at sea. They were as nothing compared to the hoarse fury of this narrow flume, undulating, piling high in the center, rushing again off to the sides, recoiling, returning, now seeming to halt like a horse on braced legs, now plunging away again like racers from the post.

Mightily and wisely worked Steen in the bows, blinded by the whiplash of the spray, cuffed and beaten by the strokes of the solid water that leaped at him. But hugely as he labored, he could not avoid all disaster. They smote a rock on the starboard. Plainly, Harney heard timbers crunch in the shock, felt them yield, like chicken bones in the jaws of a dog.

From that blow they recoiled to the farther side of the water. They reached the crest of the boiling current, pitched there as in a saddle, and then the stern of the boat flicked to the side in spite of Harney's bending the sweep in a curve as he struggled to meet the skidding motion. But all would not do. On the port side they smote, rebounded as though through air, and suddenly rode the central crest again.

They entered a passage filled with water smoke, powdered as fine as steam, indeed. It hung motionless in the air; it touched with a soft, cold breath upon the face as the scow leaped on. They were blinded, utterly, with no possibility to look ahead. Even the strongest sunlight would have been, it seemed, not bright enough to show them what lay all around.

But Harney could guess what was there before them and on either side — smooth stone face, and polished spear points, and jagged saws whose edges were just level with the surface of the water. As for the boiling of the caldron, he could feel it jumping beneath his feet.

Then, with a pitch and a lurch, they were flung forth from the hollow heart of the thunder, the blinding fog. Above them the stars gleamed. The river widened. And the last stroke of the river's fist spun them around from the rear and sent them slowly circling as they passed down the stream, even as a leaf whirls idly on the surface of a brook. Harney sighed. For the first time in hours, it seemed, air actually entered his muscle-contracted lungs. Then, with a stroke or two, he straightened the boat on its course, and they were floating idly, easily. His shoulders dropped, his head sank back loosely, he began to smile the weary smile of triumph and exhaustion.

Kate Winslow still was bailing, sending overboard bucket after bucket of liquid silver that streaked through the starlight and poured into the river. A dog began to howl like a wild wolf on the hunting trail. And that sound set the nerves of Harney jumping again until Chinook growled, and with his threat stilled the clamor.

Then Steen came aft, clambering slowly over the hoarding. Slowly he came, like a drunkard, with hanging head and arms, trailing the long sweep behind him. He was soaked completely to the skin and worn out with his huge efforts, yet when he could speak, he laughed. The laughter itself seemed like wine to him, and he cried: "What'll he do now? Run the White Horse after us? Not on this night, old son!"

They remained in a close circle for a moment, all three of them wet, weak, but vaguely happy, for they knew that they had performed almost a miracle. Other boats with loads had run the White Horse and would run it again. Other boats would even run it by night, but only under expert pilotage. But they were through. The jaws of the monster had snapped at them in vain, and now his roaring diminished gradually behind them, growing softer and softer, while the ringing passed from their ears. Utter peace possessed them. They stood closer together. They looked upon one another with that deep understanding that comes to brothers-in-arms who have dared death and seen it beaten from their way.

All things seemed beautiful and right about them. The trees stepped back in dignity from the river. The winds were still. In the quiet water at the margins of the stream they could see the small, bright faces of the stars looking back to their brothers in the sky. To make all of this more perfect, they still could hear the White Horse neighing, stamping, thundering behind them, but so distant that it was no more than the droning of a bee on a warm summer's afternoon.

"Build a fire in the stove amidships," said Kate Winslow at last. "You'd better try to dry your clothes. Then sleep, the pair of you. I'll steer."

"You? You'll steer?" asked Harney in a helpless wonder at the strength that was in her.

"I'm not tired," she told him quietly. "It's the first time in the whole journey that I've felt really rested!"

Chapter Twenty-Four

A Parting

The bank of the river was covered with berries, such high-bush blueberries as never were seen, and cranberries, strawberries, mossberries everywhere. The sun burned bright and hot overhead, thawing out the snow, sending ten million little rivulets down to join the mighty mass of the Yukon that moved majestically on toward the northern sea, unhurrying, and very still at its margins where the scow lay moored.

On the upper bank was Kate Winslow with her three dogs strung out in front of her single sled, with her diminished little pack posted on it. Steen and Harney had helped her. Chinook had come up, as usual, to look on and criticize the doings of mere humans.

For they had come almost to the end of their journey. Around the bend lay Circle City. Dim in the sky they could see a mist rising that, Steen said, came from the mosquito smudges that burned before every house. They had come within one step of the end. They had passed from that far-off region of day and night to the northland

217

where now all was day, and where afterward all would be darkness or twilight. They had crossed Lake La Barge, and nearly wrecked on its stormy waters. They had passed the ripping currents of Thirty Mile River, and ventured safely through Five Fingers and Rink Rapids. Half a dozen times they had almost been swept overboard by sweepers, but here at last they were safely arrived in sight of the little city of the Arctic.

The dangers they had passed were of small account, at this moment. Insects made the air drowsy with their humming; a bird was singing in the nearest patch of brush. All was summer — the strange, white summer of the north, starred and flushed with patches of short-lived flowers here and there.

Kate Winslow had been very business-like in hitching and harnessing her team. She was business-like still, standing with her hands on her hips and the dogs' whip with its furled lash in one of them. So she looked from one to the other.

"I know that you won't take money," she said, "or else you could have the rest of my money belt, which is still pretty heavy. You won't take thanks, either. I know what sort you are. I can only say one thing to the pair of you . . . nobody else could have done what you have done. You've beaten him! You've beaten him!" She said it with a sort of wonder. "I gave up when he paddled past the scow," she went on. "But you didn't give up."

Her glance rested on Harney for an instant, not tenderly, but with a bright, hard appreciation. Then she shrugged her shoulders, and added: "I can't say any more. It's like a dream, being here actually at the end of the trail. Good bye, Steen. Good bye, Harney!"

"Good bye," said Steen. "I'll go back to the scow. Harney ain't coming, yet. He'll want to stay here and maunder for a while. He'll have a good deal to say." He looked at Harney with one of his cryptic sneers and descended the bank to the boat, as he had promised.

It left Harney on one foot, as the saying goes, like a crane in a shallow pool. He bit his lip and glared after Steen in fierce resentment.

"What's made him so mean?" asked the girl. "So blue, I should have said. A little more, and I'd say Steen was sorry, sort of, to see me go."

She laughed at the thought even as she spoke it. Harney smiled in turn.

"There's nothing in the world that he's

fond of but his own way," said Harney. "I figgered that out a long time ago."

She canted her head thoughtfully to one side. "You don't like him a bit?" she asked.

"I like him a lot," said Harney, troubled by his own state of mind. "We've been a thousand miles together. He's never showed yaller . . . he's never stopped working . . . he's showed me the ropes. Only. . . ." He paused, adding at once: "I don't understand him, very well."

"Chinook! Chinook!" called Steen from below.

The dog turned, hesitated, then went grudgingly down the bank.

"I'll tell you one thing," she said. "If you expect to stay friends with him for long, you'd better be pretty cold and distant with Chinook. He's a little jealous of you with that dog, Joe."

"What? Chinook? I never fussed over Chinook."

"But Chinook likes to lie at your feet, not at Steen's. Chinook likes to follow you around. Chinook guards you in the woods. He doesn't trail Steen any longer. He acts as though he'd met his real master, at last."

Harney rubbed his chin. "I never thought of that," he said. "But Steen ain't small. He's big. He couldn't be jealous about a thing such as that, I tell you."

"Couldn't he . . . just," she said. And she smiled at him in a half-merry and half-pitying fashion that disturbed the big fellow.

Now, as he watched that smile and the brightness of her eyes, it came over him that perhaps this was the last time that he ever would see her again, and the thought made him sigh with open melancholy.

"What is it, Joe?" she asked him. "You look sick, really." She added: "It was that venison, the other night. If you're going to be such a greedy wolf and eat things half raw, you. . . ."

"It's you, Kate," he corrected her. "And I reckon that you know it's you."

"That makes you sick?"

He smiled a little. "It'll be my last look at you, I figger?" he queried.

"I suppose it will. Poor Joe, for your sake I hope that you'll never be tied to me for another trip to Circle City."

"That's not what you think," he surmised gloomily.

"What do I think then?"

"Wondering how deep I'm gone."

"Gone?"

"Aye, gone on account of you. Not meaning to play me like a fish on a line. I don't mean that. But wondering, sort of. It don't make a man mad to be follered by any dog, no matter how bad a mongrel."

She hesitated before she would answer him. "Well," she said at last, "you know the worst about me."

"I know nothin' about you," he insisted, "except what I've seen and heard on this here trip."

"You've read a letter," she began, "that told you. . . ."

He raised his hand. "I had no right to read it. I've been tryin' to forget ever since. You understand?"

"Joe, Joe," she said softly, "what a fine boy you are. Trying to push the horrible things about me out of your mind?"

"I couldn't do it, not entire. But now what I want to say is that I'd like to help you at the end of the trail . . . if you need help."

"Letter or not?"

He flushed. It was becoming hard to look at her steadily. His heart raced like an engine without a governor. "Letter or not," he echoed.

She smiled at him, and he, looking down at her, said deep in his throat: "Are you laughin' at me now, Kate? Or with me? Or what?"

"Smiling isn't laughing," she answered.

"But there comes trouble, and I'd better go on."

It was Chinook, who glided up the bank and, coming between them, actually pushed the girl back, so that she staggered. Then he sat down and looked gravely up into the face of his self-chosen master.

"Chinook!" called the great voice of Steen from the boat.

Chinook's head wavered for a fraction of an inch, and then he resumed his intent study of the face of his new master.

"Trouble, trouble," said the girl, stepping away and shaking her head at the dog. "It's all very well for Chinook to come between you and me, Joe, but it won't do when he comes between you and Steen. Oh, remember that, and be careful, careful."

She went back to the sled and waved her hand.

"Good bye, Joe!"

In that moment, as he waved in response, he was about to swing back toward the boat, when it seemed to Harney that he could not endure to turn his shoulder upon her, and shut her out forever. The last of his self-control disappeared with a rush like ice poured out to sea, and, freed from restraint, he strode to her with great steps.

She winced away in a singular manner

from his coming, and, turning toward him, threw up a hand before her face as if for protection. It amazed Harney — never before had she shown fear, except at the passing of her man of mystery.

"Tell me where I can find you," he said, "or I'll march into Circle City with you. Mind, I'll march in beside you."

"You don't mean it," she answered. "You're only pretending, Joe. Go back to the boat, and don't be silly." She said it sternly, with a wave of the hand that dismissed him.

"All right," said Harney. "Go ahead then, and I'll follow on. Steen!" he shouted over his shoulder. "Cast off. I'm gone!"

"Don't!" she cried. "You great. . . ." She clicked her teeth over the word that would have followed.

What would she have said, he wondered grimly. *Simpleton, perhaps, or calf, or some such pleasant word.* He was all of that, he felt. He was a blundering, sentimental, weak-kneed idiot. Then he heard the catch of her breath, like that of a person startled or half choked with resentment.

"Joe, in Circle City, find Sam Crockett, and you'll find me, perhaps. Now go back to the boat . . . quick! Or Steen will take you at your word."

He hesitated, glooming at her with a solemn tenderness and sorrow at their parting. For he put no trust in her words, or else the finding of Sam Crockett would be an impossible thing.

She stamped, the snow crunching underfoot.

"I don't want you with me on the way in!" she exclaimed. "Is that enough to tell you?"

He made a brief gesture of submission. "That's enough, I suppose," he said. "Good bye, Kate. I'll see you again . . . at Crockett's."

She spoke to the dogs, turning her back on him without another word and jerking on the gee pole, so that the light sled leaped away, and she ran on beside it with the free and swinging stride of a boy.

"Chinook!" thundered the voice of Steen from the river.

It drew big Harney about, but Chinook in person suddenly whined and seemed averse to return to the scow.

"What's in your head?" Harney asked him. "What's in your head?" Then he added with a start: "What's in her head, as well?"

Chapter Twenty-Five

To Find Sam Crockett

When Harney got back to the boat, Steen greeted him with the darkest of faces. He helped unmoor, and, as the boat began moving and after Chinook had bounded in, Steen suddenly said: "What've you done? Been stealin' dried fish to feed him?"

"Me?" asked Harney, amazed. "Stealin' fish for him? Chinook, you mean?"

"How else could you have wangled it?" asked Steen fiercely. "He's my dog, and you've stole him on the side!"

"Stole him!" burst out Harney.

The hot blood rushed into his face, darkness veiled his eyes in the extremity of his rage, but then with a great effort of the will he checked himself and said not a word. They were nearly at the end of the voyage, and, until they had gained that point, he determined that he would not have any more trouble with the big man who had been his partner over a thousand miles of trail and river. On shore, however, he would speak out.

Steen, also, said no more, and with

gloomy faces they refused to look at one another as the scow started down in the current for the town.

They saw the first of it now. There was a high bank and a row of small boats of all kinds moored at it. On top of the bank were piles of logs, ready for whipsawing.

That was all they could see, as they first moored the scow and then unloaded goods and dogs. All they heard was the familiar shuddering groan of the long saw drawn through green, wet wood.

They carted the goods to the top of the bank, from which they could see Circle City itself for the first time. It was not impressive. A fifty-foot strip ran down the river. Behind this were the log cabins of the little town, moss chinked and covered with mud to make them more impervious to the winter cold. The smudges rose from before every door to drive away the mosquitoes, whose whine now sifted ominously through the air and started the dogs snapping, snorting, shaking their heads. At one side two men were sawing. There were no other human beings in sight. This, then, was the first goal of their long march.

It was a city without sound. Even the groan of the saw was not important, or the clash of the dogs' teeth as they snapped, but all seemed half buried, lost. Somewhat as sounds come to the ear through the air of very high mountains, so they came here, faintly drifting through the air of the North-land that swallowed everything in silence.

In silence, too, Steen and Harney worked, until they had heaped the packs upon the sleds. Harney took one of the captured Indian sleds to tail on behind his own. Two went to Steen. On the other hand, four of the Indian dogs went to Harney, and only three to Steen, so that this could be considered a fair division of the spoils.

The scow was left empty, and they were ready for the start, when Harney went to Steen and said quietly: "Partner, you and me have made a long haul together. We've been a good many weeks together and done a lot, hand and hand. That's why I didn't yap back at you, yonder, a while ago. But now I gotta ask you what you meant, back there, about stealin' the dog?"

He said it gravely, but gently, and the answer of Steen was like the flash of fire. He pointed to Chinook, at a little distance, the last dog to be harnessed in the team.

"Why don't he come in when he sees the harness ready? Because you've spoiled him! By God, you've stole him as sure as though you took money out of my pocket!"

Loudly he spoke, and the two sawyers paused in their work and turned to watch and to listen.

"You're calling me a thief," said Harney, still waiting. "Y'understand that, Steen?"

"I understand English," retorted Steen. "Chinook!" he called.

The dog stood up, but did not come closer.

Steen stamped furiously.

"Now try him yourself!" he demanded.

Harney called, and at the first sound of his voice the huge dog leaped to him. Harney took him by the ruff of the mane and held him for Steen, who passed the noose of his dog whip around the husky's neck.

"Two years!" said Steen fiercely. "Then . . . this!"

He was dark red with his anger as he faced Harney, and the latter still controlled himself with a great effort, seeing not the face of Steen, not hearing his words, but instead, filled with a vision of the great white nights behind them and the stamping and neighing of the White Horse that would never quite pass from his mind.

"Steen," he said rather sadly, "I thought that we could wind up as friends. Now it looks like we can't even shake hands when we split. Is that right?"

"I'd rather shake the hand of a wildcat," said Steen. "There's more gratitude and there's more decency in one of 'em. Be on your way, Harney. I'm done with you for good. And, mind you! If ever I miss Chinook, I'm coming to find you, and I'm coming with a gun!"

He turned back to his team, and Harney to his.

Raggedly they made the start, for he was by no means an expert driver or they a combination used to his control. But in spite of his anger, there was more sorrow than rage in him. He was bewildered, furthermore, in the knowledge that it could not have been Chinook alone who had caused this outbreak on the part of Steen. Something else had been working like poison in the mind of the big fellow, and what that poison was baffled Harney.

He stopped his team near the pair of sawyers, who were about to resume work. "Partner," said Harney to the man in the pit, "I'd like to know where I'll find Sam Crockett?"

The man in the pit stared at him, then up at his fellow laborer on the platform above. "He wants to know where Sam Crockett is," he said, as though the man above had not been able to understand the question.

"He wants to know where Sam Crockett is," nodded the other. "All right."

He nodded again, and suddenly the saw was at work once more, driving up and down, pulling out a thin shower of shavings at every downstroke.

Harney wondered if the pair were mad, or if he himself were in his right senses.

"The two of you!" he cried suddenly.

The sawing paused.

"Did you hear me?" he asked. "I want to know where I can find Sam Crockett, if you know?"

The man in the pit rubbed his nose and sniffed.

"You ain't gonna find him in my pocket, stranger," he said. "All right, Bill!"

And straightway the sawing commenced again.

There was a raging impulse in big Harney to fling himself at the pitman and take the one above in turn and toss them like logs into the water from the riverbank, so that they might learn manners from the fish, so to speak.

But he had learned long before some degree of self-control. It is your inexperienced lover of fighting who plunges into every quarrel, or your bully, taking advantage of fear or of weakness. But he who has ranged the world with his fists balled and his guns in readiness generally has some measure of caution shot or knocked into him. So it was with Harney. The scars of a hundred battles were on his body; they were in his mind, also.

And now those past experiences helped him to control himself. Three or four years earlier, he would have gone for this insolently indifferent pair like a bulldog. Now he hesitated, then turned on his heel and went back to his team. He thought that he could understand this last affront. They had overheard the hard language of Steen and had taken it for granted that one who would submit to being called a thief was a natural coward. So they had treated him with perfect disdain.

He had not gone far with the team, when he heard a furious outbreak of snarling and growling and looked back to see Steen struggling with Chinook, who was making the most violent of efforts to back out of his harness.

Then, whirling, the big fellow leaped at the throat of his master. A lucky sidestep saved Steen. From a second attack he warded himself by bringing down the butt of his heavy whip over the head of the husky, and Chinook lay still, his red tongue lolling.

Dead? All that glorious power, that savage strength, that cunning, that devotion that had trailed Harney shadow-like through the woods, now was gone? He even thought, as he looked back toward the fallen form, that he had heard the crunch of the skull as the loaded whip butt went in.

Then he faced forward and lashed the dogs into a run, for he knew that if he gave one other glance behind, he would turn and be at the throat of Steen, and his life would repay that of the fallen wolf dog. He turned down the street as a man lighting a pipe came out from between two cabins.

"Hello, stranger," called Harney.

"Hello yourself, chechako," said the other, running an expert eye over the dogs, their harness, the sled, and the driver.

"Can you direct me to a gent by name of Sam Crockett in this town?"

"Crockett? Crockett?" said the other. "Humph!" He turned his back and disappeared down the alley between the two houses, while Harney, incredulous, fairly drugged with rage, stared after him.

Yet he swallowed that burst of anger as well as he could, and continued on his way. He could not explain these two affronts. He could only tell himself that a long stay in the Northland must reach the brains of men with frost. Or was there something disagreeable connected with Sam Crockett? One would have thought that the mention of his name was the inhalation of a poison gas.

One grim determination Harney made at that moment — that he would ask the question once more, politely, and then he would make Circle City think that a bomb had exploded in it if he did not receive a courteous answer.

A little farther on, he came to a saloon, and there, as at the post where all information is sure to be pooled, he stopped the team and went inside.

Chapter Twenty-Six

A Foolish Question?

It was the breath of another world, as he entered. The sour-sweet tang of whiskey was in the air. Under a rank mist of pipe smoke in a corner proceeded an amiable game of poker. In front of the bar, that ran down a side of the long room, men from the Birch Creek mines were lined up, buying drinks with pinches of gold dust. All of this was pleasant to the soul of big Joe Harney. The stove, being newly filled with wood, was making its chimney tremble with the volume of flames that roared up it. The air was warm, a little thick, streaked across with drifts of tobacco smoke at a lower level and misted above with bluish white. Beyond doubt it was a comfortable place, a place into which winter never put its frosty hand, day or night, through all the long, cold season. There was no chance for the wind to whistle in between the ponderous logs, where every chink was well stopped with moss and the crevices filled with mud.

So a warm, relaxed security filled the room, together with the poisonous fragrance of the whiskey, stealing away the minds of men and telling them to be gay, that the world was filled with good fellows, that friendship was not bought but a gift of the great gods, that happiness was a thing to be picked from the empty air, that merely to live was to be glorious. And to give a pulse to this sense, a rhythm and a harmony to it, someone sat at a piano in the corner of the place and played "The Harvest Moon" in chords, singing in a deep voice, a rich voice subdued for fear of cracking.

When Harney had surveyed the place and had a drink for fifty cents, he picked out the man who should answer his question. He had been, as he knew, the height of gentleness, of patience, and of care. But now he felt that he could indulge himself a little and stretch his elbows at the board by asking the question for the third time from the hardest-looking man in the crowd.

It was not difficult to select the man for the part. He stood out among the others at the bar as a bulldog stands out with mighty shoulders and blunt head in a crowd of dogs tall or short, fat or thin. When this man tipped his head to pour down a drink, wrinkles appeared deeply in the back of his neck, and they were not wrinkles of fat but wrinkles of power. A deep crease formed between his shoulder blades at every move of his massive arm. He was not tall, but he looked as though he could have plowed through whole football teams, tossing college heroes over his shoulder.

A most unbeautiful man he was, in addition. It was not alone his squat build, or his gorilla-like arms that dangled toward his knees, but the face itself would have been ugly even among Paleolithic cave dwellers. It was made in the dark, as it were, roughly thumbed of bone and flesh, and called "man" more by grace than by accuracy. His expression was as forbidding as his air. He stood in a corner, drinking by himself, casting a quick, suspicious eye over his shoulder, now and again, when one of the others at the bar came closer, or laughed loudly at a jest.

This was the man that Joe Harney measured with his glance and chose for his question. His eye trailed over the massive limbs and the deep chest of the other as an art lover might fondly dwell on the body of a Greek statue. It was a relish upon the very tongue of Joe Harney as he crossed the room and found the head of the bulldog thrown over his shoulder to glare at this intruder.

"Partner," said Harney ingratiatingly, "d'you mind telling me where I can find Sam Crockett?"

He saw the nostrils of the other twitch like the nostrils of a dog when a scent comes to it down the wind, a hot, reeking scent.

"You . . . damn' . . . simpleton!" said the man deliberately.

Half a pace back stepped Joe Harney. Joy played in his eye like lightning in a summer sky. "Bartender!" he called.

"That's right," sneered the other, "call your big brother, you long, drawn out piece of nothin'!"

"Bartender," said Harney again.

"What is it?" asked the rosy-faced man behind the bar.

"You might introduce me to my friend here. I'm Joe Harney."

"This here pal of yours is Mike Logan," said the bartender. "Meet Joe Harney, Mike."

"Ugh!" said Mike politely.

"Bartender," said Harney, "Mike's a little rude. I want you to watch me straighten him out a mite." And, lightly, he flicked Mike across the face with his open hand. He did not retreat after striking, but remained poised close up. It was, after all, the sort of battle he most enjoyed. And for all those ponderous shoulders, he trusted a strength that had been proved over two thousand miles of war-like men.

He heard a grunt of deep surprise from many throats, felt, like the turning on of lights, the concentration of many glances upon his face. But most of all he saw the spreading of an expression he could only call incredulous joy over the face of Mike Logan.

Slowly the latter turned. "Boy, d'you mean it?" he asked. "I ain't dreamin', or nothin'. You mean it?"

"I'm here close by, still talkin'," said Harney pleasantly.

"And whatcha intend to do?"

"Get an answer out of you if I have to tear it out with my fingers from your crop," said Harney in the same voice.

"Now, ain't that an interestin' idea," said the other, musing delightedly upon the thought. "Shake on it, boy!" He extended a great hand, furred with hair to the first joint of the fingers so that it looked like a gorilla's paw.

Harney did not hesitate. He laid his hand in that grasp, and the fingers flicked over it like iron bars contracting. Mighty was the pressure. For one long instant of dread, it seemed to Harney that his own hand must give way and fold up, the metacarpal bones crunching one upon the other under that incredible grip. But then with curled fingertips, he fought back. There was a polite smile on his lips, as of one acknowledging an introduction; on the face of Mike Logan leered a smile of brutal pleasure and anticipation, that gradually altered, as though it were frozen in place. It became empty, meaningless, like the smile of a prize fighter stunned by a blow, but still grinning in the vain hope of deceiving the referee and the friends at the ringside. So Mike Logan smiled as the digging fingers of Harney met the pressure of his hand, encompassed it, fought it, gradually surpassed it.

It was no work of an instant. For five minutes they stood opposite one another, the smile of Mike Logan growing looser and looser of lip, and that of Harney more contentedly pleasant. Moisture gleamed on their foreheads. Every man in the place had gathered about to see this strange contest. They stared. They spoke softly, registering bets with one another.

Harney could hear them laying wagers on Mike at long odds. But then the odds grew even, and finally they shifted to Harney himself. It was obvious that he was winning — the whole thick, long arm of Mike Logan was beginning to shake. Then his eyes flicked aside in a glance of infinite malice that burned at one of the wagerers. The next instant, with a curse, he strove to jerk his hand free, and slammed at the face of Harney with the other.

It was like trying to hit a wolf with a stone. The mighty arm shot over the shoulder of Harney as the latter dipped his head to the side. Then, twisting about, he jerked the right arm of Logan over his other shoulder, bent forward, and heaved all that ponderous bulk off his feet and into the air. Thunderously fell Mike Logan. The glasses jumped and tinkled upon the bar. Dust rose from the seams between the logs that covered the ground. A chair jiggled on the floor. But Mike lay still.

It was not until Harney himself had raised the loose, slipping weight of the man and half carried, half dragged him to a chair, that Mike's senses gradually recovered. The head that had fallen upon his breast reared itself again, and he looked about him like a sleepwalker, till he saw Harney and swayed forward from his chair. The fighting instinct was still strong in him, but his legs would not respond after the crushing blow that his head had received against the floor. Drunkenly he wobbled. Then he turned for the door and staggered to it, leaned there a moment, and finally managed to get into the open air.

Harney stepped to the bar. He was a little pale. His nostrils set out stiffly. But his eyes were bright as fire, so that the bartender found something to do in arranging his bottles beneath the cover of the upper plank.

"Bartender," said Harney, "I asked my friend, Mike, a question that he wouldn't answer. I'm gonna ask you now. Where do I find Sam Crockett?"

This remark jerked the bartender erect. "Crockett?" he repeated.

And like a soft echo came the murmur of the others in front of the bar: "Crockett!"

"You asked him about Crockett?"

"Yeah. I did."

"What did he say?"

"Said I was a damn' simpleton."

The bartender thoughtfully dried his hands upon his apron and then smiled upon the other customers. "I ain't in training," he said, "so I won't call you that. Even if I was in training, I lack forty pound of you, Harney. But I'll say this . . . there ain't a man in Circle City that knows where Sam Crockett is. And if there was, he would try to forget what he knew, and he would try mighty hard. No, sir, you ain't going to pry loose no information like that from me. First place, because I dunno. Second place, because I got a wife and a coupla kids back home, and it ain't worth my while to eat dynamite and call it m'lasses candy. That's all from me, Harney. Sorry. But if you wasn't just in new from the outside, you'd understand what I mean."

The others at the bar nodded in solemn agreement. They stared at Harney as they might have stared at a man trying to get through the bars into a lion's cage.

"Step up here, son," said an old sourdough. "Step up here and liquor, and don't you be foolish and start talkin' about . . . about . . . well, him that you was just mentionin'. Hey! Who let that streak of fur in?"

For the door was scratched open at that moment, and into the room came Chinook.

Chapter Twenty-Seven

A Case for Trial

He came straight to Harney, and, sitting down with his back against Harney's knees, he turned his formidable front to the rest of the world.

"Your dog, son?" asked the old sourdough who had proposed to treat.

"If he had his say," said Harney, "he would be."

The door opened again, and this time in came the two sawyers whom Harney had watched.

"It ain't Halleck or Chum Green, is it, that owns him?" asked the bartender, nodding toward the two who had just come in.

Before Harney could answer, the door was thrust open with a crash, and Steen plunged in. His gun glinted in his hand as he saw Chinook. In the rather dim light of the saloon the flash of the gun was perceptible. Its explosion dinted heavily in the ears of Harney. Chinook had flashed around behind him at once, as the bullet, narrowly missing both dog and man, spatted with a thud into the logs of the wall behind.

"Stand away from him!" thundered Steen to Harney. "You sneakin' dog thief, stand away from that dog, will you?"

Harney, hand on gun butt, waited. "If he was ten times your dog," he said, "I wouldn't budge to see you murder him."

"Then fill your hand!" shouted Steen. "I've bore a lot from you, and now I'm tired. I'm tired, Harney. D'you hear? Sidestep, damn you, or I'll slam you!"

The door crashed behind Steen's back and a worn-looking man of middle age stood within, regarding the scene with mild eyes.

"There's Harper," said someone behind Harney.

"Steen," said Harney, "put up your gun, and give me an even break. I'll handle you. I'm gonna let so much light into your brain, Steen, that you'll have one white man's thought before you kick out."

"Steen," broke in the latest entrant, "put up that gun, and don't you try to draw it ag'in, or you'll be sorry, I tell you." Steen leaped sideways, so that he could cover Harney, in a degree, with his attention, and yet get the corner of his eye upon the latest speaker. He saw, bewildered, that this was no type of a fighting man; he was not even carrying a gun.

"Is this here a joke?" asked Steen fiercely. "Are you drunk, you?"

"Put up your gun," said the other sternly. "We been laughed at and sneered at enough by Forty Mile, boys. If they ain't as much law in the U. S. A. as they is in Canada, we're a poor bunch of suckers, and I aim to show this pair of gents that we mean what we say. Come along, here, a few of you, and take the gun off of this maverick, if he's gonna try to bust down the fence!" He added to Steen: "You might bust down the fence, son, but what you ate on the other side would sure choke you."

In obedience to his suggestion, several men lurched forward from the bar, while the bartender said loudly: "Harper, you got the right idea. I'm plumb tired of never knowin' when the specks in the air is mosquitoes or bullets. Gets so's I can't tell, except by the speed they go by my ear. Harper, it's time for a miners' meeting to work out this job."

"Miners' meeting!" called another in the crowd, instantly taking up the idea. "They's enough powder in this pair to blow the half of Circle City off its base!"

In the meantime, those who advanced on Steen were partly checked by Harper. He said in his calm, authoritative manner: "Back up a little, boys. This Steen ain't going to be a fool. He'll put up his Colt and talk sense with us. Eh, Steen?"

The big man reluctantly thrust the gun into its holster. He was not one to give way before ordinary numbers, but they were not ordinary, these men who came in from the outside over the Chilkoot, down the lakes, and through the dangers of the rapids, a thousand miles of suffering to the gold fields. So he scanned those manly faces and, disdaining to retreat before them, at length he had taken the advice of Harper and put up his gun. But his dark face had grown still darker with his suppressed anger, and, raising his head, he stared venomously above the crowd at Harney.

The latter had not moved, but Chinook, when he saw that the gun was put away, came out in front of the man of his choice and sat down there, laughing with lolling red tongue at the discomfiture of Steen.

But there was no laughter in Harney. It was the end, he knew, of all friendship between him and that man who, he felt, was the most formidable in the world — unless there were a greater danger in Kate Winslow's man of the shadow. He remained now tensed and ready for any sudden effort on the part of Steen, for there was such hatred in the face of the latter that it would not have surprised Harney to see the gun once more flash into the hand of Steen to take his late partner's life even if he were lynched for the murder a moment later.

"I've come for the dog that was stole from me!" exclaimed Steen. "What kind of law you got up here in Circle City, I dunno . . . but my dog I'm gonna have, for the sake of shooting the treacherous brute's head off!"

"You'll see the kind of law that we have," said Harper. "We've got the law of a miners' meeting, and Congress, I reckon, takes our decisions to go as well as the best courts in the land. Boys, step over here and arrange yourselves around, we're gonna start this thing proper."

"A meeting!" said the others with a good deal of eagerness. "A meeting! Let's have the law on the thing, if they's a need of it."

"But," said the bartender, "I dunno that they's a need. Does Harney, over here, claim that the dog belongs to him?"

Harney half closed his eyes with a groan, and the wolf dog, at the sound, whirled from his sitting posture to confront the man he loved. He licked the big hand of Harney and looked wistfully up into his face.

"He's stole my dog, and he can't lie out of it," said Steen. "There's the best leader that ever pulled in the traces, or ever whipped a bunch of wolves into shape till they thought they was working dogs. There's a dog that can think just like a man . . . and he's been stole from me."

"If he can think like a man," said the bartender, "looks like he don't think your way, Steen."

There was a rumble of laughter at this.

"He wasn't stole," broke in Halleck, the long-nosed member of the two partners who had been whipsawing logs on the bank of the river. "I seen and heard Steen and Harney break up with a wrangle down by the Yukon. I seen Harney catch this here Chinook for Steen, and hold him till Steen had him safe. Seen Steen harness him up. Seen him tackle Steen. Seen Steen knock him out with the butt of his whip. Seen the dog later on break out of his harness after he's come to, and go streakin' down to the saloon, and into it, where this here Harney is. That's what I seen. Harney didn't steal him!"

"Leave Harney out of it," exclaimed Steen. "It's my dog. I claim him. I'll do what I please with him, and I'd like to see the man that'll stand between me and the doin' of what I want with a dog that I own!"

He said it bitterly, glaring around the room, and every pair of eyes that encountered his winced at the contact, even Harper's. Only Harney endured the stare and returned it with equal ferocity.

"Mind you, Steen," he broke in, "rather'n see you murder Chinook, because he's got the sense to pick a white man from a yaller-hearted skunk, I'll have it out with you. Now, here or outside, Steen. Hand or gun . . . or knife!" He brought the last word out through his teeth, for his anger was boiling high.

"I'll take you now," said Steen. "Outside, hand, or gun, or knife. From the day I set eye on you, I knew you were my meat one time . . . and that time's now!"

His great voice swelled and boomed through the place. Suddenly all these other men seemed to Harney like pygmies, hardly knee-high. There were in reality, only himself and Steen in the room. The others were a background, a mist through which they moved.

The voice of Harper recalled him to a more exact idea of things.

"I knew it'd be a case for a meeting," said Harper dryly. "Here's a pair that want to cut each other's throats. Here's a man that wants to kill his dog. It don't sound nacheral, and it don't sound right. What would the Canucks back at Forty Mile think about us? Tom Riley says when he was there, they called us wild Injuns down here. And if we let man murderin' and dog murderin' go on, they'll have a right to say it. They'll be right. Boys, it looks like the thing to decide is . . . has a dog got a right to pick his boss? Can he switch?"

There was silence.

"Anyway," said Harper, "we'll meet and talk it over, even if it don't seem right on the face of it, but I reckon that there's a good deal more to this squabble than you'd think."

There was a deep murmur of agreement, and instantly the court was formed. They gathered chairs and tables in a circle into the center of which Harper asked Harney to bring the dog. This he did, and with a single word made Chinook drop to the floor. There the dog remained, keeping his glance usually fixed upon Harney, but turning it in leisurely fashion to survey the circle of faces, sometimes canting it a little to the side as though he were listening carefully to some speaker and scrutinizing the words and the impulses of the human whose voice he heard and seemed to understand.

It was, in fact, the trial of a dog, and though at first it was the affair of Harney and of Steen that occupied all minds, by degrees the men passed into the background; the dog grew more and more important; and, at last, he took on the significance of an actual prisoner, a thing with body, brain, and soul, as much as any man could offer to the hands and the minds of the law.

"We'll have a judge appointed to begin with, boys," said Harper.

The bartender said instantly: "The gent that takes on this job of judge ain't likely to sleep heavy for a considerable spell, judgin' from the looks of Harney and Steen. Harper, if you got the nerve to tackle the job, it's yours, I'd say."

There was instant and general acclaim, as many voices called upon Harper to take the place as judge in this improvised court.

The man looked over the rest, then regarded the two men of the case with a calm interest. "I don't hanker after trouble," he said, "but, by Jiminy, I'm anxious to get past the outside of this matter. I'll take the job and do my best for both these gents, and for Chinook, too."

Chapter Twenty-Eight

Chinook in Court

When all was settled, the judge appointed a clerk of the court to write down a record of what passed. The clerk was not a swift worker with a pen. He sat at a table with his head sidewise and held close to the paper on which he labored, while his cheek was generally distended by the tongue that he had thrust into it. Repeatedly he stopped the operations so that he might get down the words, at the same time cursing softly or silently the difficulties of his job.

Next was the matter of a representation for the dog.

"Look here," said the judge, considering the big wolf dog with much attention, "it seems to me like Chinook ain't going to have much luck talking to us. Looks like he wouldn't say much, and if he did, as though we wouldn't be able to understand his lingo. Now, boys, here's a dog that's called by his boss the finest leader that ever tugged in traces in Alaska. And his boss wants to brain him. Who's gonna talk for him? Vic," he said finally, pointing to the bartender, "you speak up for Chinook the way you think he'd like things to go."

The bartender accepted the office with a grin. "I'll do the job," he said, "only I'd like to get introduced proper to the gentleman so's he won't take off my leg while I'm tryin' to save his neck."

This view of the thing caused a good deal of laughter, in the midst of which Harney took Vic, the bartender, out to the center of the circle and performed the ceremony of introduction, which consisted of taking the hand of the bartender in his and moving it toward the head of the wolf dog. Chinook, swift as light, took both hands in the great gap of his teeth, but feeling the flesh of Harney beneath his fangs, his head winced back, and he licked the big hand of his master in conciliation. So he submitted, presently, but with manifest loathing, to the touch of Vic upon his head.

"It's all right," said the bartender, straightening finally. "And if this here don't last too long," he went on, mopping his forehead, "I'll try to stick it out."

"The case is that Chinook, yonder," said the judge, "is accused of tryin' to steal himself away from the gent that owns him, Steen, and add himself to the gent that don't, Harney. He's accused of stealin', in the first place, of treachery, in the second. Chinook, whacha plead? Guilty or not guilty?"

The concentration of eyes upon the dog made him sufficiently uneasy to shake himself vigorously, then lie down, panting.

"By gosh, boys," said the judge, "he says, no, pretty clear! Not guilty! Write that down, clerk!"

The court applauded.

"Prisoner says, not guilty," went on Harper. "Steen, you own this here dog?"

"I own him," growled Steen.

"What's the proof you'd offer us for your ownership?"

Steen hesitated, dark with sullen anger, but he finally said: "An eight-inch scar on my right shoulder that Chinook ripped when I took him."

"Where did you take him?"

"Two years back," said Steen, "when he was a pup. I was five days out of Forty Mile, and I was mushing along without no dogs and only myself to pull my sled." He paused.

"Didn't have no dogs?" asked the judge, kindly interested.

"No," said Steen, "though I had three to start with."

"What become of them?"

"Ate them," said Steen, unperturbed.

There was a little stir in the court. There was hardly a man present who had not felt the pinch of famine, and the calm manner of Steen and the curtness with which he referred to the hard time instantly inclined all minds toward him.

"Go on," said the court. "You were pretty badly played out, and you'd ate three dogs."

"The wolves came down on me. It was winter, and pretty bad winter. They were no more than fluffs of wool and hollowness, and bones, those wolves, and they meant business. Their eyes was streaks of red, that was all." He made a pause to call up the picture. "They wouldn't tackle me for a long time, except for this here big fellow. He was only a cub then, but he was the biggest of the lot, and they were willing to go where he went. Three times I tried to shoot him, but the snow had got my eyes a little, the snow and the wind. And he jumped like a flash every time I drew a bead. Finally, as I was plugging along, head down, thinking I had them bluffed, something made me turn around, and there was the big gent, yonder, coming like a Chinook wind! He leaped and slashed me across the shoulder. He leaped to get my throat, and I managed to bash him over the head with my rifle." Again he hesitated. "That made the rest of 'em clear out. I felt the blood drainin' off down my arm and figgered that I was a goner. I never could make it into Forty Mile.

"But while I was standin' there, thinkin' about this, I got to wishin' that I had the power in the wolf at my feet to take me in. I seen that he wasn't pure wolf. No wolf ever had a head like that, and rounded ears, like the ears of a bear. Before he come to, I had a harness on him. And when he got waked up. . . ." He smiled sternly.

"We had about a day of wranglin'," he continued, "but finally Chinook agreed to help pull me into Forty Mile. That's how I got him. Does anybody wanta see my bill of sale?"

He touched his shoulder as he spoke, but the judge said hastily: "There ain't any need. Dollars is dollars, but nobody'll claim that they're as hard a price as blood. Mister Steen, you sure owned that dog . . . or wolf . . . or whatever he is! Wolves never was that size, so he must be part dog. Now, then, boys, we've got down to one thing. Steen found the dog and made him his. Got to be friendly with you, Steen?"

"No," said Steen honestly. "But after a while, he got to be interested in me. For a couple of months we played a game, him trying to cut my throat, and me trying to keep alive. He got a good many poundings, and I got a good many cuts. I never could break his spirit, and he never could polish me off. So it was a standing truce, though he learned to obey. That was where we were when Harney comes into the picture."

"Harney comes in," nodded the judge. "And then?"

"By feedin' him scraps of fish. . . ."

"You lie!" cried Harney.

Chinook leaped to his feet, his mane on end like a lion's as he heard the angered voice of the man he loved. The whole court was moved.

"Chinook says that his boss lies," interpreted Vic fearlessly.

"Go on, Steen, and shut up, Harney," said the judge. "You'll have your turn for yapping pretty soon."

"I say," said Steen, "that here was a dog that I had to watch all the time. I never was sure of him. I took him outside with me. I had him in the house with me. He never let Alaska get out of his eye. He never found a white man that he'd go near. He hated even the women. And he would've murdered the children. I used to have to keep him muzzled and on a chain. He was a murderer, every time he seen whites. But along comes this here Harney, and, after a while, Chinook begins to foller along at his heel, sit down at his feet, lick his hand, love him with his eyes. I ask you, is it nacheral or likely that Chinook would carry on like that if he wasn't bein' fed and pampered and treated fine?"

"It doesn't sound nacheral," said the judge, "but it looks to me like Chinook could digest a whole whale before he'd get friendly with the gent that fed it to him. Go on, Steen."

"I made up my mind that, if I couldn't make that dog my dog, he'd never belong to anybody. I seen Harney stealin' him away from me day by day, and I didn't say nothin'. The end of the trail hadn't come, but, when we got to Circle City, and he runs off after Harney, I made up my mind that Chinook had come to his last day, and, by grab, I mean it! Chinook dies before he pulls in another man's traces!"

This he said not with a raised voice, but rather sinking into deadly seriousness, so that every man there was drawn forward a little in his chair. Before the eyes of Harney, too, the same picture appeared that was painted in the mind of all those others who were there. They could see the bitter fight in the snow, the struggle to teach the wild beast to work in the harness, the long trek to Forty Mile, with a wounded, starved man staggering beside the sled. They saw as well the constant labor of two years to make the wild creature tame — to introduce one element of love and kindness into the nature of Chinook. The answer to all that effort was in the eyes of the great dog, green with inextinguishable hate as he looked at his master, and softening wonderfully whenever they turned upon Harney.

And this thing became, suddenly, more than the case of a mere dog — it was the tragedy of a great attempt and a great failure. With solemn faces these hard-handed men stared at Chinook, at Steen, and then at Harney — the man who had won. They waited with held breath; the very heart of suspense was in the air.

"Here," said the judge, after he himself had stared at the floor, weighing the importance of this testimony, "is the case of a gent that bought his dog with blood, and that wants to end him in blood, and I dunno that this here court has got the right to interfere. Has anybody got an idea?"

"I have . . . ," began Harney.

"Shut up, Harney," said the judge, paying no heed to him. "Shut up, and let somebody else talk. We know, all of us, what you wanta say. Has anybody else got anything to say? Why should Steen be barred from doin' as he pleases with a wolf that he couldn't turn into a dog?"

"Ask Chinook," said the bartender, in the midst of the total silence.

"Chinook," said the judge gravely, "you're standin' here a quarter of an inch from a cliff, though you can't see it, a cliff that'll drop you out of this here world of good marrow bones and dried fish and table scraps. Speak up, before I stop this here trial, and rule you into the hands of Steen."

A mosquito, at this moment, must have stung the nose of Chinook, for suddenly he began to rub his muzzle vigorously with his big paw — a puppyish action that caused the entire room to smile.

Vic leaned above him, with a hand to his ear, then straightened and said in all seriousness: "He says that he b'longs to the old U. S. A. where a war was fought to prove that all men are born free and equal. And why should he be a slave in a land where they ain't any slaves? That's what he says, and stands on."

"Vic," said the judge, "you're talkin' pretty foolish. This here is a dog. I take it . . . if he ain't a wolf . . . and dogs ain't men! Steen, I reckon that he's yours!"

Chapter Twenty-Nine

Law and Order in Circle City

To Harney that speech was a veritable thunderstroke. He had not realized until this moment that the dog meant to him something more than a mere dog. "Will you hold on, and lemme speak?" he demanded.

"The judge has given his decision," said Steen. "What could you say, anyway?"

"I can say something that'll give you a new angle on Chinook," answered Harney.

At the sound of his name upon the tongue of his new master, the big dog bounded to his feet, and, facing toward Harney, he lifted one foot and whined with eagerness to go to the man. But the order that had placed him on this spot still held him here. The great bushy tail swung slowly back and forth, and the whine, that sounded half snarl, half growl, vibrated in his throat.

The bartender said: " 'There's the man that I love, boys.' That's what Chinook is saying. 'There's the man that I love. The rest of you, why, to hell with you! I'd as soon eat you as veal. But there's the man for me. I'll work for him, fight, die for him, and never say no while there's a heart in me.' "

"Look at him, Steen," said the judge in a quiet voice. "No wolf ever wagged a tail. No wolf ever whined to come to a man for the love of him. Will you still hang to your word . . . to murder that Chinook yonder?"

Steen's face grew hard as ice. "If you had a woman that you'd loved," he said, "that you'd worked with and for, that you'd been wooin' for two years, studyin' to please, would you have her belong to another man, or plain dead?"

It was a question that struck sharply home. Heads nodded about the room in grim agreement. And the suspense increased, until men held their breaths anxiously.

"I took him out of the wilderness," said Steen, "I made him a dog, and not a wolf!"

"Then," cried Harney, "take him back and give him up to the wilderness again!"

"You're crazy!" snarled Steen. "Don't I know that there ain't a trail so long between him and you that he wouldn't cover it? They ain't enough miles and river and oceans in the world to keep him away from you, and you ask me to turn him loose? I'll turn him loose with a slug out of my gun. Harper, I'll take my dog!"

"Hold on," said the judge, "we ain't quite

through. We still gotta hear from Harney. Harney, what've you got to say?"

"I say," said Harney, "that Steen lied. I never fed him. Never once! Never patted him, at first. He used to drift around behind me through the woods, and I thought that he was waitin' for a chance to cut me down. But he wasn't. He was feelin' kindly toward me all the time."

He rumpled his hair, finding that the words came hard to him. But, with the stern need of speaking something to the point for the dog, he stepped forward a little from the edge of the circle and looked around him with the eye of a warrior.

They had seen, most of them, how this man had handled the bulk and the famous strength of Mike Logan; they saw him now as an antagonist fit for the stalwart Steen himself, so that in every man's mind there leaped up a picture of that possible battle, and a hungry wish to see it. So all men listened. They saw Harney's mental struggle, and sympathized with his lack of words.

"You want to talk about him as a dog," said Harney. "I wanta talk about him as a man. I wanta show you that Chinook has played the part of a man!"

The dog, hearing his name repeated, made as if to go forward, but, still held by the order which had placed him there, he lifted his long muzzle and let loose the long-drawn, terrible cry of the timber wolf that filled the room with terror, and yet seemed to come from afar.

Harney, troubled in his mind, desiring to be able to meet the eye of every man present honestly, went out to the place where the dog stood and laid a hand upon his head. Chinook at once sat down and looked happily up into the face of Harney. It was, at least, a happy expression for Chinook, though it was enough to have curdled the blood of an ordinary man. But yet, as one looked closer, one could see the melting of the eyes. Moreover, the bushy tail moved a little from side to side, sweeping the floor. The echoes of the wolf howl seemed to die slowly from the big room, while all there dwelt fixedly upon the man and the dog in the center of the circle.

Harney, frowning with effort, went on at last, his hand still on the head of Chinook.

"Partners," he began, "if I could show you the inside of how I feel, this would be easy, but all that I can do is to tell you the things that I've seen." He sighed. "There came a time when I went on a trail after a sled. Chinook showed me the way. We come on the sight of the sled and the men with it and eight dogs strung out ahead.

"They seen us, too, and started to light out. How could I ever catch up with 'em? But Chinook could. He went like the wind, old Chinook! He tackled the leader and killed him. He dodged through that crowd of huskies like lightning through clouds. He kept them tangled up till I got on the spot. Mind you, I hadn't told him what to do. But he knew! Was that like a dog, I ask you?

"And again up above Miles Cañon, a couple of yeggs tried to grab our scow, and I jumped onto it off the bank and knocked one of 'em out . . . but the fall knocked me, too, and I lay on my back and looked at the sky and could think but not budge, while the second crook came and heaved up a gun to batter my head in. But Chinook was there. He cut into that gent, and the crook jumped overboard. That was the saving of our scow, and everything on it. That was the saving of me.

"Partners, what can a man do that'll show him a man, except to fight for you when you're down. Well, old Chinook fought for me, and I can't forget it. Steen can! Partners, look at him! He never chose Steen. Steen grabbed him out of the woods, beat him to a pulp, made him work, but never could make a friend out of him. If Chinook could speak, what would he have to tell you?"

It was a very simple speech, stumblingly spoken. What gave it significance was that at every mention of his name, Chinook stirred and shuddered a little with pleasure at the voice that spoke it. And every man in the room stiffened a little, watching, and, finally when Harney spoke the name "Chinook," a faint tremor ran through every man. So Harney ended. He strove to find other words to speak, but they did not come. Instead, he made a few helpless, empty gestures.

"I don't seem to find no more to say, partners," he said at last.

After this, no one spoke for some time. At last, the judge shamelessly blew his nose with sounding violence.

"Steen," he said, "I'd like to know if you couldn't take a step back?"

"Not a step!" said Steen. "There's a thousand-dollar dog. Where's the law that can take him out of my hands?" He turned to Harney. "Can you buy him?" he asked. "Pay down a thousand cash, Harney, and he's your dog."

At this, Harney groaned aloud. For well Steen knew the state of his purse.

"Steen, Steen," he pleaded, "I've got a

rifle and a Colt. They're yours! I've got two sleds, and a pack. They're yours! I'll sign a note, besides, to pay you down the rest of the thousand when I've worked for it. I'll hire myself out in the mines, instead of prospectin' for myself. Will you take my promise for it?"

"Your promise?" sneered Steen. "I'll see you swing first. A thousand in good cash or dust . . . and the dog is yours! You ain't got it? Harper . . . judge . . . whatever they call you, do I get my dog?"

"It's a hard case," said Harper. "I'd rather have the hangin' of a man than send that dog to you. But . . . the law's the law, and. . . ."

At this the veteran sourdough who had offered to treat Harney earlier now spoke up. "Hold on, judge," he said. "Hold on, Harney and Steen. I got more in my belt than I need. You might pay down three or four pound of this, Harney, and welcome. There's lots more in the ground where I got it."

Steen broke out: "I don't want your money, but his. . . ."

A solid shout of acclaim drowned out Steen's voice. He saw himself swept headlong before the weight of popular sentiment, and, with gritting teeth, he submitted. The scales were brought. Harney, looking hungrily into the fox-like face of his benefactor, wrung his hands and demanded his name.

It was Dave Mayberry, at his service. Get the money back? He didn't worry about that. Not a whit.

So the sum was paid down into the money belt of Steen, who looked as though he had taken that much poison. Wildly he glared at Harney, and sternly Harney stared back.

"Hush up, boys!" called the judge. "There's one more thing. Shut up, will you all?"

Silence was restored.

"Now, the main idea," began Harper, "was to make Forty Mile set up and notice the law and order in Circle City. What I aim to say is that after Harney gets the dog, it'll be about half a day before him and Steen are at each other with knives, or guns, or bare hands. And they got the kind of hands that can kill!" He nodded to confirm his own decision, then he added: "Boys, we'll have a vote on an idea of mine. If Harney and Steen both are found dead, why, we bury 'em, sorrowin' but willin' to do our duty. But if Harney is found dead, by the old livin' Harry, we'll run down Steen, and, when we get him, we'll hang him to the first tree! We won't give him no trial. We'll just take things for granted. And if Steen is found dead, and no Harney nearby, we'll find big Harney and serve him the same way. So you two boys . . . if you want a happy life and a long one . . . had better take care of one another as long as you're in Circle City. If you wants kill each other, go jump in the Yukon together. But if you don't, be mighty careful, old sons!"

Steen, one hand propped against the wall, listened with a face convulsed with bitterness and rage. But Harney laughed as the judge put the vote, and one universal roar of applause made this odd decision the law of the land.

So were these two mortal enemies bound over to the peace and to the care of one another. The clerk, with scratching pen and swaying head, bit his tongue and labored hard to catch up. All knew that peace had been restored to Circle City for a time, at least.

Chapter Thirty

A Cup of Coffee

When the miners' meeting dissolved, it left a swirl of people going back to the bar, returning to their card games, or else stamping regretfully out of the saloon to go back to their work. But big Harney found Mayberry, who had advanced him the money for the purchase of Chinook. He wrung the hand of the old sourdough.

"But it ain't anything," said Mayberry. "Dog-gone me if I haven't had luck out there at the mines, and I expect that I'm gonna have a lot more. Why, there was only a day's work, and it meant the savin' of that dog for you. It ain't anything, Harney. Don't you think about it at all!"

He was so good natured and kindly that Harney looked upon him with an increased interest. He was one of those men who have the head of a bird set on a withered neck, a chinless head with a beak of a nose, and glittering little eyes. Out of his narrow chest rumbled a huge bass voice, wonderful to hear. This skinny man was continually wreathed in smiles. He seemed to possess some inward sunshine that made all things well for him.

"I'll find work *pronto*," said Harney. "I'll find work and get a chance to pay you back soon, old-timer."

"Come out to my diggings, if you want," suggested Mayberry. "I've got my claim out on Birch Creek, very handy. Pay is an ounce a day, that makes about seventeen dollars. You can work for me till you get a chance to locate for yourself. Does that sound good to you, Harney?"

"It sounds mighty big to me, Mayberry. When?"

"Now, if you want."

"There's no better time for me. My dogs are at the door."

"I'll have my string lined out in no time. I'm ready to go."

They went outside, where Harney's string rose apprehensively from the ground at the near approach of Chinook, but Chinook was more interested in the passage of another outfit down the street — five dogs, that looked made for speed, pulling a single Yukon sled and driven by a small man.

No, it was no man at all, but a woman's face that turned toward Harney in going past the saloon. But it was not her sex that startled Harney. It was the face itself, narrow and pale, with a great sweep of forehead above unusually deep-set eyes — the very face of the stranger who had striven to net and capture or destroy them on their way down the river. All the features were here modified and rendered more delicate, but the family resemblance was wonderfully close. Harney stared after her as she went on.

"D'you know her?" he asked of his companion, as she turned the corner of the street and disappeared.

"Know her? Why, I dunno. Maybe that's Missus Winslow. I think that's who it is."

"Missus Winslow? Who is she?"

"Why, Winslow's the fellow that's made the big strike out on the creek."

"And that's his wife?"

"Yeah. That's his wife, I think. I dunno. D'you know her?"

"I thought I did," said Harney. "And maybe I do. Mayberry, I won't be comin' out there today, maybe. More likely I'll be around here for one day, and then I'll start. They live out on the creek?"

"Not all of the time. They got a cabin over yonder in the woods, matter of fact. Pretty slick place, folks say."

"Whereabouts in the woods?"

"You go straight in, yonder. You can't

miss it. Are you gonna call?"

"I'll see you out on the creek," said Harney, and straightway rushed off in pursuit of the girl.

She had glimmered away into the edge of the woods and disappeared as he came into the open behind her, but Harney went on at full speed, with Chinook ahead of him as though he recognized the trail. So they came to the edge of the woods, where Harney paused again and looked around him in sudden alarm. For if she were, indeed, related to the man of the river, then there was danger connected with her as surely as there is danger in the paw of a wildcat.

He went on more softly, keeping to the side of the well-defined trail that had been broken through the woods. He was greatly excited, for he felt that if his eyes had not deceived him, and if she actually were blood kin to the man of mystery, then he was, perhaps, on the verge of making all manner of important discoveries. But the more important they were, the greater dangers would shroud them.

The woods opened suddenly into a small clearing, and there he saw a cabin heavily built of great logs, and looking as though it could laugh at the cold and the storms of a thousand winters. In front of the house the woman was rapidly unharnessing the last of the dogs, and at the sight of Chinook they came with a rush, all five to circle about him and strive to cut him down.

He, warily erect, placed himself at the back of his master and waited for the attack.

It was not delivered, for the woman was instantly after them, cutting right and left with her long-lashed dog whip. They scattered under the strokes, and she watched them fly, laughing a little and nodding.

"Too much wolf," she said. "But a mighty good thing for them that they didn't come within grips of Chinook."

"D'you know this dog?" Harney asked her.

"That's Steen's dog, of course. I suppose everyone knows about Chinook. Only, I've never seen him act so chummy before."

"He's taken charge of me," Harney told her. "Are you Missus Winslow?"

"Yes."

"My name is Harney. I've heard that Winslow has struck it big up at the mines."

"He has a good claim or two," she nodded.

She seemed perfectly matter-of-fact and open, and yet there was that about her that kept him more than a little uneasy.

"Then he's the sort of a man that might need an extra hand?"

"Why, of course, he may."

"I'll go look him up and ask," said Harney, "because I need a chance at a job until I've paid off the price of this dog."

"Ah, you've bought Chinook?"

"Yes. For a thousand."

"He's worth it," said Mrs. Winslow. "Come in and have a cup of coffee before you start back. My husband isn't here. He's up at the mines, and he'll be glad to have you, of course. Good workers are hard to get. The people up here would rather slave for themselves, naturally."

He followed her into the cabin. And as he walked behind her, he told himself that he must be carefully, carefully on guard, every moment he was near her. Trying to put things together, he wondered to find that she was Mrs. Winslow. Unless, to be sure, there were two men of that name in Circle City — brothers, perhaps, of whom the one had married Kate and the other this woman. However, Harney was certain that he was on the trail of important information.

He found the cabin on the inside both big and comfortable. There were some bearskins on the floor, some homemade but very comfortable chairs, and an array of pots and pans hanging against the wall just behind the stove. The banked fire of this now was roused, and soon the stovepipe was trembling and roaring, choked by the flood of ascending flames. This heat penetrated the damp and the chill of the room. Above the waistline, the air became almost hot, though there was still a chill dampness, like a cold bath, about Harney's feet. But that was to be taken for granted in Alaska, unless a strong fire were constantly maintained.

"The woods here, they keep things pretty damp, I suppose?" said Harney.

"But they give us plenty of fuel," replied Mrs. Winslow. "And besides, it's delightfully quiet here, as you can see for yourself."

Harney stared at her. Of course, there was quiet here, but where did the Northland lack quiet? Even the town itself was a city of silence where the snow muffled all footfalls, and where all sounds seemed shrunk to ghosts of reality. But this family needed silence, enjoyed the arctic quiet. He had to look down at the floor for an instant to compose himself so that his astonishment should not be too visible, but luckily she was still busied at the stove, preparing the coffee.

"But don't the loneliness bother you a good deal?" he asked her.

"Loneliness?" she said. She paused in measuring the coffee and clinked the iron spoon meditatively against the rim of the pot. "No, I'm never lonely," she told him at last. "There's always plenty to do."

"With your hands, yes."

"Oh, and with your head, too," she assured him. "I'm as busy as can be."

She laughed, as she said this, an odd note coming into her voice, and, as she laughed, it seemed to Harney that she became no longer beautiful, but wrinkled, aged, turned ugly. He would have called her thirty, the moment before. But all at once she was forty, at least. He had an unaccountable desire, also, to look behind him toward the door, as though danger might be entering from that direction at this moment.

But the coffee pot was already on the fire, and soon it was hissing and simmering, while Mrs. Winslow came to a chair near him and chatted good naturedly and with the freedom of the North. He answered freely her questions about himself, and his reasons for coming to Alaska. Until at last the coffee boiled, and she poured out two cupfuls.

She tasted her own cup as she handed him his. "It's bitter," she said. "We don't get the real thing up here. But, anyway, it will be a hot drink for you."

He thanked her, and drank it off, scalding as it was, then looked up to find that her eyes were fixed upon him, coldly meditative and still.

"Not so bitter, either," he said politely, "though it has a funny taste. I'd better be starting on, I suppose."

"Just as you please," she said, and turned back to the stove.

He rose, with an odd sense that his head had turned light and his knees weak, when he was restored to himself by the sudden shrieks of a woman in some adjoining room. It was a wild, fierce sound as though she were in agony. In the midst it stopped, as though stifled by a hand.

"What . . . what on earth . . . ," stammered Harney.

Mrs. Winslow seemed shut away from him behind a thickening veil. Now he heard her voice breaking heavily upon his ear, like the sound of voices that thicken and boom on the eardrum as ether begins to subdue the brain.

"You're curious about her?" asked Mrs. Winslow. "Well, you'll be with her in a little while."

Chapter Thirty-One

With Tied Hands

The veil before the eyes of big Harney grew thicker, his knees more flabby, but the horror of that voice which had rung at his ear and the sense in his own mind of what was coming to him gave him sufficient force to keep erect. He turned toward the door that seemed to waver from side to side like an image in water. He reached the latch of it, and heard the deep, anxious growl of Chinook on the outside. Then the drug gripped his brain like fire. His hand fell. Dimly, as noises in high mountains or visions seen through heavy fog, he heard the woman crying: "Help, Sam! I gave him enough to floor twenty, and he's still going . . . !"

Thereupon hands seized upon Harney. A whirl of darkness covered him. He vainly reached for a gun that was too heavy to be drawn. Or did it stick in the holster? Then he fell. The last thing his stubborn brain was aware of was that he was being dragged, that someone was cursing the bulk of him. He realized this, and with an odd certainty he was sure that he was being hauled toward his grave, to be flung in and covered with wet, cold, stifling clods.

When he recovered himself a little, his first impression was that he was choking, then that his brain had been battered, and finally he could open his eyes. At first he thought it was a great star, like ten Jupiters massed together and burning in a black sky; then it dissolved into a meager ray of light coming through a chink. He tried to sit up, but rough ropes gripped at his arms and legs and kept him immobile.

Here he heard the voice of Mrs. Winslow saying: "I don't think he'll pull through. I don't see how he can. My hand slipped when I was putting the stuff in."

"Why didn't you change it?" asked a man.

"If I threw that cupful out, I was afraid he might suspect something."

"You're so logical yourself, Sylvia," said the man, "that you suspect everyone else of being the same way . . . logical and wide awake. However, it may be simpler, after all, if he doesn't wake up. What do you think, Kate?"

Harney's brain, by that word, was dragged suddenly back into the realm of full consciousness. He waited, tense with eagerness, amazed, and the familiar voice of Kate Winslow answered: "He'll wake up."

"Will he?" said the man.

Then a shadow leaned over Harney. "He looks about dead," said the voice in Harney's very face. "But perhaps you're right, Kate. However, although you know him very well, you don't know how much Sylvia handed to him in that coffee."

Mrs. Winslow said: "Kate had made him into a great god. He can't fail, according to her."

"But still you see him here, Kate?" said the man.

Kate did not reply.

"We might as well go in and have something to eat," went on the man whom Sylvia called Sam. "I think they'll be reasonably safe here, and we can talk about their future. Give another pull on that rope that holds Kate's hands, will you, Sylvia?"

"They're tight enough," she assured him. "Her hands are already blue."

"So tender hearted, Sylvia?" said Sam.

Harney glanced out beneath his eyelashes, as the man leaned over and jerked hard, until there was a muffled exclamation from Kate. It made the hot blood leap into his brain, but in another moment his body went cold again. For, as the man straightened, Harney saw his face, and it was that of their man of mystery, he who had passed them on the river. Sam, they called him. Sam Crockett, therefore, he must be. That very instant his guess was confirmed.

"They've come so far, and done so very well," he said, "but poor Sam Crockett was beginning to worry a good deal. However, this reminds me of the old fable of the wishing gate . . . the two little children who searched for it all day through the woods and finally sat down right under it. So tired, however, that they didn't know where they were. Can't we say, in the same way, that our young friends hardly know what to do now that they are here?"

"But, oh, Sam," said Mrs. Winslow, "if those big hands actually had dropped on you!"

"They would have paralyzed me at the first grip," said Crockett calmly. "But you see that they didn't drop. What about Steen?"

"If Harney disappears, Steen will hang for murder."

"Heigh ho, the holly!" exclaimed Crockett. "That's true, also. The miners' meeting arranged that little detail, I'm glad to say. Harney dies from . . . exposure, shall we say? Drink and exposure, of course. Our dear little Kate vanishes in the cruel North-land. Mister Steen is hanged for the death of

Harney. And there you are, Sylvia. The whole party of these brave adventurers, who set out nobly to fight against great odds . . . what's become of them?" He laughed again.

Then they left, and, as the door closed behind them, Harney rolled to his side so that he could look across the room and see the girl. It was a little chamber stored with barrels and boxes — food supplies, no doubt — and against one of these boxes the girl was now wriggling to a sitting posture that made it plain that she had not been so tightly bound as Harney.

The moment she saw that he had turned with his open eyes fixed upon her, she cried out — a sound that died suddenly, as she realized that she might be overheard. Then breathlessly, with canted head, she listened toward the door. But nothing happened. In the other room, they could dimly hear the clanking of the ironware around the stove as Mrs. Winslow, no doubt, cooked the supper.

Kate looked back at Joe Harney then, with all the coldness, all of the complacent assuredness gone from her face. It was seeing her in a new guise, it was seeing her for the first time, as it seemed to Harney, and he dwelt half sadly and half joyfully upon the picture. She who had been masculinely strong now melted like a child before his eyes. Her lips trembled. The tears stood bright, ready to fall. He saw her face flush and the working of her throat. Always with the certainty that it was for him that she was grieving and not for herself.

"I gave you his name," she said at last. "Ah, and I should have guessed that somehow you would be able to find him, no matter how many of the others had failed. Joe, can you forgive me?"

"I forgive you dead easy," he replied. "It wasn't the name that brought me here, but the sight of Missus Winslow's face. That fetched me along. She looked like the sister of him."

The tears that had threatened to fall were controlled. But Kate's eyes remained softer, and whereas in the other days he had felt that she was looking through and through him with a cruel ease, now she dwelt on him hopelessly, as a child at an old man — something beyond comprehension.

"She is his sister," she said. Then she added: "Joe, here there are two of us, and there's something that we can do."

He smiled and shook his head.

"I've heard of ropes being rubbed in two," she said.

"So've I," answered Harney. "They can

be, too . . . in a couple of weeks of good hard work. I've heard of people bursting ropes, too. But that doesn't work out very well, either. There's enough hemp wrapped around me to keep me from catching cold, Kate. And there's enough to moor a ten-thousand-ton ship in a high wind. No, nothing but a knife will breeze me out of this anchorage, Kate."

"Are you dreadfully sick?" she asked him. "For all your smiling, Joe, you're white as a sheet."

"I feel," said Harney, "like I'd just been stepped on by an elephant . . . that he'd been standin' on me for an hour. Outside of that, I'm all right and coming stronger every minute. They've tied you in knots, too."

She shook her head, dismissing such an idle thought.

"Sam Crockett was here with me . . . then I heard your voice in the next room, I thought. And suddenly I hoped that it wasn't too late, but that I could warn you what sort of a place you were in. That was why I screamed. . . ." She grew paler, remembering that moment, then shook her head. "It was no good, Joe. He clapped his hand over my throat and told me he'd strangle me. It looked as though he meant to do it. And then they dragged you in. They dragged you in, and let you fall like a lump . . . like a sack . . . like a loose, dead thing. . . ." She closed her eyes and took a sharp breath. "Forgive me for what I've brought you to! We have an hour before us, perhaps. Joe, what do you want to do? Rage at me? Denounce me? I don't care. I'll listen and never speak a word back."

"I've told you my story," he answered her. "I want to hear yours. I want to know who the Winslow is to whom you're married. That'll make a beginning point. And after that, it'll make me tolerably happy just to hear you carry on and chatter, if you got the voice to stand it."

"Who's the Winslow who married me?" She looked at him with the faintest and most weary of smiles. "I should have told you long ago," she said. "But I was stubbornly proud and foolish. Partly because you'd read the letter. Partly because my pride was hurt that you could think such things of me. But . . . it wasn't a husband that wrote the letter to me. It was my own father, Joe."

Harney writhed in a sudden and involuntary effort to spring up from the floor. He relaxed after a moment, panting with excitement and effort. "Your father, Kate! Father? A letter like that?"

"He'd learned to hate me . . . to be afraid of me," she said steadily. "That was why."

"But he denounced you, Kate. He wouldn't have you near him."

"Would you want a daughter near you, if you thought she had tried to murder you?"

"Hold on!"

"That's what he thought."

"Murder?"

"He was sure of it. He took poison out of my hand."

Harney groaned. "You don't have to explain," he said. "Only. . . ." Then he broke in: "But this other woman . . . ?"

"She's Sam Crockett's sister. She's my father's second wife. Does that explain anything to you, Joe?"

"Everything!" he said savagely. "And me lyin' here with my hands tied."

Chapter Thirty-Two

A Strange Story

That story which Kate told to big Joe Harney in the rear room of the Winslow cabin would stay in his mind forever. He, with numbness and cold creeping through his body from the biting grip of the ropes, lay on his side and watched her face with an almost childish intentness, as men do when they strive to draw out more than the spoken words can say.

Her mother had died when she was very young, she said, and for ten years her father had lived without a woman in his house. But, only two years before this moment, he had married again, taking as a wife Sylvia Crockett.

The new wife in the house was looked upon with a good deal of horror by Kate, although she controlled her feelings and tried not to allow her emotions to show through. Nevertheless, Sylvia had discovered that she was hated.

"How?" asked Harney. "Though, I suppose, she could read minds if she wanted to?"

"She didn't have to," said the girl. "Men

don't watch faces as women do, Joe. They don't have to. They can speak their minds more boldly, and they can express themselves more in action. But women are taught to grow up with a smile. They're taught to speak softly, Joe. And so they learn to read one another past the surface indications. I knew that she hated and suspected me from the first, but I hoped that she wouldn't ever guess how I felt. But, one day, she looked through me as though I were glass. I gave her one glance unguarded, and she knew everything that she needed to know."

"I dunno," said Harney, "that I can follow the drift of this. I never heard of looks meaning so much. If a man's glum in the morning, it don't mean that he's glum all day."

"Because men don't have to pretend all the time. They can act more naturally. But when a woman's sham is put aside, then you can guess at the real truth about her."

"Maybe you can," agreed Harney. "How did she surprise you?"

"In the simplest way in the world. She had a caressing way with father. Did you ever meet him?"

"No. Never."

"He's big, rough, and likes to have people think that he's a sort of caveman and tyrant.

As a matter of fact, he's as soft-hearted as can be. And the caressing ways of Sylvia were what unnerved him and made him marry her in the first place, I'm sure. You see, whenever he looked at her, there was a smile. Whenever he made a joke . . . and he's full of very poor ones . . . she was ready with a laugh. She never had heard them before. How I used to despise her hypocrisy!"

"But never your dad? He never understood?"

"Why should he? He's like a child, unsuspicious, straightforward himself, and never wanting to believe anything bad of others. Poor Dad.

"Well, on this day he had told a story. I think I can remember it. It was about a man in Arizona who had been sitting up very late drinking with some friends, and this night he had a great deal too much. They were a rough lot, these friends of his, and they had taken as much red-eye as he, so in the early morning they decided to tar and feather him . . . and did it. He woke up in the desert on the red-hot sand with the sun over his head, burning him, and as he sat up and looked at himself, he burst into tears. 'In Hades, and a bird!' he said.

"Well, I suppose there's enough of a point

to that story, but it was Dad's favorite, and he told it every month, at least. I couldn't look anything but sour when I heard it, and, yet, at the finish of the story, I heard Sylvia break into hearty laughter. Dad laughed with her, as usual, and she looked around the room, as if she were inviting everyone to join in.

"That was when she met my eye. I know that my face was hard with contempt for her and suspicion of her, and her glance went straight into my very soul. The shutters were wide open, and she could see the whole house, I suppose. And what she saw there made her blink and look down at the floor. The laughter died on her lips. She managed a smile, but it was a frozen affair. From that moment I guessed that she understood how I felt, though I didn't dream how dangerous she could be.

"I think it was about a month or so after that, when I saw Sylvia walking in the garden with a man who looked very much like her. He had the same pale, narrow face, and the great wide forehead, and the dark, deep-set eyes. I was at the window of my room on the second floor, and, as I leaned out, he lifted his eyes and stared at me. I'm not a nervous sort, but that look of his frightened me. It had a calm, impersonal quality, as if I weren't a human being at all, and he were estimating me. In fact, I got away from that window as fast as I could, with an ugly feeling that I had been eavesdropping, or that they would suspect me of it.

"I didn't see the man again for a day or so, till I was walking down the street with Father and we passed the same man. He drooped his head a little and hurried past as though he didn't want to be recognized, but Father stopped and looked at him. Father gazed after him with a sort of horror on his face. 'There goes the worst scoundrel in the world and the coldest-blooded villain. That's Sam Crockett!' he exclaimed.

" 'Is he Sylvia's brother?' I asked.

" 'Good heavens, no!' said father. 'Sylvia has no relatives alive.'

"I couldn't help saying . . . 'I saw him walking in the garden with Sylvia the other morning!'

"Father turned gray, and set his jaw, but he didn't say anything more to me. He did to Sylvia, however. She had told him that she had no relatives, and he taxed her with it. He hated lies . . . he still hates them. She tried to explain it away. There must have been a frightful scene. I think she told him frankly that she was afraid that anyone would connect her with Sam, and that was exactly the reason she had refused to tell him the truth about her family. I know she wept, or pretended to weep a good deal.

"But Father wouldn't forgive her. I think he decided that they must be separated, and, when Sylvia heard that, she was desperate. Or perhaps she had been waiting all this time to find out how she could get rid of him and decided that there would be no better day than this.

"She pretended to have a nervous breakdown and went to bed. The next morning, I cooked breakfast for Father, and prepared a glass of orange juice for him. I remember that it was a bright morning, with the sun streaming in through the kitchen window and striking through the glass of orange juice on the table, filling it with sparkles. Father had just come into the dining room, and I went running in to say good morning to him. When I came back to the kitchen, I noticed that the door to the backstairs was open, but I didn't think anything of that. I carried the drink of orange juice to Father, and he took a small swallow of it. He pushed back his chair at once and said that the stuff had an unusually strange taste. I'll never forget the way he looked at me as he said it. He wouldn't touch another thing for breakfast, but put the orange juice in a bottle and went downtown.

"I thought it was rather strange, but still I didn't suspect. However, he came back in mid-morning. He had had the orange juice analyzed, and in it there was arsenic . . . enough to kill even a man as big and strong as he. He never is a man to mince words. He told me at once that he didn't know what evil possessed me, unless it were because I wanted to get rid of him and have my share of his estate at once.

"I did the worst thing I could have done. I was angry that I should be suspected, and terribly hurt, of course. So I played the proud part and refused to explain anything, though I did tell him about the open door to the backstairs. He gave me one grim look and went upstairs.

"A little later, I heard a dreadful scream from Sylvia's room. I ran up and opened the door. She was lying in Father's arms. She had fainted, or pretended to faint, when he merely mentioned what had been in the orange juice.

" 'If I am not the blindest man in the world,' he said, 'she's had nothing to do with this. How could she? She hasn't the nervous strength to walk across the room, let alone go down the stairs and back again.'

"I stared at them, not able to speak, because I saw that she had been able to convince him at one stroke. She would have been an even greater actress on the stage than a murderess in plain life. But that was the end of me with Father.

"Afterward, he came to me and swore that he would forgive me if I would explain what had made me hate him, or how he had scanted his duty to me. And he wanted to know if this was the result of my wanting so desperately to go East?

"I simply denied everything. He studied me for a long time. Then he said . . . 'Whatever else happens, I'll tell you now, Kate, that I'll never suspect that poor woman upstairs. She loves me, I think, more than she loves herself. Heaven forgive me! Is it her fault that she has a fiend for a brother? Kate, confess that you thought you would take this chance of getting rid of me when there was an excellent opportunity of putting the blame on poor, sick Sylvia? Who else would be suspected except the wife that I was planning to divorce? I had already talked to the lawyer about it. She would have hanged for your crime, and the whole property would have fallen into your hands.'

"That was what he said, and I was tongue-tied. I've thought since of a great many things that I could have said, but I didn't say them. And a week later he was gone from the house and left me alone in it. He took Sylvia with him, of course, and came up here to Alaska. I'd been up here with him one winter before, when I was much younger, and I would have been glad to come again.

"I followed him with letters. I couldn't find my tongue when he was talking to me, telling me about his suspicions, but I found it again in writing to him. Well, no answer ever came from him except the letter that you read. What happened, I don't know. I tried to point out in my letters that I never had bought any arsenic in the town, and that I could prove I never possessed any of it. But nothing seemed to make any difference, and the one letter I got was the one you read. After I had read it, it didn't take me long to make up my mind. I packed and started for Circle City . . . and on the way I luckily found you, and so I got through the first traps of Sam Crockett. But when I left you, that was the end of me, as I half suspected it would be. They caught me and brought me here. And you've followed me. Heaven forgive me for your life, Joe."

Chapter Thirty-Three

Chinook Smells a Rat

She had not finished the last words when the door to the other room jerked open and Sam Crockett stood before them with a long-barreled Colt hanging in his fingers. His eyes glowed as he surveyed his two prisoners for a moment, and, then, stepping quickly inside, he shut the door softly behind him. At the same instant, Harney heard a deep, strong voice in the next room — the voice of Steen. It was audible because the door had not been pushed securely home by Crockett, and the latter now stood with his hand upon the wooden knob, listening intently.

He only turned his head and his glowing eyes upon his two prisoners to whisper: "Not a word . . . not a breath from you." And he twitched up the muzzle of the revolver to give point to his remark.

There was no need of such a gesture. As plainly as day, Crockett meant business, and that business was murder. Only he had spread the mouth of his trap to include Steen.

And Steen's voice, in the meantime, was

saying in the other room: "Hello, Missus Winslow. Good morning to you."

"Is it morning?" she answered cheerfully.

"I dunno," said Steen. "But it always seems like morning up in this end of the world. Don't it? When it's not night, I mean?"

"No, it's like dusk to me," said Sylvia Crockett. "I mean, when the day's sliding down into the evening. Will you have some coffee, Mister Steen?"

"You know me, then?" asked Steen.

"I saw you come in when you won the race from Forty Mile last year."

"Chinook won it, not me," said Steen frankly.

"Oh, there's a dog! You still have him?"

"No. He belongs to Harney. D'you know Harney?"

"Harney? I never heard of him."

"You will soon," said Steen grimly. "He's the kind that gets heard of, I can tell you. He came up from the coast with me."

"What sort of a man?"

"My size. Better natured."

"They can do with your size in Alaska, Mister Steen. You'll have some coffee?"

"Thanks. I'm a tea drinker, Missus Winslow. You've got a fine snug place here."

"My husband's a great builder."

"And digger, too," said Steen. "They tell me that he's taking out a ton of the stuff."

"He's getting along," she assented cautiously. "I'll brew some tea for you, Mister Steen."

"Thanks," he said. "About that Chinook dog, that you were mentioning. . . ."

"Yes?"

"Ain't been around here today, has he?"

"Chinook? No. What would he be doing around here?"

"Why, I dunno. I thought that maybe he would be. Missed him from town."

"Thought you said that he belonged to a man by name of Harney just now?"

"He does, but I want to keep Harney under my eye, and where Harney is that dog'll be."

"Oh, Harney's a chechako, is he?"

"Pretty green one, at that. He ain't been by, I suppose?"

"Harney? A man your size?"

"Yes. About my size."

"When I was coming in from the town, I saw a man . . . a big man . . . and a big dog at his heel, walking across past the timber."

"Very big?"

"Well, you can't tell so well when there's a distance between you and a thing. But I'd say it was one of the biggest dogs that I ever saw. The man was big, too. Not so big as you, I would have said."

"It's Harney, then," said Steen. "What could he be doing off in that direction?"

"Gone to pick up gold off the top of the snow, maybe, or maybe he expects to find it hanging on the trees."

"He's not a fool, even if he's green. He's as hard as they come, this Harney."

"Oh, is he?"

"You'll hear more about him one of these days."

"Maybe I will. Here's your tea, Mister Steen."

"Thanks," said Steen.

Harney listened, drops standing on his face in spite of the cold close to the floor. He looked at the girl and saw that her face, also, was constricted with anxiety, while Sam Crockett watched them both with a thin-lipped smile of malice. He could afford to trust to the efficacy of his sister's potions. Their strength already had been tried out upon big Harney himself.

"You're not drinking your tea, Mister Steen," said Mrs. Winslow presently.

"I burned my tongue a while ago, and I have to be a little careful now."

"It's a painful thing, a burned tongue."

"Ain't it? Not up to boiled new potatoes, though."

"No, they're regular stoves to hold the heat. Here's a biscuit, if you want it."

"Thanks, I'm not hungry. About Chinook, though. . . ."

"Oh, the dog?"

"Yes. Not the wind. But about Chinook. I came along this way hoping to find him."

"I've told you what I've seen and what I haven't," she said, a little asperity breaking into her voice.

"I know you have. However, the fact is that I followed Chinook's trail right up to the door of your house."

Harney started, and he saw the face of Crockett grow paler and the nostrils flare. Never before had he seen murder so clearly defined on any human face.

"Up to the door of my house!" exclaimed Mrs. Winslow. "Why, man, that's a hard thing to believe! Chinook? But what does it mean?"

"I dunno," said Steen, "but I'd take it ordinary to mean that, nine chances out of ten, the man was right in this house."

That caused the heart of Harney to leap again. He must have stirred upon the floor, because Crockett turned suddenly upon him and threatened with the leveled revolver.

Mrs. Winslow had managed to bring out a pleasantly musical laugh.

"You people," she said. "How could he be here? I've been all over the house since I came home."

"Have you?"

"Yes. I missed a bag of prunes, and they weren't in the storeroom."

"Which is the storeroom?"

"There at the back," said Mrs. Winslow reluctantly.

"I'd like to see how you lucky people stack up the food for the winter," said Steen.

"You can see if you want, but it's no use. Nothing but barrels and boxes and such things."

"Is that all?"

"Yes. Just the way the things came up the river on the steamer."

"I'll see some other day, then."

Undoubtedly Steen was playing for time, in some manner. But his reflections and attempts were cut short by the long-drawn howl of a wolf, sounding strangely out of place in the full of the daylight, and horribly close to the house.

"There you are," said Steen at once.

"What is it?" she asked. "It sounds like a wolf at my door!"

"Does it?" said Steen. "I'll tell you a

better thing than that . . . it's Chinook."

"Chinook again!" she exclaimed impatiently.

"Oh, he must have some idea back in his mind," said Steen complacently. "Can I open the door?"

"I don't want snow and mud tracked all over the floor," she insisted quite sharply.

"Aw, but I want you to see a champion," said Steen.

"I've seen him already. I hate dogs!" she exclaimed.

"I'll sweep out after him myself," insisted Steen.

The hinges of the outer door creaked. Then the vast growl of Chinook rumbled through the room.

It gave to Harney his first actual hope. Not that he could attribute more power to help to the dog than to Steen, but somehow it seemed to him that there was more than mere physical power in Chinook, more than mere dog cunning. He loomed large in the mind, but somehow it seemed to him that he could understand when Crockett shook his head more grimly than before and glanced over his shoulder with a hunted look. Surely with Chinook on the trail there was no escape and, together with Steen, he was a formidable force.

"What a terrible-looking brute!" said Mrs. Winslow. "But here, puppy! Here's a scrap of fish for you. Look, Mister Steen . . . he won't touch it. I'll wager that he's gone mad. He won't eat. Do get him out of the house for me!"

"He won't eat. He's thinking about the man he wants to find, Missus Winslow. D'you see? A good dog's like a good woman. Only one man at a time in his heart. Don't get near him, or he's likely to take an arm off you. His bite is like the stroke of an axe."

Strong nails were heard clicking on the floor of the larger room.

"You ain't seen Harney?" repeated Steen.

"No, no!" exclaimed Mrs. Winslow, nervousness breaking into her voice at the same moment. "I don't see why you keep harping on that man's name all the while. But . . . you'd better drink your tea before it grows cold, Mister Steen."

"The tea can wait," said Steen grimly. "I'd always rather watch a dog on a trail. Is he after a cat, maybe?"

"There's no cat in the house. Maybe he smells a rat, though."

"Now, there's an idea," said Steen. "Maybe he smells a rat and is after it." He spoke with a certain significance.

The next moment there was a loud sniffing at the base of the door, followed by the unmistakable whine of the great dog, half whine, half deep growl, and the sound of his nails being drawn along the crack in the door.

Chapter Thirty-Four

Danger Everywhere

Waiting for no more, Crockett leaned heavily against the door. He thrust it home and pushed the bolt across.

"Hello," Steen was saying. "Didn't that door move? And what does Chinook want with it?"

Then the closing of the door shut away all sound of his voice except a murmur.

Crockett, in the meantime, stood at full pause, uncertain what he should attempt, although the flare and the fall of his nostrils and the malignant eye he cast on his prisoners was a reasonable indication of what he would have liked to do.

Kate Winslow, wonderfully calm as usual, interpreted aloud for him.

"Kill them! That's what I want to do. Blow their brains out . . . leave them here . . . and get away. But what's the good of that, eh?"

"And why not good?" asked Crockett in a fierce whisper, moving until he stood over her. "Why not good? The satisfaction of clearing you out of the way, pretty Kate,

307

would be about enough for me. More than enough."

"You don't love me, Sam, do you?" she asked him, opening her eyes as though childishly hurt.

"You've forced everything from the start," he told her, actually weighing the gun in his hand. "Every trouble that we've had has been because we've had to dodge you . . . and the hulking loafers you've picked up!" He cast a venomous side glance at Harney as he spoke.

"But if you want to finish us off, as you'd so love to do," she suggested, "there would be all manner of trouble. Steen would surely find the bodies. Then think of the ugly scandal that might follow? And trails in the snow . . . and Chinook with the nose of a bloodhound . . . you wouldn't want to get into such trouble as that, old fellow, would you?"

His face worked as he listened to her. "After all," he said, "the money's not in you. And without much haste, I still have plenty of time to finish off the job where it pays to finish it." He laughed down at her as he spoke, and she shrank beneath that ugly laughter.

A heavy hand struck at the door. The bolt jarred and crashed in its sockets. Crockett sprang across the floor to the outer side of the room. There he fitted a key into a lock that opened for him a narrow side entrance. Through this he slipped, closed it behind him, and turned the key from the outside.

Harney was already shouting, as soon as the menace was gone: "Steen, Steen! Get the woman! Get Missus Winslow! We're both in here . . . Kate and I!"

He thundered with all his might, but Steen already was at work. Two crashes against the door followed. The first made it spring out at top and bottom. The second cast it down with thunder upon the floor, across which Steen lurched, unable to control his impetus.

Big Chinook, behind him, flashed past and instantly was lying on the breast of Harney, and was lovingly licking his face.

But Harney cried again, and again: "Steen, Steen! Get Missus Winslow! She's half the battle. Get her, Steen!"

The other, with an oath, and a single wild glance at the two bound victims, whirled back into the broken doorway. But it was only as the outer door of the house slammed heavily and sent a booming echo through the place.

Steen came back. "I should have nailed her the minute that Chinook began to stalk this here door," he said. "I was a fool . . . was there someone else here? Who tied you? What happened?"

"Caught by Sam Crockett and his sister. That's his sister out there . . . Missus Winslow."

"I'll get her now, then!" cried Steen, spinning about again.

"Don't, you chump!" shouted Harney. "They'll shoot your head off if you show so much as a nose outside the door. But pull this dog off me and cut my hands loose."

Steen was instantly at work. First the girl was freed and lifted to her feet, which she stamped while rubbing her hands together for the sake of restoring circulation. Then she hobbled toward the main room of the cabin.

Harney was liberated next. He was even worse off than Kate. His big limbs would hardly operate for the time being, and he had to thrash his arms to get the numbness out of his muscles.

He growled out his story to Steen in a moment, and the other answered: "I followed Chinook. There ain't two tracks like his. Now where for it, Harney? Where does the game lie?"

The girl came back into the doorway to hear.

"The game lies up at Birch Creek or beyond. Wherever my father is," she said.

"Father?" grunted Steen.

"The husband we talked about, that was her father," explained Harney rapidly. "She's been crooked out of his house by Sam Crockett and his sister, who's married to him. And there you are. They're trekkin' now for Birch Creek, wherever that is, to polish him off. Kate, is that the story of what's going to happen?"

"That's the story," she assented.

They looked at one another.

"Have you tried the front door?" asked Steen.

"No."

"I'll try it."

"Take care. It'll be like touching off some powder!"

It was exactly like that, for when Steen cautiously jerked open the door — himself remaining well out of sight on the inside of the room with its shadows over him — there was a blast of bullets from what seemed like at least half a dozen repeating rifles. Steen kicked the door shut again, just as a random slug bored a hole through a big copper pan behind the stove, making the puncture with a great *clang*.

The big man came back, as Harney

kneaded the sore places of his legs where the ropes had bitten almost to the bone. And they held a council around the central table.

"What will Crockett do?" asked the girl. "Will he go up to Birch Creek to . . . ?"

Here she paused, and Harney had respect for the pallor that spread over her face.

"Or will he stay here and box us up and keep us sealed until he is ready to peel us out and kill us off?" suggested Steen as the other alternative.

"What sort of safe men has he got working under him?" asked Harney. "D'you know that, Kate?"

"Well, you've seen some of them."

"The ones I've seen were Injuns, half-breeds, and whites no better than the others. Sluggers, yeggs, gunmen. Whacha think, Steen?"

Steen did not answer for a moment. His attention was riveted upon the girl, of whom he suddenly demanded: "Why did you do it?"

"What?"

"Make fools of us. Make perfect fools of us! Couldn't you trust us that far?"

"I felt," she said slowly, "that I'd better be like a man on that trail. Not a very big man . . . but a sort of a man. That was what I was trying to be."

"She was trying to be a man," said Steen, with his habitual sneer and still never taking his eyes off her. "She was trying to be a man," he slowly repeated. And, out of this remark, he seemed to extract a great significance, for he broke into harsh-sounding laughter.

Harney struck him on the shoulder, impatient. "What's the use of talking about that?" he asked. "We got our job here, haven't we? Why turn back into the past that way?"

"Look here," said Steen. "Suppose that you was mighty sick and expected to die, wouldn't you want to know the name of the disease, if you could?"

"Why, I suppose so. You must be crazy, Steen, to want to be talking this way. Minutes, why, they may mean everything now."

"Sure they may, to her," said Steen. "But why to us? We're settin' pretty here. We got log walls that the bullets ain't likely to go through. We got a storeroom clogged with eats. Why be in a hurry, I say? Let the time roll. No, she's the thing that will get us out."

"I've never begged any man for help," Kate asserted proudly.

"Kate," said Steen, almost in disgust, "you don't ask it because you don't have to ask. You was born to use your eyes, I guess?

Harney, she's the disease that's gonna get us out in the cold, and she's the disease that's gonna kill us!" He pointed at the girl.

Harney, crimson with shame and rage, struck down Steen's hand. "Are you drunk?" he asked.

He expected Steen to fling himself at his throat, but, instead, Steen lolled back against the wall and laughed.

"I know what I'm talking about. It ain't her fault. She understands, Harney, better than you do. If you doubt it, look at her now."

Harney, in fact, looked across at Kate Winslow and saw her pale, indeed, but by no means offended by the brutal bluntness of Steen, who now lurched suddenly to his feet and struck his hands together.

"But what are we going to do, Harney? What'll we do? What can we do?"

"Sit still, here. I'm going to make the rounds of the house," said Harney.

He left them at once and climbed the ladder at the corner of the room, leading up to the attic of the house. The attic itself was low, with big beams sweeping close to his head, but it was a useful storage room, and as such it was now stowed. Among the piles he worked his way in turn to four small windows that peeped from the four sides of the house. Through these he spied, getting a sufficient angle to enable him to tell something about the assailants. No doubt many of them were entirely out of view, but, even as it was, he was able to see six men about the place. It made him shiver when from the last window he spied three of them in a row. Indeed, it seemed strange that even Sam Crockett could have assembled so many men in a country that was chiefly poor in hands.

He went back to the gap in the corner of the ceiling through which the ladder descended and there, pausing, first glanced down to make sure that all was well beneath him. What he saw was Steen seated with head partly averted and eyes upon the floor, while beside him was the girl, saying at that moment in a voice sufficiently loud for him to hear: "We have to slip away from him. Never let him know. We must go, go. I don't care about anything else."

Chinook, waiting at the foot of the ladder for his master, now growled, but instead of looking up, Kate Winslow merely walked rapidly across the room and disappeared into the same storage chamber where she and Harney had lain before.

Chapter Thirty-Five

A Flight Through Fire

There could have been no more subtle and cruel blow to Harney, for he had felt that one vast problem was almost settled. Kate cared for him, he could have sworn, in a deep and important way, for, when they had lain prisoners together, surely her eyes had given to him love for love. Or had it only been mutual sympathy that is bound to exist between two companions in misfortune?

At least now he heard her saying clearly that she wished to be away from him — away with Steen. Steen, the sullen monster, the very figure of gloom and scorn, he who had heaped such insults and difficulties upon her during the entire trip — it was with him, now, that she wanted to go, and shift poor dull, honest Harney behind her.

So thought Harney as he crouched at the head of the ladder — then climbed down, with bitterness in his heart and with sullen hatred for both the man and the woman. Old maxims drifted through his mind. The more a man abused a woman, the more contented she must be. She followed the hand that beat her. *How true it was!* he thought.

He reached the floor and turned to face the pair of them, but they seemed too involved in their own thoughts to pay any heed to him. She came back from the little storage room with an anxious face.

"If we threw open one door," she suggested, "and started to shoot from it, might that not gather them all together? And then we could break out in the other direction. . . ."

"Wonderful," sneered Steen. He actually clapped his hands and nodded at her in his sardonic applause. "In other words, she suggests that we make a feint in one direction and run in the other. Well, a clever trick like that would sure paralyze their brains. They couldn't fathom that! They'd all run toward the sound of firin', wouldn't they? Just like good soldiers."

Harney wondered at the indifference with which she endured this outbreak from Steen. It did not seem to wound her pride, but she went on instantly: "Then there's the possibility of tunneling under the side of the house and getting. . . ."

"Through froze-up ground?" said Steen. She sighed.

"Besides," he went on, "whatever we do,

has to be quick. You know what they're doing, Kate."

"I can guess, Andrew."

It was the first time she had used his first name; one would not have thought that she knew it, and Harney was unpleasantly disturbed.

"They'll head up for Birch Creek," said Steen, "and, when they get there, they'll most surely throw out their nets for your father. He's the goldfish that they wanta get the scales off of. And they got mighty little time now."

"You mean they'll kill him, Andrew?"

"Why not, if that would let her and Crockett get the lootings of the mines up there? Don't they say that your old man has about half a million dollars' worth of dust up there, ready to be shipped down? Well, they'd be glad to take charge of that for him, if he was to die. It wouldn't take them long to clean it out and get away with it, and what's to prevent a wife from takin' charge of her dead husband's property? Why, nothin', I guess. It'd be hers, and Crockett's, and nothin' to hold them back, except that we should get loose from this house, d'ye see?"

He made a short, fierce gesture to point his speech, and the girl closed her eyes.

"If only there were night so that we could slip out by stealth."

"This here is summer," said Steen with his bitter grimace. "This here is the season that everybody prays for. Well . . . I'd rather have the winter, for my part. A man can get used to the dark, but not to the light that's always pressin' against your eyeballs. You can see . . . so can everybody else."

"If we made a break altogether," she suggested desperately. "We might get through."

"Not Harney nor me . . . and they'd catch you, afterward."

She paused as she heard this, still thinking hard, but finding no solution. Then she whirled on Harney. "You have an idea?" she suggested.

He nodded.

"Then what is it, for heaven's sake?"

"Start your idea," said the gloomy Steen. "It ain't going to be worth hearing. Because we're cooped up and trapped here. But start the idea, anyway."

"I can run," said Harney.

"Good for you," sneered Steen.

"The pair of you go up into the attic and get to the window that looks toward Circle City. When you look down through that, you'll find that you can get a couple of glimpses of these gents behind the brush and the snow. Draw your beads and start shooting. When that happens, I'll yank open the door on that side and bust out. They'll have your bullets to think about, and, when they see me, they may get a little rattled and shoot crooked. Well, if I get through to the trees, they'll begin to stew. They can't afford to have me bust away to Circle City. I could find help there and come back with a band. So the whole bunch of them are pretty likely to swarm over to where I've gone.

"Now, then, after they've started in that direction, the pair of you stop firing, and run down the ladder. Break out through the front door and hike for the woods. Hike fast! I got no doubt but that you'll break through, and then you'll have the woods to dodge through and to keep you from bein' seen. Your trail won't amount to much in a few minutes . . . listen to the wind comin' up! And it'll drift the dry top snow into all the holes."

He was proud of his plan and paused now for admiration.

Steen merely said: "There's a ghost of a show that way."

"A show for us?" said the girl. "But what about Harney? What about him, with the fire of the whole crowd centered on him?"

"He has luck," replied Steen calmly. "Besides, I can't think of any better way of doing this here thing. If you want, I'll take Harney's place and go back toward Circle City to draw the fire. It makes no difference to me."

The girl looked curiously at them both. It was one of her impersonal moments, such as Harney had seen in her often before, when she was entirely trying to sum up the facts about a man and not to invest the slightest degree of sympathy in him. He could not for his life have told which of the two she preferred to see enter the greater danger.

So he said bitterly: "I made the plan, and I ain't a quitter. You do your own job, Steen, and I'll 'tend to mine. So that makes us equal. Are you ready?"

"Wait a moment," urged the girl. "There may be some safer way."

"There's no other way," insisted Steen. "Think it over for yourself, and you'll see that Harney has the only idea that we've hatched up to this time. How'd you happen to think about it, son?"

He looked without enthusiasm at Harney, and the latter shrugged his shoulders.

"Go up there where I told you," he insisted. "I'll be ready at the door, and

Chinook'll go along with me. That'll give 'em two targets instead of one, and they'll be lucky if they hit me."

Steen went straight up the ladder, but Harney thought that the girl had hesitated a moment at the first rung, turning toward him as though she still had something to say. However, it remained unspoken, and presently she was climbing up the ladder rapidly after the big feet of Steen.

For his own part, he went to the storage room and tried the door. It was still locked, and from the outside, but a heave with a crowbar readily snapped the bolt that fastened it shut. Then he put aside his rifle, for it would be too heavy a weight for him to handle while he was running at full speed. He stood ready, revolver in hand, prepared to thrust the door wide, while Chinook, eager as a hunting dog, stood by with laughter on his fierce face, now and again sniffing at the base of the door as though he knew what lay on the farther side of it and rejoiced in the danger to come.

The fusillade above began at this moment. From the outside of the house, Harney dimly heard curses, and then one prolonged shriek of agony. He did not need to be told that someone had been badly hit. He waited for another moment and then felt a war cry like the whoop of Indians rising in his throat.

It formed against his teeth, his lips, as he dashed the door wide open and sprang out. Wildly he yelled and lunged straight for the nearest trees. As for the wolf dog, he hung back only through an instant, and then flashed into the lead, bounding high into the air with a yell such as Harney never had heard from man or from beast — a yell to inspire terror, a yell of joy.

He heard confused exclamations, callings through the brush on either side, but yet he had followed half the distance across the open before rifles began to spit. Two bullets went past his face like the rising shadows of the dead that are said to whir upward at the moment of death, a whisper, and then no further speech through all the millenniums to come. Like the very voice of death they were at the ear of big Harney, and he dodged like a teal when the marksmen are firing.

On his left hand, also, guns began to chatter. Chinook, already in the shelter of the brush, turned back toward his master with bristling mane, ready to help. And so, in another moment, he was inside the line of the trees and was safe. Safe for the instant alone, however. For the bullets still crackled like a roaring fire through the branches of the trees and shrubs around him, and he could hear voices calling in the wildest alarm, one of them pleading with the rest to get between the fugitive and the way to Circle City. He heard that, but did not stir from his place.

He knew, beforehand, that he could not get back to the house, but he was not sure that he could not double back into the woods, on the trail of the two fugitives. There they went now.

"*Yah—e-e-e-e!*" yelled an excited watcher from the front of the house. "Two of 'em comin' this way! Help!"

Guns barked in that direction, then a voice of triumphant thunder pealed through the air, and he knew that it was Steen, glorying in his triumph.

Chapter Thirty-Six

On the Snow Trail

The wind was every moment stronger, a thing that promised to cover the crunch of footfalls in the snow. The sky was streaked over by low clouds that looked like puffs of smoke, then like the haze that settles at the top of a room among the beams when a fireplace will not work. This also would help in making visibility very much lower.

So Harney decided to circle the clearing as rapidly as he could. He kept just inside the rim of the trees and traveled fast, with lunging strides. On his right, he saw two hurrying figures, slackened his pace to let them get by, and then turned with an oath of self-denunciation for one of the two, he was sure, was the great Sam Crockett. He was certain of it as soon as the men passed, for the nearer one had a way of walking with his head jutting a trifle forward, and that was very characteristic of Crockett. More than all this, there was a certain atmosphere that exuded from the man, and even at a distance, the blood of Harney was chilled. He whirled, therefore, gun in hand, but the two already were out of sight in the dimness of the woods.

Something like a tiny cold hand touched his cheek. It was a flake of downward-fluttering snow, and, when he looked up, he saw the dim streaks everywhere wavering down. He could have shouted for joy. The wind, the snow on its wings, would help the three of them enormously to escape through the hands of Crockett's men. Furthermore, Crockett himself was going in the wrong direction, and at this he wondered for a moment. Then it was clear. First Crockett would strive to draw a line through which the fugitives could not break back to Circle City and the ample succors there, and, having done this, he would sweep forward, confidently, to scoop them up on the way up Birch Creek.

Harney delayed no longer. However sound the scheme of Crockett might be, his own first task was to rejoin the girl and Steen, even though she had declared to the latter that she wanted to get away with him, *alone*. It filled him with a sullen rage to think of such a plan, yet he went on at full speed, around the rim of the trees, with Chinook scouting before him, swinging back and forward, and from side to side.

Once he leaped back to Harney and stood

riveted in place. Harney stepped behind a tree just in time to avoid a man who floundered past, head down, and instantly disappeared in the increasing darkness of the trees and the storm. Then he went on. Sometimes, when his shoulder struck a low branch, thick showers of white fell down and powdered him over. Sometimes he slipped, where the surface snow had been scoured away and a glassy crust remained exposed. Yet he made good time, swiftly rounding the clearing and striking across the line in which the two fugitives must have traveled from the front door of the big cabin.

He found the sign at once. The wind and the drifting snow already were marking out the prints, but they were still faintly legible as he hurried forward. If he were in doubt, Chinook would solve the case for him. He seemed to understand at once what was wanted and glided away on the trail before his new master. So Harney gave his might to the task, forging ahead with a resolute swing of his whole body, such as gives distance to a stride.

He left the trees. A dull, swampy flat appeared before him, pricked with a few stunted spruces, here and there. His vision of this became clearer when the snow ceased falling for a moment, and the wind no longer beat into his eyes. Then it was that he saw the two before him — Steen looking like a giant, and the girl like a child, rapidly making their way against the wind. But if he could see them, might not Crockett's men see him from behind with equal ease. He glanced back, but nothing in the shape of human life was visible there, so he plodded on again with the same space-devouring stride.

He came so close that he could hear the crunch of the snow underfoot of the others before him, but neither of them looked around. They knew that he was there, and yet they would not give him so much as a word of thanks or of congratulation after the successful working out of his scheme. Was it true, then, that they wanted to escape together, alone?

He pulled up beside them. Neither of them turned an eye in his direction, but with set faces they went forward, Steen breaking trail and the girl following him. It was more than wonderful that she should be able to keep up with the pace on this march, for Steen was not sparing himself, and yet she moved with the greatest ease, almost as though she had mysterious wings to help her forward.

Harney fell in behind Steen to beat out a better trail for her, and with a wave of his hand he sent big Chinook to the rear to scout for them. Still not a word was spoken, but all was labor forward.

Two, three, four hours they worked with nothing said and without a single halt. Only, from time to time, Steen would slacken his pace a little for the sake of resting their legs a trifle. But on they went, endlessly, while Harney moved up to the lead every hour to break trail, and then fell back when his time was ended.

It snowed in bursts, then grew quieter. When the snow fell, the wind generally was blowing. Almost as though it were snatching this great soft burden of white flakes from some shelf in the sky and fluttering it down in an endless succession of white wings that waved from the zenith to the ground. Sometimes the snowfall was so thick that they hardly could make out the way, and it was at one of these times that Harney blundered into the edge of a slushy marsh, burying himself waist-deep in the stuff before Steen could grapple his shoulders and drag him back.

Steen snarled like a wolf at him. "Use your eyes, you! Use your eyes!" he said. "D'you see what you've done now? You've cost us half an hour, maybe, sneaking along the edge of this here marsh!"

Harney did not make a retort. There was plenty that could have been said, but there was no point in the saying, for whatever energy they had should be husbanded for the common purpose.

Steen ordered him to the rear and himself reassumed the guidance of the party, a task in which he moved either with wonderful skill or with singular insight. For never once did he bring them into any difficulties.

They were making good time. By miracle, as it were, the girl was holding up, and still from the rear there was no sign of the approach of an enemy.

It was after all this that Harney, while traveling in second place, looked back and saw the girl lagging. She smiled and nodded at him, and increased her pace at once, but he guessed that she was far spent, and that thought instinctively forced his glance back to the horizon behind her.

There he really saw them coming at last. It was not one knotted group, but first, far to the right, he saw the dim streak of a long dog team with men beside it. To the left appeared another, disappearing behind a hummock of snow. Directly to the rear came the main guard, with two dog teams and a whole cluster of men.

"Steen! Steen!" called Harney. "We're followed fast, now! There's four dog teams and a whole damned army right behind us!"

"Am I blind? Ain't I seen it?" said Steen. "Keep on!"

Harney glanced back again, and this time he could see the head of the girl jerking with effort every time she raised her feet. She made a great burst and came up close to him.

"Joe," she said, "it's no good. I can't keep up. Besides, it's me that they want, not the two of you. Go on. Say nothing to Steen, and he won't notice that I've dropped back."

For answer, Harney said sternly: "Here! Take off that belt."

She obeyed, unquestioning.

"Throw an end to me."

He caught it over his shoulder. "Now pull on that," he said, "and we'll manage the thing in some way through to the end."

She caught the end of the strap, and he saw a fierce, unresisting hope spring into her face again.

Very light was the pull, at first, but it grew heavier and heavier with the passing of the moments. Now and again he looked back, ostensibly at her, but really to mark the approach of the dog teams. They must have been doing anywhere between five and seven miles an hour, even where the snow was soft, and it was no wonder that Crockett had been confident that they were in his hand, no matter how comparatively far they fled afield. They had gone fast and far, and it seemed a bitter pity that all they had done should be given up in this manner, while they were caught by the reaching hands of Crockett.

Rapidly the teams on the right and left forged ahead, each accompanied by three men — doubtless with rifles in the packs upon the sleds. Swift teams — light sleds — picked villains for the company, beyond question.

There were still more in the main body, who plodded in the rear, but even so were swinging along at such a clip that every man plainly could be discerned in outline — one of them with that forward-thrusting head which marked Sam Crockett in person.

There was a heavy jerk upon the belt, then it was released. Harney, glancing back, saw that the girl had slumped into the snow and lay with her face buried in her crossed arms. He was on his knees instantly beside her, calling.

And she answered, her voice stifled by the

muffling of her arms: "It's no go! I can't keep on. Besides, it's me they want. It's me they want. Let me be, Joe. Go on. Go on. Save yourselves."

"Get up, Kate. Will you get up?" he pleaded.

"It's no good, I tell you. I'm done up. Go on, Joe. I won't blame you. I'll only thank heaven that ever I met with such men as the two of you."

He glanced desperately to either side. Already the outskirt dog teams were advancing ahead of them. They were hopelessly pocketed, but still there seemed nothing so bad as to wait here and surrender. He picked her up, and turned on the trail at once with his long step, while her voice panted and fluttered at his ear, begging him to put her down, and to end the battle.

Chapter Thirty-Seven

Succor in Sight

When he picked her up, Harney had one rather staggering revelation. He had thought, as he watched her gliding over the snow, climbing, drifting through the landscape, that she was a veritable sylph, an airy creature, a slender child. As a matter of fact, he was lifting a good, solid hundred and forty pounds at this moment, besides the wrappings of the heavy clothes. Strong men can carry such a weight, but not forever. Certainly he could not carry her in his arms, and yet he kept her there as long as he could endure the burden in this manner. For it seemed to the somewhat childish brain of Harney that as long as he bore her on through the snow in this manner she had become his, surrounded by his arms, surrounded by the joy that grew up in him. Sometimes he staggered, and then he laughed, drunkenly, and went straight on with a stronger step.

He could look down at her and see without being seen, for her head fell helplessly back upon his shoulder, and the arm about his neck was limp. So great was her exhaustion that she moaned as she breathed. Many a man would have given up the struggle long before this, but she had gone on when steps were separate and complete agonies. It was strange to see her with her eyes closed, the intellectual strength, the criticism, the mockery, the satire melted from her face and only her weakness remaining, only the woman. But a hundred and forty pounds! Tenderness could not lighten the load for long.

He saw big Steen come striding back of him. He came with a dark face more clouded by fury.

"You sneak in . . . to take advantage," said Steen in a fierce murmur. "Give her to me!"

But she recovered her senses, as it were, at that moment, and slipped to the ground.

"I can go on for a while longer," she said. "If you'll help me a little."

She took an arm of each of them, and they went forward, the girl swaying between them. But now and again she raised her head and looked up. It was always at Steen that she gazed; it was always for Steen that she smiled.

Harney watched, incredulous; his heart seemed to be turning to lead in his breast. But then he told himself that he could understand clearly enough. For what was he, after all, to pretend to the notice of such a girl as this, clever, graceful, beautiful enough to take the eye of any man? Steen was the one for her, of either of the two — Steen who had no equal. Steen the Hercules, the warrior.

And if he, Harney, would have taken equal battle with Steen without fear, as he accepted it at their first meeting on the ship, still he felt that there was a great margin of difference between them, with the advantage of intelligence, experience, dignity all on the side of his companion.

So it was that the girl turned to him in the end. He could understand why she did so, but it did not decrease his bitterness. He looked back and to either side. They were traveling surrounded by their enemies. It was simply vain folly, he felt, to keep on, except that to pause and wait for death was intolerable. And he was almost glad that this day would see the end of them all.

The sky had grown almost clear; the only clouds appearing high up, a very thin translucent veil. Straight ahead of them was a gathering mist upon the horizon, a bluish mist that coiled thicker and thicker, throwing up spectral arms, to which the heavens put down other arms as in greeting, so that the mist grew continually.

The pursuit now grew suddenly excited. Those to the rear increased their speed, and on either side the dog teams were turned in at an angle, so as to cut off the retreat of the three.

Steen brought them to a halt. "Here's the end," he said.

"There's no end for you, Andrew and Joe," she contradicted. "Go on to either side. They won't follow you as long as they can have me for the asking. Go on to either side! Why should we all go down together? If you get away . . . you may be able to help me, afterward . . . from the outside, when. . . ."

Steen raised his hand. "Talk sense," he ordered. "We're due to stay here. Joe, un-limber your gun. If they come close enough for a Colt to reach them, we may pepper a few of 'em before this day's ended." He laughed a little, the fierceness rising in his voice and in his face.

Spotted on three sides of them, the groups of the enemy were equidistant points on a circle. They converged only slowly now, and, as they came, a gunshot clanged from the rear, followed by a rattle of several weapons.

"They're gonna take no risks," shouted Steen, bracing himself to a sudden gust of wind that smote them with staggering force. "Harney, you take the ground!"

They went down, all three, burrowing into the snow, while Chinook, after a leap into the air and a howl, imitated that good example, and burrowed into the snow at the side of Harney.

At this, the gunfire broke out all around them. They presented only hummocks of snow, indefinite forms, but the plunging rain of the rifle balls knocked through the snow as through a mist and whipped all about them.

They were advancing, too, which gave them a better chance with every step, except that the light was now falling. The reason was obvious. That horizon mist had advanced with a wonderful speed until it was rolling now, from the center of the sky to the earth, still blue with darkness, still putting up arms. But these arms that on the horizon had appeared like indistinct mists were now huge masses of impenetrable clouds. Half the sky was obscured, and now the wind that had blown before in gusts leaped on them with a wild scream.

There appeared beneath the solemn and rolling blue of the storm cloud a mist of shining white. It was the dazzling load of snow sucked up from the earth by the force of the wind and whirled on high. It came nearer. The sky was rapidly turning dark. And now the rifle fire was a steady roll, and they could hear men shouting orders, directions, cursing.

They well could curse. Once Harney and once Steen rose on hands and knees from the snow and took pot shots at the nearest enemies. Whether they struck the target or not, it was a sufficient warning to keep the others back. The popping of the rifles became like the distant clapping of hands, overwhelmed by the howling of the wind.

Then, like the falling of a great wall, with rumblings, roars, and buffets, the wind reached them. Bewildering white lashed across their faces. Thunder cannonaded over them, and then lightning cracked the sky across.

A hand gripped the shoulder of Harney in the murk of that dirty twilight. It was Steen, his face close, his lips parted. Not a word could Harney hear, making out only a murmur, but he could see the pointing hand, and he rose.

Together they drew up the girl. One on each side of her, they supported her in the darkness, in the merciless smitings of the wind. So they staggered onward, reeling together from side to side, like a trio of drunkards uselessly striving to give one another help.

Something arose before them, blurred, stumbling. It sank back into the snow, and there was a snake tongue of flame from the muzzle of a gun. They paid no heed, as though the force of that wind were great enough to turn back bullets. In fact, there was hardly freedom for them to think in the roar and yell of the wind. And the man who had dropped into the snow and fired at them, shot no more, as though he, too, realized that he could work no harm with his weapons.

Rapidly the storm changed. It began to cuff them from behind. It began to lighten their feet. They went with staggering lurches and uncertain starts. Sometimes, when the wind failed a little, they were lurching backward. Sometimes a flaw of it struck them still from in front. But they made good distance with the gale behind them. And for long miles they continued in this manner, until the girl suddenly sank to her knees. There was nothing more in her to respond to the urging of her will, and together the two men carried her on.

More fiercely than ever the wind screamed behind them, pressing on them with hands of lead, then making them light as figures of straw. Then, as suddenly as it had rolled upon them, the storm rolled away, leaving the sky not gray filmed, but sparkling bright with the light of the long summer.

They looked back hopefully, but also with dread, and they saw their dread fulfilled, for across the snow came two sleds, as the passing of the storm unveiled them, making in their own direction and gaining every step.

"It's the end," said Steen. "We've had two busts of luck, but we won't have a third one. We'll put her down here and make the last stand, Harney."

Harney, however, had followed the retreating gloom of the storm, and now he pointed ahead with a hoarse shout. For as the mist cleared in front of them, a long, low building appeared, with smoke curling from the top of it.

Steen glanced in the same direction, and then whooped joyfully.

"A way house!" he shouted. "Whoever has the luck here, has a ton of it. A way house! Step out, old son. We've still got more than half a chance!"

It gave their aching and suffering bodies fresh strength. Their blood seemed to stir again, their muscles grew supple, and, carrying their burden between them, they hurried on. Behind, they could see the dogs trotting, whipping the sleds over the newly wind-scoured surface of the compacted snow. So clear was the air that they could even see the whips curling in the hands of the drivers.

But all that speed and all that united effort was too late. The way house drew closer. It seemed to the tired eyes of Harney to change its place and float nearer, helping out their tired legs. The smoke that floated above it was a flag of peace, as it were, and he found himself laughing weakly with relief.

So they reached the door. It opened on a long, low room, with rows of bunks all around it and a deacon seat beneath them. Harney saw one window, an open ventilator to keep the air fresh, a dirt floor, a dirt roof, the logs of the walls made proof with moss. There was a stove burning red hot at the top. Two or three groups of people were already inside. And suddenly it seemed to Harney as though civilization were worthwhile after all, comforting, warm, a succor for the weary and the distressed. He slumped against the wall, weakly, barely with force enough in his arm to shut the door behind him.

Chapter Thirty-Eight

Black Shadows

There were two such way houses between Circle City and the mines used by travelers, particularly by freighters, going to and fro with their dog teams. The long bare houses furnished shelter, wood, and beds, nothing else, for travelers were expected to carry their own food with them and to do their own cooking. Those who already were in the place, cooking or eating, received the newcomers with wonderful placidity. They looked over the three, and then one of them rose, as though he silently had been delegated by the rest of the tired, hungry men to do the courtesies of the place to these exhausted late arrivals.

It was a grim-looking sourdough who approached Steen, as the latter laid the girl on a bed of bare poles. In the autumn, when it was possible to get hay, the beds were deeply and comfortably covered with it, but, as the year wore on, the hay was constantly taken to stuff into moccasins, with the result that by this time there was not a straw upon the beds.

"The kid's kind of tuckered out, eh?" said the sourdough, glancing at Kate's limp form. He proffered a cup of hot tea that he had brought over.

"This'll do him good," he said. "Windy weather for travelin', and the young kids like this one oughta have sense enough to stay at home. . . ." He had leaned a little as he spoke, and suddenly the wan face of the girl turned toward him, delicate, inescapably feminine. The sourdough turned upon Steen a glance of mingled contempt and envy.

"Give her this," he said, handing over the tea. "How are you fixed for grub, the three of you?"

"Blank," said Steen.

"Blank?" growled the other. "Countin' on the way houses?"

"My poke ain't empty," answered Steen. "Besides, this is no pleasure trip."

This amount of explanation seemed to be sufficient for the sourdough, who now went off to the stove and prepared another meal with expedition. Harney, making for a bunk, lounged into it with his back resting against the wall, his arms hanging, his hands dangling. He watched with a dim eye where Steen was working over the girl, bathing her face and rubbing her hands until she was

344

sufficiently revived to drink the tea. And now she was smiling up at Steen with returned color. She was flirting with him, Harney could have sworn, with the abandon of a bird on a sunny branch.

She would have no care for the man who had carried her and tugged her so great a portion of the way. It would be only Steen who mattered — he who had the strength for the last effort. So thought Harney, and bitter was his soul within him. Yes, even now she raised her head and smiled toward him vaguely, dimly, as though he were a picture on a wall, barely recognizable.

His strength came back to him slowly. Another might have been totally prostrated by the effort he had made, but perfect condition told. Gradually, his heart beat with a more assured stroke, and his breathing was deeper. Finally he was able to sit up, and last, there was the food. Appetite had come raging back upon him, and the steam that went up from the kid that the sourdough brought him looked to Harney like incense for the gods.

The door was kicked open then, and the squat, enormous form of Mike Logan appeared in the opening. He stood there a moment, regardless of the howls of protest about cold air that roared at him from the men about the stove.

Then he strode in slowly, taking step by step as he surveyed the people in the way house. Not a doubt for an instant remained in the mind of Harney that this was one of Crockett's men. If he had doubted at first, the doubt would have been removed when he marked the manner in which big Mike Logan strolled down the hall until he noted Steen and the girl. Then he paused, stared at them, and, whirling about, his eyes encountered those of Harney. He crossed to him with a smile of cruel satisfaction and stood there, looking down at the shaking hands with which Harney held the kid of food.

"You poor sucker," said Logan. "You poor stiff! You're done for, and I'll have the eatin' of you!"

Harney did not even look up. He only looked at the great feet of the newcomer and said nothing, for he felt the truth of Logan's words. The strength had run out of him. It had leaked from the tips of his fingers and from the soles of his feet. There was nothing left to him except the shape of his body.

Logan lingered for another instant.

"You've had all the luck today," he said grimly. "Tomorrow, we clean you up. They ain't gonna be a scrap left of the three of you. But you, you're my meat. Remember that. Think about that, will you?"

He went off, and Harney breathed a little easier as the fellow departed. There was no doubt that he would do as he had been bidden and think of the warning and the warner. When he looked up from an empty kid, he saw Mayberry pulling off his gloves and stamping his feet beside the stove.

Mayberry also! Could he be one of the men of Crockett? He was reassured when, a moment later, the eye of Mayberry fell upon him, and the older man came straight to him and shook his hand.

"Hello!" he said. "I didn't know that you'd started on so soon."

"I didn't know that you were coming up so quick," answered Harney.

"I decided to get up here and give things an overlooking," said Mayberry. "There ain't any way to run your mine except to do it yourself. A straw boss is only a man of straw, most of the time, and so I came up here to put a little stiffening into the boy that's handling my claims. What made you start? Are you anxious to get to work on the creek?"

He was a very good-natured fellow, continually smiling and nodding as he talked, and Harney listened to him with quiet pleasure.

"Maybe I'll get a chance to work for you soon, Mayberry," he said. "But the fact is that just now I'm tied up with another job."

"What job, son?"

"Why, a personal freightin' job, as you might say."

"Freightin'?" cried the other in surprise. "I didn't know that you had a team."

"I have, though."

"With Chinook to lead, eh?"

"That's right, and two to foller."

"Only a three-dog team?"

"That's it, Chinook, and this foot, and that foot."

Mayberry, understanding, laughed in a deep, husky bass that seemed too deep and too large for his body.

"I won't ask questions," he said. "You understand your own affairs. Sounds mysterious enough to have something to do with a woman though."

He went back toward the stove, and Harney sat up with a revived strength. The food, the friendly good-natured words of Mayberry, now made him almost his old self, and he was able to go over to Steen and the girl.

Steen had made himself wonderfully useful. Above all, he had arranged a warm bed for Kate by getting from several of the other drivers in the way house bits of tarpaulin and old sled robes. There were even a few bits left over, with which Steen and Harney could attempt to make themselves comfortable.

Kate could not look at anyone but Steen now. It seemed to Harney that, no matter how close he came to her, or how often he spoke, her glance always wandered toward the other big man and dwelt on the dark, Egyptian face.

What emotion Steen felt on account of this steady and deep devotion, Harney could not tell. The man's face was like stained granite, it never altered. But once, when Steen thought he was unobserved, it appeared to Harney that the eye of his companion softened, grew gently luminous as it dwelt on Kate Winslow. It was enough for Harney. It was like seeing a wolf dog wag its tail. It was like hearing a wolf bark.

Suddenly Harney knew that Steen was in love with this girl as profoundly as he himself could be. And if she were not in love with Steen in return, then all signs failed, and the language of gestures, attitude, looks, had no meaning.

He spoke a few words to them both. The girl answered him in monosyllables; Steen answered him not at all, except at last with a dark, impatient look, and so Harney went to bed.

He had to accept another favor from Mayberry before he was asleep. The latter vacated a bunk near the stove, and invited Harney to take it.

"I got a sleepin' bag," he said, "that keeps me roastin' even in the snow, so what do I need to be so close to the fire for? You take this place, kid. It'll make you sleep good, and you ain't got much to put around you."

Harney did not argue. Fatigue was spreading like poison through his body. It knocked at his brain like a hand at a door, and, when at last he had lain down on the bare poles of the bed with a meager wrapping of fur rags and tarpaulin about him and the glow of the stove in his face, he had only to open the door to that knocking, and instantly he was unconscious, fallen like one from a height into deeps of sleep, and deeper and deeper into the same dark water.

So he lay for long hours, the hands of that profound slumber rubbing the agony from his overlabored muscles and restoring his brain. He slept no longer with a frown and with set jaw and puckered mouth, but relaxed, happy.

Now he had a dream that he was passing over a meadow toward a garden gate through which he could see the warm flames of many flowers of yellows and golden, scarlet, crimson, rose, of purples, of violets, all mingling together like a brilliant smoke. He came straight up to the gate, but, when he strove to look in more closely, a shadow appeared, blocking the gateway — a shadow like that which a man casts on the wall when he stands before an open fire. He could dodge this way, and lean that, but the shadow still cut off his sight of the lovely garden.

Vague unease and distress rose in the heart of Harney, and suddenly he opened his eyes and saw above him the pools of shadow across the ceiling, felt the warmth of the stove oddly blocked away from him, and then was aware of something gleaming just beside him, rising into the air.

It was a knife gripped in a man's hand, and behind and above the hand there was the face of his companion, his benefactor, his generous helper of Circle City and now again at the way house. It was Mayberry!

Chapter Thirty-Nine

Good Friend Mayberry

The shock of that sight rendered Harney instantly awake. It gave him a chance to see again, and more vividly, the contorted resolution in the face of the man beside him, the beastliness of murder writhing on the features of the sourdough. He saw the knife come to its height; he saw the left hand of Mayberry stretched out toward his breast, as though to guide the down stroke to a correct target. He saw the raised right arm stretch as Mayberry rose on tiptoe for the stroke.

Then Harney moved. It did not take much of an effort. It was merely a quick stroke with his right arm that staggered Mayberry backward with a faint grunt of terror and surprise. He did not fight back. The wakening of the giant was enough for Mayberry, and he turned to flee just as the long arm of Harney shot out, and the great hand picked him off the floor by the nape of the neck. He was crushed to the floor upon his knees, his eyes popping with fear, his mouth agape as he gasped for fresh air. Slowly Harney relaxed his throttling thumbs. He even ventured a glance around him, and made sure that this swift segment of a tragedy avoided had not wakened a single one of the sleepers.

Most of the men lay snoring, their bodies flaccid with weariness and slumber. Once in a while, there was a childish murmur of complaint, and he knew that was the voice of Kate, speaking confusedly in her sleep. But no one roused. No one groaned or stirred, half awake.

He said to his captive: "Mayberry, they ain't a soul that knows. They're sleepin'! If they wake up, they're gonna find you settin' here peaceable and quiet on my bunk, talkin'. They'll not need to know what you've said. Y'understand?"

Mayberry, staring before him like one stunned, said nothing for a time. But at last he muttered: "I deserve everything that's coming to me. I got it all coming to me, Harney."

Said the latter: "Back there in the saloon, Mayberry . . . they'd got to you already and told you to do everything that you could do for me?"

"You mean the money for the dog?" asked Mayberry.

"Aye, and the drink before that."

"D'you think that I'm as low as that?" asked Mayberry slowly. "Well, maybe I am.

I dunno. I dunno. Look what I would've done this same night."

He pressed both hands over his face and drew them slowly down. He seemed rather weary than in any agony of remorse. Except for the uneasy quivering of his hands, Harney would not have known that his captive was desperate.

"The drink money . . . the money for the dog," said Mayberry, "of course, all that was my idea. And that was what started the brain of . . . of him, working."

"You mean who?"

"That I won't say."

"I figger that you will."

"You be damned then," said Mayberry. "I won't say a word."

Force would be easy to use, but, instead, Harney used appeal. He said gently: "Partner, you played white with me. I owe Chinook to you. I'm not gonna try to force talk out of you, but . . . a minute ago I was a quarter of a second from bein' a dead man. Now I'm settin' here and askin' you why? What did I do to you, man?"

"You to me? Nothin', nothin'."

"I must've done, somehow. It ain't likely that you'd be after me unless I'd harmed you, some way. How did I step on your toes, old man?"

"You never done nothin'," Mayberry assured him. "It was in the cards that I was to cotton to you right off and like you fine. And it was in the cards that I was to show my liking and do a couple of pretty good turns for you. Well, that was the cause of all the trouble, you can see."

"No, man, I don't see."

There was a rift in the side of the old stove, through which a single red ray glided out and fell upon the face of poor Mayberry as he talked, turning his head rapidly from side to side, and sometimes shuddering throughout his body in the excess of his shame and of his grief.

"Why, when Crockett or his spies seen what happened, they figgered that I was the man to use on you. I'd have your confidence. So they used me, of course, right *pronto*."

"How could they make you, Mayberry? You're not the kind that's easy bought. They couldn't get together your price."

"Couldn't they?" asked Mayberry with a soundless, sardonic laughter. "I'll tell you, man. We all got one price, only it ain't always in hard cash. They's some of us that have a price in bein' flattered and smoothed down . . . and they's some that get their head turned by givin' 'em a chance to kick the other boys in the face . . . pay some men notice and you never gotta raise their wages. Get a young girl to smile at an old man . . . get an old man to praise a young one. They's hundreds of prices, son. And one of them is the price of being respectable. I been respectable for thirty year now. But I wasn't always. I wasn't always."

He made a brief upward gesture, as though resigning himself, as though casting upward in smoke the evil of his youth that now had overtaken him.

"Crockett knew about it. He knows about everything, I guess. So when he come down on me, I figgered that I had to do what he said. It was you or me. I figgered that I couldn't give up what I'd done. I'd won through. I'd got to a landing place. I was out of the dark. There was enough stuff stacked up on my claims to keep me easy the rest of my life in God's country. I told Crockett. I begged him to take a split on what I had and not ask me nothing, but he wouldn't listen. More'n money, he wants you dead."

Harney listened, absorbed, with pity rising in him.

"And Steen?" he asked. "Steen was to go next?"

"Steen?" said Mayberry. "I dunno about that."

"I should've thought that Steen would've been the first," persisted Harney. "It beats me. I don't understand at all. Why was it me that Crockett wanted you to get first? Didn't he say Steen?"

"Steen?" said the other impatiently. "Why should he worry about Steen when he's got you out of the way?"

"But Steen . . . why, everybody knows what Steen can do," said Harney, more amazed than ever.

Mayberry looked sourly at him.

"I dunno nothin' about it," he said, "and I wish to heaven I knew less. All I can say is what I heard from Crockett . . . that you'd given him more trouble than any ten men in his life. It was you that throttled a mad dog that was about to tear her, you that made tracks to keep her from a gang of his boys that was about to pick her up, you that trailed the sled that was carryin' her off afterward, and fought three men for her. It was you that stopped the pair that was stealin' the boat . . . and her in it . . . and what you've done since then. I know myself and wouldn't have believed that any man could manage it, except that I watched with my own eyes. If you wanta know why he wants you first, them are some of the reasons, I guess. As for Steen, he's big enough, and he's hard enough. But the hoss with the most heart is the one that gets my money to carry."

"The hoss that has the heart . . . as though Steen didn't have heart to burn," murmured Harney.

"I'm telling you what Crockett said to me. Why should Crockett be wrong? He never is wrong, man."

Mayberry grew silent, his glance fixed apparently upon the stove, but really upon the distant future, as Harney easily could guess. It was well enough to call off all accounts, now that the other was so genial and gentle, so oppressed by the sense of his sin. Yet Harney could not forget the convulsed face that had appeared above him.

He said at length: "Mayberry!"

"Aye," the other said dreamily.

"I'm not gonna ask you a question. I'm gonna tell you."

"All right."

"You've killed a man long before tonight."

Mayberry did not stir, made no answer.

"That's what Crockett had on you. You've killed a man, and I'll lay my money . . . that you did it with a knife."

At this the other started with a faint groan. "You can say what you want," he said. "The cards are in your hands. But finish with me quick . . . or let me go to bed. I can't stand to talk to you, man. I can't stand the sound of your voice, even."

He turned his head away as he spoke. But it was not hard for Harney to guess why. The sight and the sound of Harney reminded the other that he had planned to take the life of this man. And he turned with a shudder of self-disgust from the picture of what he might have done.

"Very well," said Harney at last. "I've never been quite so near before. But we'll let it go. So long, Mayberry. I'd like to say that it's all right. Anyway, it's right enough for me to let you go."

The other rose without a word of thanks, without speech of any kind, and, crossing the room, dropped onto a bunk and lay stretched there, face down, with his arms hanging over the side of the poles, like one utterly exhausted — and such Harney could guess him to be. The very soul of Mayberry must have been weary for the strain of the past few hours. Aye, from the very moment when Crockett had assigned the brutal task to him.

Harney stretched himself and watched the light of that undying day of the arctic summer pouring steadily in through the window. He stood up, and scanned the sleepers. Then he went to the place where Steen slept and touched his shoulder.

"Kate," whispered the sleeper. Then he wakened and sat up, thrusting himself high on his great arm. At Harney he scowled fiercely.

"What's up?"

"You've slept long enough," said Harney. "We gotta start."

"She'll never make a day's march unless she's rested up."

"She can ride on the sled."

"What sled?"

"Why, son," said Harney, "I got a good friend here, by the name of Mayberry, and the way that things stand between us, I reckon he wouldn't refuse anything that we ask him. He'll let us take the same team and sled that he used in getting here."

Chapter Forty

The Whip Hand

The sound of the pick spatted sharply out of the pit, almost like a clapping of small hands, and Sam Crockett paused at the edge of the woods with his sister.

"I hoped that we'd find him in the hole," he said. "And there he is. Where's that gun?"

"Here," said Sylvia. "But be easy. He has a pair of ears, I tell you."

"They'll be plugged with more than cotton in a few seconds," said Crockett.

"The other way's better," she insisted. "A lot better."

"You're talking nonsense," he told her. "Besides, the stuff's not right. It didn't work on Harney."

"He's an ox, not a man," said Sylvia. "I thought he'd never go down. He fought like a fury against it. But my dear husband is nearly fifty, and he wouldn't last."

"Fond of him, all right, aren't you?" sneered the brother.

"Don't dislike him," she replied calmly, "but I'm sick of him."

"Which adds up to about the same thing. Here I go. . . ."

The sound of the pick ceased, and, as Crockett stepped out, the head and burly shoulders of Winslow appeared above the edge of the prospect hole. For, not content with his valuable claims already established, Winslow had come here apart to dig in the seclusion of the stunted forest. He had found nothing as yet, but his patience was not easily exhausted. Now, at the end of his shift of labor, he climbed from the prospect hole and made for the tent that stood close beside it. Crockett, at the first glimpse of him, had faded back among the trees. There he stood, frozen in place behind a trunk, while his sister remained equally turned to stone, one hand stopped mid-gesture.

Within the flap of the tent the big shoulders of Winslow disappeared, then Crockett whispered to his sister: "A pretty close call, Sylvia, eh?"

"It means that the luck is with us, today," she said.

"Unless Harney comes through in time," he said.

"Harney? He's used up. He was staggering like a drunk when he went into the way house. He'll never be able to get through with a dozen men watching him.

Never in the world, even if old Mayberry doesn't slip a knife into him."

"That was a pretty idea of yours," said her brother retrospectively. "But we have our job ahead of us now. Harney, that dolt of a Harney . . . that great square-headed hulk. The deuce's own luck has been in him. If Harney were out of the way, I'd go after Winslow rough handed."

"Go after him anyway," said Sylvia. "He's nothing to me. As for Harney, his luck's used up. Wait a minute, Sam. I'm going into the tent first to talk to the old boy. I'll pave the way for you. You're a repentant man that wants a new start in life. And if you won't get it through him, who will help you? You hear, Sam? While we're talking mealy mouth, like that, you ought to have a safe chance to polish him off. That's the only way you'll be able to get at close range, and I don't trust a revolver at long range."

"Soft and tender and clinging, you are," he commented. "But right, for this time. Go on in."

She was almost to the tent when Winslow appeared with a skillet in his hand. He dropped it into the snow in his surprise at seeing her.

"Sylvia, Sylvia!" he exclaimed, "what under heaven brought you back here?"

"The big house was so frightfully lonely," she moaned. "You'd never guess how cold and still and wretched it is without you, dear."

"Humph!" said Winslow, a man not easily stirred by his emotions. "You've been there many a time without me before this. There's something else you want, Sylvia. Let's hear it."

He stooped and kissed her forehead as he spoke. Plainly his mind was on the business of cookery at that moment, and the whole interest of his soul was in the prospect hole that he was digging. This abrupt and casual questioning made Sylvia flinch. But she answered with an apparent frankness.

"You're always right. It was partly the house . . . but it was mostly Sam."

"Sam?" he said blankly.

"Yes," she replied.

"Who do you mean?"

"The man you told me never to speak of again. My brother, Sam Crockett."

He picked up the skillet, turned it thoughtfully, then looked back into her face. "I'm sorry," he said, and his manner of saying it would have been enough to stop any other person than Sylvia Crockett.

She, however, persisted. "He's been abused by everyone. The world's against him, dear. But that's no reason why a big-minded man like you should be. Sam, come speak for yourself."

Crockett glided out from among the trees and stood before the other.

There was no difference in their size, except for the breadth of Winslow's shoulders, but the latter was imposing as a lion, and Crockett was like a smooth-stepping panther, easy, flexible, swift.

He bowed slightly to Winslow, as he came before him.

"I never should have done this," he said. "Never should have let Sylvia persuade me to do it. But the fact is that I've been desperate, Mister Winslow."

"You've been broke, do you mean?" asked the miner.

"Not broke," said Crockett, with a smile so open that his face lost its shadow and became almost charmingly frank. "Or broke in a sense, if you wish. Spiritually broke, sir."

Winslow nodded. "Go on," he said briefly.

"The fact is," said Crockett, "that I've been a bad man. A very bad man."

"I know it," answered Winslow with equal gravity.

"Do you?" answered Crockett, a little disturbed because this confession did not alter the situation a trifle.

"I know nearly all about you," answered Winslow.

A gust of wind picked up a thin glitter of snow and hung it in the air about them. And behind them, the trees bowed, swayed, and groaned and clashed with the force of the squall. Only Winslow appeared unmoved, for both the Crocketts, as they heard the noise, started and looked behind them.

"A thousand bad reports about me, I know," said Crockett, looking on the ground. "But I think there's some good in me, too. Mister Winslow, you're a man who could give me a fresh start. I don't care where I go. And you have interests in China . . . you have friends everywhere. If you sent me with a new name and your backing, I'd be able to start a new life."

Winslow looked him straight in the face. "Bunk, my man," he pronounced.

"Mister Winslow," said Crockett, lowering his voice suddenly with appeal, "I want to ask you how you can have this attitude toward me . . . when my sister is your wife?"

"What has that to do with it?" asked Winslow bluntly.

Sylvia Crockett, with an imperceptible

nod to her brother, slipped to one side, uncoiling the long lash of the dog whip that she carried. Presently she was behind her husband.

"It has this to do with it," said Crockett. "If there's the same blood in us, how can she be all good and how can I be all bad?"

"Crockett," said Winslow, "I married a second time because I was a very lonely man. I'm fond of your sister. Perhaps she's told you that I've never pretended any boyish devotion or love. We live amicably together, but sometimes I feel that our happiness is founded on sand. Shall I tell you why? Because of you! I know your character, and I know your career. Everything comes handy to young Crockett. Green goods, salted mines, wallets that are fitted a little too loosely into pockets, diamonds that shine a little too brightly on a woman's hand, old-fashioned safes that a can opener can crack, even new ones that need nitroglycerin and yellow soap to blow them, smuggling of Chinamen over the border, smuggling of drugs, also. And when I've named these things, I've only skipped lightly over the smaller sins."

There was a light cracking sound in the woods behind him, and Crockett jerked his head over his shoulder, but then decided that it was the wind only and the giving of some bough as another brushed it. The gust died down. The arctic silence fell softly over them.

"Are there bigger things against me?" asked Crockett in a sad voice.

"Slightly larger."

"Such as what?"

"The betrayal of old friends, Crockett. That's one thing."

"You're very hard on me," murmured Crockett.

"I have to be hard now that I have you before my face. And the thought of you has been a constant poison in my life since I married your sister. All these things are against you, Crockett, and worse things besides."

"Mister Winslow, you make me out a monster."

"Crockett, I fear you are. A monster and a murderer, as well. I almost think that I can see it in your eyes now, as I tell you the truth about yourself."

"In my eyes?" said Crockett.

"Why do you look on the ground, man, if there's any honesty at all in you?"

"Well," said Crockett at last. "I can look you in the eye as well as any man, for that matter." And he raised his head suddenly and stared fully in the face of Winslow.

"By heaven," said the latter, "there is murder in the heart of you, or else I'm a blind man." He drew back a little as he spoke, and that movement was the signal for which his wife had been waiting. Over him she flung the long, tough lash of the dog whip, and, jerking the noose tight so that it bound his arms to his sides, she twisted the two ends together.

He was helpless before them, and in the hand of Crockett dangled a Colt, gleaming blue and bright.

Winslow did not struggle. The instant grip of the lash upon his arms convinced him that resistance was useless. He closed his eyes and muttered: "Sylvia, too. Oh, heaven, that I have blinded myself to what I have almost guessed a thousand times."

Chapter Forty-One

"Well Done!"

That speech appeared to give the keenest pleasure to the great Crockett.

"You hear that, Sylvia, old girl?" he asked. "He's suspected that being my sister you were the same breed of danger?"

"I hear," she said, her voice brusque, harsh. "But finish it up. Make an end of it, will you, Sam?"

"She wants speed," said Sam Crockett, his dark eyes brooding over the miner. "The dear girl has nerves, you see, and it disturbs her a little to see you go under. But it don't disturb me. Not a bit."

Winslow considered the speaker gravely.

In the first struggle he had grown flushed, then pale, but now his ordinary color had returned. He was gravely calm, observant.

"Crockett," he said, "I know what you want now . . . to wring words out of me, just as the Indians used to love to wring yells out of a victim. But that's not the stuff I'm made of. I agree with my dear wife. You might as well finish your work at once. You'll get no exclamations out of me."

"Won't I?" said Crockett. "But that's a challenge, old fellow, and challenges appeal to my heart and soul, I tell you. To do the impossible. There was the president of the First National at Claitonville. He said it would be impossible to wreck his safe. Impossible! That was the word that stung me. 'Fame is the spur, *et cetera.*' Therefore, the bank lost its money, and the president lost his life. Disturbed vanity caused him to commit suicide. Now with you, Winslow, you're sure that nothing can cause you to exclaim . . . and yet perhaps a mere word or two about your daughter. . . ."

"Sam, will you stop it?" demanded his sister.

"I have no daughter," said Winslow. "Therefore, it makes no difference to me what you say."

"However . . . ," began Sam Crockett, when Sylvia interrupted again: "Sam, this very minute Harney may be slipping up on us."

The thought alarmed him enough to make him leap back and whirl around, but he saw only the tall, dark face of the forest and snow dust mounting up.

"Harney is beaten for once," said Crockett.

"If we must talk, who is Harney? Some

honest policeman?" asked Winslow.

"Harney," said Sam Crockett, "is the most extraordinary man I ever have met. I have been beaten, I have been baffled before . . . sometimes by luck, sometimes by men, but never more than once by any one man, no matter how often luck assisted him. Harney is different. Harney, I should say, is the ordinary bulldog, the common man, the genius lacking brains, such as the streets are filled with, such as covers the range. Nothing but courage and a strong body were given him. And yet Harney has beaten me, baffled me, traveled a thousand miles in spite of every odd I could bring against him, endangered all my plans, and finally rushed me so much that I have been forced to adopt this crude, this stupid method of disposing of you in order to rake in your present or surface profits."

"An interesting young man, but if he's a fool, how can he have done so much?" asked Winslow.

"This Harney," said Crockett with considerate thought, "who has nearly maddened me, crushed me, prevented your 'natural' death by slow poison that would have made dear Sylvia the 'natural' heir . . . instead of becoming Missus Murderess Winslow at a stroke . . . this fellow, Harney, who has done so much in spite of his small equipment of brains is a man inspired by a woman. Think of that, Winslow! Inspired by a woman!"

"By the love of a woman, I suppose you mean?" said Winslow.

"Exactly! By the love of a woman. Of what woman, you may ask?"

"I do not ask," said Winslow.

"You must, however," said Crockett, "because the woman in question is that same daughter whom you have disowned, rubbed out of your will, erased from your life."

Winslow raised his head as a bull raises its head in front of the herd.

"Yes," said Crockett. "Cleverly playing him as an angler plays a fish, she has permitted him to tow her upstream, as it were, over the rapids, through every danger, twitching her through my very own fingers. . . ." He extended his hand and closed the fingers slowly, venom in his face. "And all for the sake of your dear girl, Winslow. Doesn't that change your heart toward her?"

"Crockett," said the captive. "I told you that your words would leave me totally calm and cold. They do."

"Ah, and do they?" said the criminal.

"They do. Death is not particularly bitter to me, either, because there was never a man who stood more alone in the world than I do now."

"Not even curious as to why she came all this distance?"

"Not a whit."

"Not curious to know what supported her through all her march, nerved her through terrible dangers, enabled her to bring two men into her service . . . two giants among men . . . and let her float like a bubble past enough dangers to have wrecked another Napoleon?"

"Not curious," said Winslow soberly. "She was inspired by the same guilty cunning that makes a beast of prey persevere on the track of a dying moose."

"Winslow," said Crockett, "like most honest men, your prejudices are contemptible and your ignorance a vast well of darkness. Do you still think that your daughter dropped the poison into your morning orange juice?"

Winslow stared and said nothing.

"Because she was straight-eyed, intelligent, clever with her tongue, ready with an answer, never cornered, elusive, independent, full of wiles . . . because she was these things, you were ready to suspect her.

You never in your life were at ease with her. Not after the first time you found her eye on you, and a faint smile on her lips."

He paused, as Winslow colored.

"No," said Crockett, "that girl was worthy to have made a wife for me. For the sake of such a prize, I might actually have become honest, except that honest neighbors are such dull ones. However, Winslow, she didn't please you. She wasn't the moon-faced, calf-eyed, clinging-vine type. She wasn't the helpless, hopeless, brainless variety that softens the hearts . . . and the minds . . . of common men like yourself. In a word, she was an unsatisfactory daughter. And in the end, it was perfectly easy for you to accept against her the testimony of a stranger in your house despite a score of years of experience with your own daughter. Bah!"

Winslow, at this, drew a short, deep breath, but he set his teeth over the words that were about to break out.

"However," said Crockett, "lest you should die with any misconceptions, let me tell you that it was not my sister, it was I, who slipped through the door from the backstairs and dropped the little addition into the glass of orange juice."

The breast of Winslow heaved.

"You follow me, my clever fellow?" said Crockett. "And, therefore, you may follow me still further when I suggest that to intelligent fingers there is such a thing as interrupted letters, and forged ones to take the place of the real. . . ."

"Ah, heaven," said Winslow, his strength suddenly breaking, his head falling. "She was honest and true, and I have been the blindfolded dolt in my own house."

"Exactly," said Crockett cheerfully, his eye seeming to collect strength and pleasure from the dejection of the miner, "and that which supports this girl across the arctic is one of the oldest emotions in the world, one of the simplest, the purest . . . filial love, old fellow. In spite of your letters . . . bludgeonings with words . . . in spite of her pride . . . she had no grievance against you, Winslow. She didn't go mad, either, knowing her own innocence, and the lies you were believing. She simply came three thousand miles to try a last time to talk to you in person. But she comes too late. Not too late, however, to have given life a trifling new taste on your palate, Winslow, I take it?"

"Yes, it's true," said Winslow. "I would pay down my life blood, drop by drop, to see her for one moment and beg her to forgive me. I would kneel at her feet. If heaven sees me, I am kneeling now."

As he said this, he raised his hand above the venomous and sneering face of Crockett, and above the sight of the forest, and up to the pale, bright sky of the North, and reverence and sorrow for the moment so met in his expression that his face assumed a grandeur of patience and of grief.

Crockett brought him promptly back to earth. "It's a man's duty," he said, "to teach the weak wits and the fools. But I think that I've taught you your lesson, Winslow. Are you ready for the period to be put to our little talk?"

"I'm ready," said Winslow, looking back into the face of Crockett. He looked beyond him, however, in the next instant, and his expression altered in a singular manner.

The gun in the hand of Crockett had not yet risen when a great voice rang hoarsely out from behind the trees: "Crockett! Crockett! Throw up your hands, and drop that gun! There's two of us have you covered!"

It was now that the greatness of Crockett appeared. He neither changed color nor winced at the shock of those words that meant that his schemes were snuffed out — his life, perhaps, with them. He looked upon Winslow with a slight smile as he said: "You see that I'm right, Winslow? A rare girl and a pair of rare men that she's brought along with her . . . a good sled dog and a good leader, we might say, eh?"

"Crockett, damn you!" boomed the voice of Steen, who had spoken before. "Will you drop your gun?"

"Presently," said Crockett, and, as he spoke, leaped sidewise, spun, and started angling for the trees at wonderful speed, the gun speaking from his hand as he raced.

His sister, darting back across the clearing, disappeared in the opposite growth of shrubbery, but such luck was not for Crockett himself.

It was Steen who brought him down; it was Steen who finished him with a second shot as he rolled himself vigorously toward the sheltering shadows of the woods.

When they reached him, they found him almost gone. He only lasted long enough to open his eyes and recognize his destroyers with a quiet smile. Then, in spite of the fact that Steen's well-aimed bullets had cut him down, he raised his hand with a wave toward Harney.

"Well done, my boy," said Crockett, and, as his hand fell, he died.

Chapter Forty-Two

To Give Him Life

What Joe Harney felt as he leaned against a tree and looked down into the dead face of Crockett was the weight of his own hands. They had been tensed for the battle; his whole soul and body had been made taut for this crowning effort, and, now that it was accomplished, weakness and sluggishness ran through his veins like water.

There was a veil before his mind, also. It was only dimly that he saw Kate Winslow in the arms of her father. And the sound of their voices broke faintly on his ear, like the sounds that pass through the roaring of cascades, inarticulate, heard, but meaningless. He saw that she wept, but this seemed to have no meaning to him. He saw the tears running down the rugged face of Winslow himself, and this he looked upon with the uncomprehending eye of an infant.

Ever and anon, he looked around the scene, saying aloud, softly: "This is the place. This is the place."

It was almost as though he had seen it before. But the journey of Kate was ended here, and Crockett was dead. His shadow was removed, that had lain with such sinister darkness over the paths of all of them. And this was the end of the labor.

It seemed to Harney that the separate fatigues of the long way now descended upon him with united force — the toiling over the pass, the races through the snow, the furious shooting of the rapids. All of these perils ached once more, numbly, in his brain, and all of these fatigues were lead in his body. Idly he watched the wind rippling the hair of the dead man; idly he watched the living smile that goes with death and looked down to his own hands, heavy, feeble, useless.

An electric presence came beside him. It was big Steen, and he turned and looked Steen in the face. Was he seeing him for the first time? Or was it true that Steen had grown thin, his eyes deep-set, his mouth cruelly taut? So it appeared to Harney at this moment.

He smiled in a vague, childish way at Steen. "I guess it's finished, Steen," he said. Then he fumbled in his mind: "You did some pretty shooting, old-timer."

"If I hadn't shot him, you'd've been able to run him down," said Steen. "That was what mattered. Finishing him one way or the other. He was a dead man, the minute you laid eyes on him here. Me, I didn't count. It was you that he thought of when he kicked out. You know it, too."

"I know it?" echoed Harney, amazed.

"You know it perfectly well."

"I know it?" The face of Harney grew hot, and the blood leaped through his body. "What are you drivin' at, Steen?"

Chinook slid up and looked with cold, green eyes upon Steen, as though he realized that danger was coming out of this man.

"Her, too," said Steen. "She counted on you all the time."

"You mean Kate?"

"That's who I mean."

"She ain't looked at me for two days."

"You dolt!" said Steen with disdain. "I was thinkin' that what I was about to do was a sort of a shame, but I can see now that it's necessary. I gotta remove you. There ain't any place for a blockhead in this little old world of ours. Harney, you come with me."

"Where to?"

"To the finish of our trail."

"I dunno what you mean by finish, Steen."

"Don't you? I mean, to the finish of one of us, and let the other go on and get her if he can."

"Her?" said Harney. "Kate?"

"Her," said Steen.

"You mean that you want her, Steen?"

"Ain't I been mad about her from the first minute that I seen her?" said Steen.

"Why, man, you swore that she was no good, and that she'd make nothin' but trouble."

"She's made it, ain't she? Joe, when you first come over the skyline, I figgered that I'd found a new kind of a man. I was aimin' to make you my partner, permanent, but I knew, when she come along, that she'd be the bustin' up of everything."

"Hold on, Steen. You mean that she knocked you over, and you ragin' ag'in' her all the time?"

"What else do I mean? Of course, I mean it. Who could've looked at her once without seein' the truth? She was made for the paralyzin' of the brains of men. She was made for it. I seen it at the first look, and it turned me sick."

"Meanin' because it would bust our friendship up, Steen?"

He said it with wonder, because he never could recall the time when Steen had appeared or acted as a friend, there had always been a cloud on his face.

"Bust up our chance of friendship," corrected Steen. "Me that had gone alone in the world, it meant something to meet a man-sized man. But I seen that I couldn't want her without you wantin' her. I seen that a bust was comin'. I was kind of glad when they snaked her away from her tent. It rubbed out the problem."

"Would you have let her go then?" asked Harney.

"I would! She's the kind to make a good memory, not a good wife. She has too many brains. But you went out and got her back, and that started the crash. There was no help then. There had to be trouble. She had to pick between the two of us."

"They's a lot of other men in the world outside of us," said Harney.

"They's only one man now," said Steen.

"Meanin' you?"

"Meanin' you!"

"I tell you, she ain't looked at me!"

"Because she wanted me to string along and work hearty. That was why she turned the cold shoulder on you. But now you're gonna be blotted out."

"By you, Steen?"

"Aye, by me. I licked you once. But I wouldn't take advantage afterward. You'd saved me out of the sea."

"Luck beat me that day."

"You still got a heart?"

"To break you in two," said Harney fiercely. "If it's trouble you want, Steen, you see me. You're crazy," he went on. "She's played me along like a fish on a line. You can't see that, because you don't know her. And I do."

"Do you, son?"

"I do."

"There's plenty places here in the woods where we could finish this out."

"Wherever you please."

"Foller me then."

Steen turned his back and stalked off among the trees. He covered several hundred yards before they came out into a narrow opening in the woods, where the ground was level, free from snow, and only littered by a few fallen branches, most of them half rotted and torn down by the last storm. Around this open space, Steen looked carefully.

"Are you ready?" he asked.

"Ready," said Harney, peeling off his heavy coat.

Steen imitated him. They faced one another.

"Look at Chinook. You want him to help?" asked Steen with a sneer.

"Go back!" Harney commanded.

The big dog had been dragging himself closer on his belly. Now he flattened himself against the ground and wagged his tail.

"Away with you!"

Chinook whined, appeal in his eyes.

"He's smellin' the fight," said Steen. "He's got as good a nose for trouble as any buzzard. He always had."

"Get!" cried Harney, and at last Chinook rose and retreated to the verge of the trees, where he lurked behind a tree trunk, shaking himself as though he had just dragged himself clear of the water.

"You got him, too," said Steen slowly. "There's been two things that I've wanted. Chinook. I got him, but he never was mine, and you come to sneak him away from me. Kate . . . and you follered her around like a slave, till she got used to you." His voice turned to iron. "What'll it be, Harney? Pick your way of fightin'!"

"Guns," said Harney, "are welcome. But they make a noise. And we want peace here, eh?"

"Yeah. We want peace," assented Steen.

"Knives is silent," said Harney. "But . . . how much time have you spent in Mexico?"

"Never been there."

"Then," said Harney, "I would be takin' advantage of you. I been there. I've learned the ways of knives."

"All right," said Steen. "And what's left then?"

Harney held out his big hands. "These, Steen."

Steen started, a fierce light of joy coming into his eyes. "Joe," he said, "remember that I met you once and beat you!"

"Luck beat me that day," said Harney. "I'll take you with these, and ask nothin' better."

"It's a finish," said Steen.

"It's a finish."

"Till one of us hollers enough."

"Till one of us hollers enough," echoed Harney, his lip curling in disdain at the thought.

"Or . . . till he's dead?"

"Yeah. Till he's dead."

"Then heaven help you, Harney. I hope you won't be too proud to holler."

"Watch yourself," said Harney.

"It ain't fists alone this day. Remember that. It's anything you can do with hands."

"Aye. Strangle holds, too."

"Are you ready?"

"Ready," said Harney.

"You was jealous because she hadn't noticed you," explained Steen. "So you got me off here into the woods and then you tackled me."

"That's what you'll tell her when you've stretched me out, Steen?"

"It's gonna be my sad duty, kid."

"Then," said Harney, "here's something to give you a little life." And he struck Steen lightly across the face with his open hand.

Chapter Forty-Three

The Way Home

The big dog watched from the shadow of the trees. All his movements were in sympathy with the battlers. Sometimes he crouched, digging his big talons into the soft ground. Sometimes he dragged himself forward on his belly a few feet. And sometimes he crouched back. Now and again he made ready to spring. But a moment later he was sitting erect with lolling red tongue from which saliva dripped. So Chinook alternately shrank and approached, but eventually he was sitting still and laughing at the progress of the battle.

For the master was victor. He could see the hard-handed Steen reeling under blows. They closed, writhed. The arms of Steen were plucked away. He was smitten full in the face and staggered, hands down.

"Are you through?" said Harney. "Are you through, or d'ye want me to finish it? Because finish it I will if you ask for it."

Now Steen had fought the greatest battle of his life, and he was beaten. He could see the defect through one eye; the other was blinded by the drops that drained from a wide gash over his brow. There the hard knuckles of Harney had bitten to the bone.

He had tried all his tricks. He had tried all his wrestling wiles. The ground was gouged deep where their feet had stamped and scraped. But the strength of Joe Harney had seemed to grow as the battle grew, and now he laughed as he looked at the face of Steen. All the madness of battle which is the oldest rage of man stormed and raged in his veins. It was that laughter that gave him new power, while the gloom of Steen was like a weight upon him.

So Steen looked and knew that the laughing man had beaten him, and Harney felt the fury of destruction burn to the tips of his fingers that yearned for the throat of Steen.

"I'm not through," said Steen. "I'll break you in two still!"

"D'ye mean it? Are you askin' for it, Steen? Because if you are, may heaven have mercy on you, because I won't. You've snarled and snapped like a wolf. You've hated everything, includin' me, and now it's your time to go down. D'ye hear me, Steen?"

"I hear you, and damn you," said Steen.

Harney came at him, not rapidly, but as a

boxer closes on an opponent, with dancing, uneven steps, so that the enemy cannot gauge the progress of the attack with accuracy.

Even Chinook knew that the crisis had come. He stood up, half crouching, tense, trembling. He went forward to what he felt was the limit that he might not pass, the irremovable boundary established by the spoken will of his new master. Cross it, he dared not. No matter how he yearned to add his teeth to the fight, and so swiftly end it with slashing strokes, yet all his love of Harney was less than his fear of that man. So he waited there, taut, on the boundary.

As Harney came in, Steen, leaning one hand against a branch of the tree behind him, felt that the last moment of his life had come. He gripped the branch hard, and under his strength felt it crack. That was suggestion enough for his desperate mind. He ripped it away with a sudden jerk, raised the jagged club that now armed his hand, and, as Harney rushed in, he struck.

That, Chinook saw, and half his length he advanced across the verge of the clearing, with a horrible snarl in his throat. Then he saw his master reel, fall, and support himself with one hand while the other was at his stricken head.

Chinook hesitated. All his soul urged him to break in upon the battle with his decisive aid, but man is mysterious. His ways are not to be forecast or foregathered, and he smites good actions and bad with a whip of fire. Only, to that scene of disaster, he felt that he must bring some other human aid and, turning away, he raced. A backward glance showed to him how Harney had rerisen, staggering, and was driven unsteadily back before the attack of Steen.

Then speed blinded the wolf dog. The forest crowded past him, a legion of shadows. The open flared dazzling on his eyes, and there was the woman whom his master had touched, had talked to. His scent was still upon her, faint, but distinct to Chinook. Therefore, she was a friend, and with her human hand she might do what he dared not try.

She shrank from him with a scream, for he came on her like a raging demon from the woods — but Chinook caught hold on her skirt and drew her toward the trees.

Who has not seen a stunned and beaten boxer reeling in front of a furious and victorious enemy, but his very reeling disappoints the blows of the conqueror. So it was with Harney before Steen.

The smashing blows of Steen grazed and glanced from his head and body, twisting him this way and that. And always down his head flowed the tide from the blow that had descended upon his skull, that had stunned and paralyzed him, body and brain.

This, like a flag, challenged and urged Steen on. Desperately he struck, before the daze of Harney should vanish, and those loose hands become once more terrible. But though the head of Harney swayed back, though he pitched here and there with the powerful strokes, still no solid finishing blow could be landed. And Steen, at last, ran in with wide-open arms and gripped his man.

Let it be said then that he felt less elation than horror as he felt the huge body of Harney yield under his grasp. The rigid might that arched the chest and ridged the limbs of Harney now was gone. He was like pulp in the grasp of Steen. And Steen paused, feeling the life of this man in his hand. Once before, his own life had been about to slip into the ocean, and this was he who had saved him. He thought of that, and of the strong man who had marched with him across the snows, and struggled with him down the dangers of the Yukon and its lakes. But he thought of the lovely face of

Kate, and instantly he was all steel.

And he shouted at the swaying, contorted face of Harney: "Are you through, Harney? Have you got enough?"

He saw the other steady a little, and with a far-off look Harney rallied himself for the end. In place of an answer in words, he managed to get one weak arm free and struck the hand futilely into the iron face of Steen.

Steen laughed. He thrust his right arm behind the shoulder of Harney. The right hand he curled across, until it gripped the big throat of the man, now soft as the throat of a child. Then, exerting his full pressure, he bore backward, and Harney collapsed under the strangle hold.

Together they crashed to the ground as two forms slid from beneath the trees into the open — Chinook and the girl just behind him.

Her cry came before her upon Steen, and he gave back before it as though he had been clubbed in turn.

He had not yet come to his feet when she threw herself on Joe Harney. He saw her arm pass under the head of the fallen man. He saw her touch the purple-stained lips and cherish the battered face with her hand. In agony she listened for the heartbeat —

heard the flutter of it — and at last raised her face to Steen.

"You black-faced fiend!" she cried at him. "You murderer! You coward!"

"Kate . . . ," he said, and would have come a step closer to her, but Chinook, snarling like a fiend, was crouched before him, ready as a snake to strike.

So Steen looked gloomily upon them both, and slowly backed away. There was murder and there was a frightful grief in his heart, but he could not take his eyes from them.

The dog, too, had dragged himself beside his master, and licked the wounded face. A face disfigured, a face swollen and battered by many blows — never a handsome face at best. And yet the girl hung over him as if he were a prince from a fairy tale.

Another shadow came through the shadow of the trees beside him, and he turned with a start toward Winslow. The latter looked calmly at the wounded face of Steen and again at the group on the ground. Then he nodded.

Steen knew that whether from that one glance or from what Kate had told him before, Winslow understood perfectly.

"We've left the old heroic age, it appears," said Winslow. "We've come to sentimental times, it appears, Steen. But children, dogs, and women are apt to lean toward the simple hearts which are capable of blind service. Eh? Or, in the words of the old song, the longest way 'round is the sweetest way home. Or have I quoted that correctly?"

About the Author

Max Brand is the best-known pen name of Frederick Faust, creator of Dr. Kildare, Destry, and many other fictional characters popular with readers and viewers worldwide. Faust wrote for a variety of audiences in many genres. His enormous output, totaling approximately thirty million words or the equivalent of 530 ordinary books, covered nearly every field: crime, fantasy, historical romance, espionage, Westerns, science fiction, adventure, animal stories, love, war, and fashionable society, big business and big medicine. Eighty motion pictures have been based on his work along with many radio and television programs. For good measure he also published four volumes of poetry. THE MAX BRAND COMPANION (Greenwood Press, 1996) edited by Jon Tuska and Vicki Piekarski provides an excellent guide to Faust's multitudinous fiction of all kinds as well as his life and times.

Born in Seattle in 1892, orphaned early, Faust grew up in the rural San Joaquin Valley of California. At Berkeley he became a student rebel and one-man literary movement, contributing prodigiously to all campus publications. Denied a degree because of unconventional conduct, he embarked on a series of adventures culminating in New York City where, after a period of near starvation, he received simultaneous recognition as a serious poet and successful popular-prose writer. Later, he traveled widely, making his home in New York, then in Florence, and finally in Los Angeles.

Once the United States entered the Second World War, Faust abandoned his lucrative writing career and his work as a screenwriter to serve as a war correspondent with the infantry in Italy, despite his fifty-one years and a bad heart. He was killed during a night attack on a hilltop village held by the German army. New books based on magazine serials or unpublished manuscripts or restored versions continue to appear so that he has averaged a new book every four months for seventy-five years. Beyond this, some work by him is newly reprinted every week of every year in one or another format somewhere in the world.

The employees of Thorndike Press hope you have enjoyed this Large Print book. All our Large Print titles are designed for easy reading, and all our books are made to last. Other Thorndike Press Large Print books are available at your library, through selected bookstores, or directly from us.

For information about titles, please call:

(800) 257-5157
To share your comments, please write:

Publisher
Thorndike Press
P.O. Box 159
Thorndike, Maine 04986